WAXING GIBBOUS

by

CHRISTOPHER D. ROE

authorHOUSE

AuthorHouse™
1663 Liberty Drive
Bloomington, IN 47403
www.authorhouse.com
Phone: 833-262-8899

Published by AuthorHouse 01/18/2022

ISBN: 978-1-5049-6731-0 (sc)
ISBN: 978-1-5049-6732-7 (e)

Print information available on the last page.

Any people depicted in stock imagery provided by Thinkstock are models, and such images are being used for illustrative purposes only. Certain stock imagery © Thinkstock.

This book is printed on acid-free paper.

Wrap Around

Last Evening

How deeply you sleep, my child. How deeply indeed! It wasn't my intention to awaken you so abruptly, but if I had left you alone, you would have slept for much longer. From the time you had fallen asleep at half past nine last night, you never once stirred; not even to pick up the comforter from the floor to cover yourself as the dark of the night cooled the bedroom down to sixty-seven degrees. I must say, I didn't mind the blanket covering us for a spell. It is the one your Grandma Jane made for you last Christmas, isn't it?

Isn't it?

You hear me, don't you, child?

Alice?

Thaaaaaaat's better. Yeeeeees. It's good that you vocalize, although you will no longer be able to do so. I'll not risk the chance that you might alert your family downstairs if you were to have a sudden burst of strength. You lie still now, and let me have my say. It's better when you don't fight it. Struggling makes your weakness seem so...apparent. Is that too big a word for you, Alice? I mean to say that when you fidget...now I know you know that word, Alice, because your mother tells you all the time to stop fidgeting at the table. When you fidget, I can see just how easy it will be to conquer you...to overtake you... to make you mine.

1

You're trying to speak, child. Your intonation suggests it is a question. Please repeat the question, Alice.

I have control of your mouth now and therefore you cannot communicate vocally unless I will you to do so.

Our minds are connected. Think your question and I will hear it.

You want to know who I am?

In time, child...in time.

Only know that I am eternal. I have no beginning and no end. So you know you cannot deceive me or defeat me. Just accept this as your fate.

I've been your constant companion for many years, so much longer than you can imagine. I remember your infancy. I remember the day you walked your first steps across the living room, held first by your father until you achieved a wobbly yet sustainable balance. And then inch by inch you made your way across the room and landed in the bosom of your doting mother. I was there on your first day of school when Missy Laurel, the little girl who sat behind you, kept pulling one of your pigtails, and how after the third tug, you began to cry.

I was there.

I saw it.

I was with you when you lost your first tooth. You were watching television with your parents and baby brother, Brandon. You were six. Your mother had just brought out a bowl of fruit for an after-dinner snack. You took a pear and bit into it, which caused one of your top front teeth to come loose. Allow me to recall an even finer detail, girl. It was your right front tooth, wasn't it, Alice?

Y-e-e-e-e-es, it w-a-a-a-as.

I was there with you last summer when you and your best friend, Bethany Rogers, found a half-dead turtle lying at the side of the road. He'd been hit by a Nissan Sentra. How do I know this, you ask? Because I saw the animal get hit and heard his shell split wide open. I see all, child. As I've mentioned, I am eternal and omnipresent. I watched as you and Bethany took a large rock and smashed in the dying turtle's head. Was that to spare him from further misery? Or did you enjoy killing him? You don't need to answer, Alice. I can read your thoughts. I know that the two of you wanted to save him from any more pain. You have an abundance of compassion, girl. To that I can only say that I've never seen perfection among human beings, and you are no different.

I was there with you every night since you were almost one year old, staring at you as you slept. Never taking my eyes off of you.

Never.

Watching you take in every breath, studying your eyes with every blink.

Even during the stormy nights when you and Brandon slept in your parents' bed because of your silly fear of thunder.

I watched all four of you.

I mostly watched you, but the other three were in my sights as well. However, none of them captivated me as did you, little Alice.

But where are your mother and father now? They're not here with us, and they won't hear your wretchedly weak moans, because, soon, even your feeble whimpering I will control. I know. I see. It's a little after eleven. In about eight hours, your mother and father will begin to wonder why you're not down for breakfast. They won't come up to check on you for another twenty-two minutes after that. This I know and this I've foreseen. Therefore, my time is short. I have only until the new phase of the moon and that is to come this night. The moon shall tell me when all is ready. When it glows in the heavens fuller than not, then and only then will you finally be MINE! That leaves me counting the hours until my power can take full possession of your body. I say, may the great cyclical celestial event come to pass on this, the first night of Luna's subsequent phase!

I count the hours until then! Not that I worry in the least about your parents discovering me. Or what they can do to me. They will not be aware of my presence. To them you will look like a very sick child: one who no longer has the ability to talk and whose body temperature has inexplicably dropped to ninety degrees. So have no faith in them. They cannot help you, even if they were to achieve the impossible and discover me. Let them try to take you from me! There's no time, really. The union between your body and my spirit is almost complete. It's taken weeks to get to where I am now within you. So they can bring a priest! They can try an exorcism! NOTHING can stop me now!

I do rather enjoy mocking the worthless ritual of exorcism, but I find it a bore before too long. I'm not alone in this, you see. Any demon will tell you that. Oh, yes, Alice. Whimper all you want, but that is what I am.

A demon!

That's good, child. Cry. It weakens you all the more.

No, I am not a ghost. Ghosts are the wandering souls of your kind. I am what you would call an entity.

NEVER YOU MIND WHAT MY NAME IS!

Only that I am undying, and that my spirit has neither had a beginning, nor will it ever see an end. I see how that frightens you.

Good.

I need you scared. I need to feed off that fear until you are at your most vulnerable, and I shall explain. You have a will that has been hard to penetrate. Yet, when I revealed myself to you last night for the first time; it frightened you immensely. So much so that your hope in everything you trusted all but vanished for a spell! Up until this point, throughout all the years I have followed you, throughout the course of your life, you had never yielded as much as you did last night.

Ahhhh. The fear is building in you with each word I mutter.

Excellent.

But still this is not enough! You need to be broken!

Now then. You will be still and silent over the next several hours and listen while I tell you three stories. These narratives were carefully chosen, especially for you. They all have something in common. Would you like me to tell you why I've chosen these particular stories for you, my piglet Alice? It's quite simple, really. Knowing you as well as I do, I am aware that you have many fears. Didn't I say that I needed to build up your fear to its absolute limit before I could completely overtake you? Well, now, out of all your fears, there are three that most terrify you.

Three stories for three fears.

Your heart! How it races now! Be mindful of your breathing, child. You're no good to me dead.

Now then, I shall continue. These stories are sure to plunge you into a virtual hell and will terrify you more and more with the passing of each word I speak. In fact, it will be perhaps the easiest thing I've ever had to do to own your body after the end of my third tale.

And know, my child, that there is one more thing. Each one of these stories is true! Yes! They have their place in history. I want you to know that so as to increase your terror. These people live or have lived. Remember that these places are real and that what occurred is as real as you or me.

I know this. Believe me. And I know it frightens you. Do you remember all the times you were ever scared? Do you?

Well...I do, child. I remember everything you've ever done every second of your miserably happy life. Any time you were frightened, you were always reassured that it was imaginary; whether it was the horror film your sitter Bambi dragged you to so she could see her boyfriend Cole; or her nighttime story about the three gremlins living in your closet; or the Halloween costume of the neighbor's son; or the neon apparitions in the funhouse that made you wet your pants. You always took comfort in hearing the words, 'It's not real, Alice. It's made up.' Let me assure you that nothing about these stories is imaginary.

You are thinking, 'how do I know they're true?' Remember, child, I am omnipresent! I am everywhere. I see all. I know all. It's not so hard. Your mayfly existence could never grasp how I know what I know, that of which I am capable, or what I can see and have seen. Every one of these narratives I have witnessed firsthand. So, before you even think of telling yourself that they're only stories so as to provide a false sense of comfort, remember these words I am telling you now! My only hesitation is that I will terrify you to the point where your heart will stop; stop from the very knowledge that what I relate to you has truly happened. To know that you live in a world where such things exist!

THEY ARE TRUE!

I have never seen you so terrified, Alice. Excellent. However, believe this or not, your present fear is not nearly sufficient! You need to be pushed to the brink of suicide if I am to enter your body. I must break your will to live. I must break your hope; your faith in your God. I must do all this within the time I have left.

Why must I hurry if I have no fear of anyone or anything?

Foolish child that you are!

If I am to break you, I must keep you clear of any hope. If your parents were to enter the room, then some, not all, but some of your fear would subside, and that will only delay the inevitable. A minor setback to be sure, but a setback nonetheless. I have waited too long and want this too badly to waste any time unnecessarily. I know I shall not fail this time. It's taken me ten revolutions of the earth around her solar parent to get this far with you, and last night I came the farthest I'd ever been! I spoke to you and finally you heard me! Oh, how long I have waited for this moment! To enter a human body! I have waited eons! Thousands of years for my match. And YOU are that match. I have this one chance, and I shall not fail!

Now stop your petty resistance. Lie still and listen to my words as they pass into your lovely ears and bury themselves deeply in your brain.

The first of my tales I call...

The Metamorphosis of 2012

1

"An ugly bugger that thing is!" Robbie Taylor heard himself say out loud as he turned off the engine to his Mustang. His comment was in reference to the strange gray insect that had been clinging to the passenger-side window. "What is it?" he said, hearing his own voice raise one octave. "Looks like some kind of mosquito on steroids." By this point, Robbie couldn't care less if the King of Prussia had been spread eagle on the hood of the car. Too much had happened to the young man over the course of the afternoon and none of it was good. He'd just pulled into the driveway of the mid-sized suburban colonial outside New Haven, Connecticut, that he'd purchased just one year earlier. The day was waning and he'd had a fairly miserable last several hours. At six minutes to two he left the office of Whiting, Whiting, Chilton & Foresby where he worked as a paralegal, practically three whole hours before quitting time. Regardless of any head start he might have had that fateful Friday afternoon, he didn't make it onto the expressway until about a quarter after. Had it occurred to him to switch on the AM radio and listen for the Shadow Traffic Report, which came on every ten minutes on the threes, he would have avoided I-95 all together, and instead would have taken the service road the entire eight-mile stretch from the exit near his office to the one not far from his home in Hawham.

Robbie had only gotten as far as the East Haven service stop, which was only about a hundred yards or so from where he'd entered, before noticing all three lanes of stationary cars braking, illuminating an ocean of bright red as far as the eye could see.

"FUCK!" he shouted, and then quickly composed himself after glancing to his left. He saw a little boy, who bore a striking resemblance to a young Macaulay Culkin, occupying the shotgun seat of a car beside him in the left lane. Robbie smiled at the boy, hoping the child hadn't heard his profanity. Then he offered the boy a wave of his hand and followed it up with a nod of his head toward the traffic ahead of them as if to say, '*Hi there, kiddo! What's up? This sure does suck the nipples right off your GI Joe action figures, don't it?*' The boy didn't make any attempt to respond amicably, but did offer Robbie his middle finger, which Robbie couldn't help but notice before quickly turning away in an attempt to pretend he hadn't seen it.

He reached into his empty breast pocket for a cigarette. This was nothing more than a force of habit, as Robbie Taylor had quit smoking two weeks prior. Whenever he felt a sudden rush of adrenaline, whether it be his cell phone ringing, showing *unknown caller* on the screen, or his deadbeat drunken Uncle Gerard showing up unexpectedly on his doorstep looking for money, basically anything he wasn't ready for, he'd reach into the breast pocket of his dress shirt, and pull out a smoke from the hard pack of his Marlboro Reds.

Not the right moment to be left without a butt, wouldn't you say, Robster? He thought, trying to convince himself he was cooler and more composed than a minute before. However, as he looked left again, this time expecting to see the little boy mooning him,

Robbie noticed a different car had moved into place and the vehicle in which the boy had been sitting was now ahead of Robbie's by two car lengths.

He let out a string of obscenities as he realized his lane was the only one still not moving. He extended his left arm out the window, resting a sweaty armpit on top of the thin rubber cavity inside the door that housed the driver's side window. With his index finger pointing left, Robbie made a gesture to the vehicle behind him that he wanted to move into the middle lane. This car, which Robbie perceived just in time through his rear-view mirror, did the exact opposite of what he had hoped, and sped up to pass Robbie's blue Mustang.

Another obscenity escaped Robbie Taylor's lips as he slammed his palms down hard onto his steering wheel. He suddenly felt a shooting pain radiate through his wrists and up into his forearms. He let out one more *FUCK* before finally deciding to accept his indefinite immobility. He took a deep breath and reached for his sun visor. He remembered putting his *Aerosmith's Greatest Hits* CD up there the Saturday before, with the intention of listening to it during his ride to Newport with a few college buddies. All week long he had forgotten to take the CD back into the house.

As he began to pull down the visor, the cars ahead of him in his lane began moving. He instinctively responded in anxious haste by nearly flooring the accelerator, which in turn caused all nine CDs he'd kept wedged between the closed sun visor and the roof of his car to come cascading down onto him. Two hit the bridge of his nose, another nearly poked him in his eye and the rest slid onto his chest. One fell into his shirt that he had partially unbuttoned for ventilation.

Startled by the deluge of digital music, he slammed both feet on the brake pedal and, in a split second, his neck whipped back and the Mustang lunged forward. He'd been rear ended by the car in back of him.

"FUCK! FUCK! FUCK!"

Robbie Taylor jumped out of his car and channeled the remainder of his anger by slamming the door shut as hard as he could. It certainly worked to alleviate the stress he'd been feeling, for Robbie instantly felt somewhat calmer than a moment before. He walked toward the area of impact and surveyed the damage. The white Mercedes Benz that had hit his vehicle was now about three feet from his fender. The driver of the Mercedes was a middle-aged woman with short blond hair. She wore a large straw hat, a blue and white horizontal-striped blouse, white slacks and white shoes with low heels. Her earlobes and fingers were adorned with various pieces of gold jewelry, which all suggested that this lady had expensive taste and most likely socialized in quite wealthy circles. Robbie noticed a string of expensive pearls about the woman's neck. This last item particularly grabbed his interest because she kept tugging at it as if it were there only to offer her comfort and security. Based on his first impression of her, he thought she could be the cruise director of a five-star luxury liner for the recently-retired. It occurred to Robbie that if he were dead broke, there wouldn't be a more ideal person to be rear ended by; unless the Queen happened to be in New Haven County, Connecticut that day.

"Oh, just look at that!" the woman said, putting both hands on her hips and stomping her foot once on the asphalt. "I honestly didn't see you break. Are you all right?"

Robbie gave himself the once over, slapping his upper chest hard and then the insides of his thighs, just around his crotch. Then to check his back, he leaned forward before swaying backwards.

"Yeah," he said, trying to seem out of breath, although he wasn't the least bit winded. "I am. Are-Are *you* OK? I mean, that was a pretty nasty bump we took."

Both drivers observed their respective fenders. With the exception of the license plate bracket and frame of the Mercedes having been cracked off at the top, there wasn't the slightest bit of damage done to the vehicle. The blue Mustang, on the other hand, was not so fortunate. The impact had dented the center rear bumper, which in turn caused the edge of its left side to protrude outward on the driver's side.

The drivers behind the Mercedes began leaning on their horns, which quickly grew into a symphony of *beeeep-beeeep-beeeep* in the standard key of F. This reminded Robbie of the first and only time he and his father had taken the Circle Line around Manhattan Island when Robbie was just twelve years old. All sea vessels, including the one on which Robbie and his father were sailing, saluted the Statue of Liberty as they sailed past Liberty Island. Robbie looked over the woman's shoulder to wave the other cars over to the next lane, and the first car behind the Mercedes did just that.

As Robbie was busy directing traffic, the pleasing scent of expensive car leather hit him. He observed the woman who'd rear-ended him bend over and go head first into her car. She arched her back, making her behind appear to undulate. Robbie took a few seconds to study her ass.

Plump and shapely. Not bad for an old broad.

She opened her arm rest and pulled out a tidy black leather-bound checkbook. With a flick of her thumb she opened it up to the next available check and removed a pen with her mouth that she had lodged inside the case. Robbie thought that if the Women's League of New Haven, of which he was sure this lady must be a member, had witnessed this behavior, they would consider it to be a breach of etiquette and a prime example of blatant unladylike comportment. She dropped the checkbook onto the hood of her car and, beginning to fill out the next check, used her free hand to scratch the back of her neck.

"We don't really need to go through the insurance, now, do we?" she said, putting her sunglasses on, which told Robbie that she was completely unscathed and was getting ready to buy him off. "The damage seems to be utterly superficial."

"Utterly." Robbie repeated, eying the checkbook like a vulture. But it was fleeting, as Robbie's practicality returned to him just as fast as it had left him. "Really, Miss," Robbie began, looking down at the checkbook and continuing in a fainter voice like he were merely reciting a script from memory that required no tone or effort. "I don't think we need to…I mean, I think we should call the police."

She reacted suddenly to the word *police*.

"POLICE? Oh! No, no, no. That isn't necessary." And with that, she ripped out the check from the book and handed it to Robbie. The deliberate and continuous manner in which she removed the check made it curl slightly. To Robbie, it had sounded like playing cards fluttering against the spokes of a bicycle wheel. "Now, you just fill in your name and go to your bank and cash it. I'm willing to pay for the damage done to both cars, so why even bother to go through the insurance? Insurance companies are nothing but blood-sucking leeches anyway. You get in one little fender bender like this and they make it out to be like you did it on purpose. In fact, it's a wonder they don't just come right out and say it!"

Robbie examined the check, thinking: *Damage to both cars? Lady, I think your license plate will survive.*

The name in the top left-hand corner of the check read: *Irvin & Elaine Meredith.*

Friggin' Jews. he thought. *Always throwing around how much money they got. But I'll tell you, Robster, this is the first time I ever saw one of 'em throw their money at someone like she is. Take it, Robster. Take the money and run like a goddamn wetback headed for the Texas border.*

He immediately noticed the amount she'd written on the check. *Fifteen hundred dollars, payable to: blank.* When Robbie, now finding himself beginning to drip with perspiration, turned to face her, he jumped back as Mrs. Meredith was close enough to plant a kiss on his wet salty lips. She gazed at him, mesmerizingly. Robbie could see through her dark lenses that her eyes were wide.

"Are you *sure* you're all right, sir?" she asked him, digging a primly-manicured digit into the collar of her shirt and giving her neck a steady series of scratches. "Perhaps I can follow you back to your home, just to be certain you're ok."

"No," said Robbie, uneasily, but trying his best to sound convincing, "really, truly, I'm just a bit shaken up but I'll be fine."

"Are you *certain*?" asked Mrs. Meredith again, this time leaning somewhat closer.

"Mrs...uh, Meredith, is it?" he replied, as he glanced briefly down at the curled check. "I'm fine. I guess I should be asking *you* if *you're* all right."

She withdrew just as a warm breeze came through. She slowly brought one hand up to her straw hat to make sure it was still planted firmly atop her head.

"Fine," she said, dismissively.

Is she worried I might sue her? he reflected. *Maybe you should, Robster. Fake an injury. Whiplash! That always does the trick. Goddamn, is Connecticut a no fault state?*

Robbie turned back to his car and was suddenly hit with a fowl stench emanating from what seemed to be the air around Mrs. Meredith. At first he thought it might have been the woman's breath, but he hadn't smelled it until now. What's more, Mrs. Meredith had already returned to her car, now feverishly scratching the nape of her neck. Although it was from a distance of fifteen or so feet, Robbie saw something protruding from the back of her neck as she turned to put her checkbook back in the armrest. It was approximately one inch long, black and thin. If Robbie hadn't known any better, he'd have testified that it was the stinger of a massive bee lodged in the woman's skin, but instantly dismissed the hallucination.

Robbie Taylor turned to walk back to his own vehicle. He looked left and observed the traffic moving more freely now, despite his and Mrs. Meredith's cars blocking the right lane, not to mention the constant gawking from the long line of rubberneckers as they passed. The acrid air lingered in Robbie's nasal passages as he slammed his driver side door shut and started his engine. He equated it to rotten seaweed, as there was a hint of ocean decay in the air as well.

Robbie looked through his driver's side rear-view mirror to inch back into traffic. It wasn't hard this time to get into the center lane as the cars began to slow down considerably as they approached the back end of Mrs. Meredith's Mercedes. With a more prudent foot than earlier, Robbie accelerated into the middle lane and again looked behind him, this time using the rear-view mirror.

"Oh, great!" he exclaimed as he saw a group of dark clouds approaching ominously from the west. They moved in swiftly. "I guess ball's off for tonight."

He was part of a junior baseball league in the greater New Haven area, which had been given permission in the summer months to play all its games in the practice field at Yale University. Robbie Taylor's team was the Bruisers, sponsored by Jansen's Bait & Tackle, and their uniforms were a piss yellow. A giant fish hook acted as the "J" in "Jansen", which was emblazoned in red in the center of the shirts. Although he sounded disappointed by the prospect of not playing ball that night, Robbie thought twice about it. He figured that after the day he'd had, coupled with the weeklong heat wave, he didn't feel like standing in the outfield and sweating through his cotton uniform; even if ball didn't start until just before dusk.

The smell continued to offend his senses to the point that now he was tasting it. He slowed down and the vehicle behind him began honking angrily. He saw through his mirror that it was no longer the white Mercedes, complete with expensive, pleasant-smelling leather and damaged license plate cover, but rather a black Lincoln Town Car with Jersey plates. Within seconds, the Lincoln pulled into the passing lane to Robbie's left and revved its engine as it sped by. Robbie read the Lincoln's license plate. *UCR45H*, but for a quick second, Robbie read it as *UCRASH*.

"Jeez! I need to get my ass out of the path of that stench." He rolled up both windows and turned on the air conditioner to maximum power. Within seconds, the car was filled with the odor.

"OH, HELL!" He shouted and fumbled for the circulate button below the on/off switch. Robbie turned on the AM radio to 1570 at 2:33, just in time to get the traffic and transit report. He opened his window to let the cool stink within the car's cabin escape into the hot, still foul air outside; yet this did little good.

"GOD! What *is* that?" he growled, and it quickly occurred to him that in all the time he'd been taking that same route home, he'd never before noticed any smell like that on I-95.

The radio frequency went fuzzy enough to where Robbie could no longer make out what the reporter was saying. He smacked the radio's LCD, knowing that wouldn't do any good, but it served to relieve a bit of the frustration he'd built up in the short while since leaving the office.

"*Eastbound Connecticut Turnpike is a mess,*" proclaimed the reporter, and Robbie shot the radio a glance as if to say, *Sure sweetheart, now that I can't exit.* "*Due to a jackknifed tractor trailer at Exit 64 in Westbrook knocking out the right and center lanes. Delays stretching back all the way to Exit 51 in East Haven. Police activity is heavy at the scene and all lanes are subject to closure.*"

No sooner did he hear *subject to closure* than Robbie once again had to slam on his brakes. The back brake lights of the cars in front of him in all three lanes were once again illuminated. In an instant, the sky opened up, and, as if fifty thousand Olympic-sized swimming pools had been tossed up into the air and turned upside down, it began raining torrentially. Within seconds, hot steam began to rise all around the stationary cars as the rain cooled the scorching asphalt. To Robbie and the other drivers it seemed like a sudden and mysterious fog were beginning to form.

"YOUR MOTHER'S A BAG LADY!" he shouted at the radio and then simply closed his mouth and expanded his cheeks like a puffer fish while cocking his head back against the headrest of his seat. Still, even with his air conditioner on and the vents closed, Robbie continued to sense that distasteful smell of putrefying marine life, although now it was mixed with the scent of tar emitting from the smoky blacktop.

"Christ!" he growled. "So much for getting home early. I'd have been better off leaving at quitting time and walking home."

At around four o'clock, Robbie, still on the verge of nausea, disdainfully surveyed his surroundings as if to scold this particular stretch of I-95 for smelling so putridly. His eyes slowly made it down to the bottom of his passenger-side window, where he saw what appeared to be a long, slender piece of gray twig. From his vantage point, it didn't look like it could be anything more than that. It was too big and narrow to be a cigarette butt (as well as the wrong color), and too small to be any of the myriad of items he could think of that could be that color, size and shape.

Perhaps if it hadn't been raining, Robbie would have leaned over toward the passenger-side window to see exactly what it was. There didn't seem to be anything else to do while sitting it the sea of traffic in which he found himself dead center. He also found it strange that even with the downpour, this object remained completely inert. It looked jammed between the window and the weather stripping, and he dismissed its motionlessness as being due to just that. As his eyes left the strange gray object, he took note of a motorcycle cop standing at the side of the road beside his motorcycle. The officer did nothing to move the traffic along, nor did he seem to be checking for motorists not wearing their seat belts. In Robbie's mind, this cop was being paid to do absolutely nothing. What made this sight more remarkable than not was that the heavy downpour didn't seem to bother the policeman in the least.

OK, chief, thought Robbie, *you'll let us know when Noah shows up with his ark and we'll all file in two at a time.*

A car carrying a little girl in the backseat was crawling alongside the Mustang. Robbie noticed the child nearly covering her entire face as her eyes narrowed. He assumed this to be the child's repulsion to the smell with which he was also afflicted. Yet oddly enough, the stench, as bad as Robbie found it, didn't bother the officer whatsoever.

How is it that this dude is not smelling what we *are? We're in our cars with the windows up for God's sake and it's almost unbearable.*

Robbie looked at the motorist in the car behind him through the Mustang's rear-view mirror. This man was pinching the sides of his nose and visibly trying to hold his breath as he extended his chest outward. Robbie then observed the motorist in the car behind that of the little girl. That motorist had his face nearly entirely covered with the crook of his arm while his occupant used both hands to cover both her nose and mouth, as if in pious supplication.

That's right, sweet stuff, Robbie thought, *pray for this stink to go back to Jersey where it belongs.*

The traffic was at a standstill for a total of three hours, and once it started moving again, it took fifteen minutes to drive one mile to the next exit. By then, the foul odor had somewhat dissipated, yet as faint as it had become, was still apparent. Robbie didn't get to his own exit until almost a quarter to six. By then the traffic had almost completely subsided and the drenching storm, which had been pounding his and everyone else's cars for the last two hours, had finally abated to nothing more than a slight drizzle. Robbie pulled into the driveway that extended all the way to the back of the house. He could still detect the foul odor, perhaps because it had lingered in his nose for so long that it simply set up shop in his nostrils. He even thought about performing his own version of Islamic Ablution, albeit secularly, inhaling cold water through his nose.

He groaned and extended his chest forward to relieve the pressure on his lower lumbar from sitting in a car for so many hours. He stayed there and stared through his window as the windshield wipers continued moving back and forth on the highest speed. It didn't dawn on Robbie to turn them off, even though there wasn't sufficient rainfall to keep the wipers working on even the slowest speed. Robbie could scarcely believe he was finally home, and the relief he felt carried him away into a state of meditation-like nirvana.

About a minute passed before Robbie snapped out of his near catatonic stupor and went to turn off the ignition. As he lifted his arm, he heard a tap at his passenger-side window.

Tap-tap-tap.

At this point, the Mustang began to idle louder as its coolant system kicked in.

This time, Robbie leaned closer to the passenger-side window to find out what the hell this thing was. As he began to slant over to the right side of the cabin, his seat belt locked and Robbie stopped dead, his head jerking forward unexpectedly. As he inhaled deeply in frustration, the stench grew more profound.

He grew anxious now, and in a show of frustration jammed his thumb down on the seat belt release button and shook off the over-the-shoulder strap. The heavy metal buckle slammed against the window with enough force to shatter it.

"What in the world?" Robbie said in a low, raspy voice. As he brought his eyes closer to the grayish thing, it suddenly took shape. He saw its two large dark gray eyes, void of any life; its silver fur, its narrow extended legs and its long black stinger protruding from the insect's nasal cavity.

Robbie observed the creature for a few moments, trying to make out what it was. He had never seen anything like it before. When he'd first realized it was a bug, he thought it to be a mosquito. But he knew very well that the bodies of mosquitoes are much more slender, and their stingers are not as long and pronounced.

As the seconds grew into a full minute, it would have looked to the casual observer like Robbie and the insect were staring at one another. But something began to trouble Robbie the more he thought of it. This…*thing* appeared to be doing more than just staring at Robbie; it seemed to be *watching* him.

2

Robbie didn't find it difficult to fall asleep that night. The culmination of a week's worth of heat-induced exhaustion, sitting in bumper-to-bumper traffic for four hours-and all the emotional exertion that came with it-made it no surprise that insomnia was as unlikely that night as finding a virgin in a French whorehouse. He was so worn-out by a quarter past seven that Robbie could only collapse onto his bed, clothes and all, without so much as turning down the sheets. His feet hung off the side of the bed and his right arm, which would go limp and then numb before too long, was tucked neatly under his ribcage.

Before he drifted off, Robbie could hear a noise coming from the solitary window of his bedroom. It was a slow and random tapping, and just after he'd heard it, there came a mild, albeit less-than-refreshing breeze, originating from the window, just behind the partially-drawn venetian blind. He turned his head drunkenly and quickly realized that he'd forgotten to close the window and turn on the central air. He'd locked himself out of the house earlier that morning, but luckily his bedroom window had been absentmindedly left slightly open. He had to resort to breaking through the screen to get back inside. As he fell hard onto the wood floor of his bedroom, he noticed a few superficial scrapes on his hand that were a result of using his fingers to slice through the taut mesh that kept the screen sealed and impenetrable.

"I'll replace it after work." he told himself. "Home Depot is open until eleven on Friday nights."

Here it was now, Friday evening, and Robbie, already convinced that he was ready to call it a night, made a decision that would change his life over the course of the next few hours.

No way in hell am I getting up. he thought. *I don't care if I wake up tomorrow and find my balls three inches deep in sweat. Screw the window, screw the central air, screw comfort, and screw my balls too, I suppose.*

The last thing Robbie remembered was the venetian blind tapping intermittently against the window's ledge. If he hadn't been so tired, his brief attention to the opened window might have also reminded him that he'd forgotten to replace the screen.

****

Not long after he crashed did Robbie awaken to what felt like a pinch behind his neck. He instantly answered it with a swipe of his hand. He soon noticed, however, that he'd been lying in a pool of his own sweat. The satin bedclothes were sticking to his body. What's more, when he moved his head in reaction to the sudden sharp pain, the satin pillow on which his head rested seemed to peel away from his moist cheek like Velcro.

Christ. he thought, *did I put the heat on? Or am I in hell and just don't know it yet?*

As groggy as he was and with the pinch to his neck leaving a dull but still-present sensation, Robbie ignored his discomfort as best he could and soon found sleep again. He dreamed he was lying on his stomach on an orange inflatable raft in the middle of the swimming pool his parents owned behind their four-bedroom house down in Fairfield. As he slumbered on the rubber object, he felt the steamy sun sear his skin from head to toe. Even the downturned half of his body was sweltering hot. He then dreamed of being paralyzed in that same position as a swarm of hornets exited a hive in line formation just beyond the pool deck. Their destination: the back of Robbie Taylor's neck. He dreamed that each of the nearly two hundred bees took turns jabbing him uniformly in the back of his neck. With each jab came a searing hot sting whose infliction included an excruciating pain that resonated from the entrance wound all the way down to the tips of his toes. With each shot of pain Robbie contorted his face into a grimace that suggested suffering. But as badly as the stings hurt and as hot and uncomfortable as the rest of his body was, he either couldn't move, or just gave up the will to try.

Three hours later, he awakened, concurrently turning onto his side and immediately feeling the small of his back go into spasm. This was either a result of sitting for hours in his car or sleeping in an awkward position. He drowsily reflected on the dream he'd had hours before and thought of the pain behind his neck that he'd felt throughout the nightmare. The pain was gone and so he dismissed it as having been imaginary, a manifestation created in his sleep. He brought the fingers of both hands down to just above his buttocks, and softly stroked the spasming muscles of the small of his back. No sooner did he round his fingers slightly up his back than he swiftly withdrew his left hand in reaction to what felt like a prick to the tip of his index finger. Robbie got up and immediately felt his legs turn to jelly. As he went for the light switch, he began locking his knees with each stride. Flicking on the light switch, he brought the tip of the finger in question up to his eyes and examined what looked to be a spot of blood, perfectly round, beginning to pool out of the skin. Had this spot of red found itself between Robbie's eyebrows in lieu of one of his ten digits, he could have possibly passed for a Hindu.

What the fuck? he thought and gently squeezed the wounded fingertip, knowing very well it would cause the blood to escape quicker and perhaps trickle down to his knuckle. The bathroom was a stone's throw from the master bedroom, located just on the other side of the living room, opposite Robbie's bedroom. He had hesitated to buy the house at first because he'd been hoping for one of those homes whose floor plan showed the bathroom inside the master bedroom. However, Robbie could only find this layout in condos and townhouses throughout the greater New Haven area. With houses in this part of the state being as old as they were, pre-1960's colonials and ranches, Robbie wound up opting for a colonial-style home. A dozen somnambulant paces to the bathroom was the price Robbie conceded to pay to realize his dream of owning a home.

He got to the bathroom without even once bumping into any furniture, a feat he'd never before achieved. The cold tap ran dutifully under the lesion and the slight throbbing that Robbie had begun feeling instantly subsided. He reached into the medicine cabinet for the small tube of Bacitracin and mistakenly grabbed the tube of Crest before angrily dropping it in the ivory basin. He reached into the cabinet for a second time and pulled out the correct remedy. He spread a thin layer of the antibacterial ointment onto the prick hole, which began to bleed out again, and he hastened to cover it with a small adhesive bandage. It didn't dawn on Robbie to check to see why he'd punctured his skin until he looked at himself in the bathroom mirror.

****

Robbie pitched his cell phone nervously from one hand to the other as he paced his bedroom. Although he was dripping with perspiration due to the excessive heat and humidity, he paid it little mind. His singular preoccupation at that moment was the haunting image he had seen in the mirror. He stopped pacing and dropped his phone onto the edge of the mattress, and the phone bounced up and fell onto the floor. The hard plastic casing made an unnerving sound as it hit the parquet and this further increased Robbie's anxiety.

He brought his hands to his face and felt for what had sent him into a state of near panic. He sensed the dozens of tiny prickly cilia protruding from his soft pink flesh. Despite his gentle touch against the coarse hairs, they registered waves of discomfort and subtle pain through his nervous system. He was immediately reminded of the minuscule injury with which he'd been afflicted just minutes before.

"What the fuck is happening to me?" he cried. "Holy Christ, am I fucking dreaming this?"

For a moment, Robbie tried convincing himself that he was still dreaming. But the way those hairs felt along his visage were far too genuine to be imaginary. As reality set in, Robbie despaired and stumbled back a few steps and, in so doing, his backside collided with the end of his sleigh bed. This mild impact startled him and he quickly pulled his fingertips away from his face, practically shredding the nine previously unscathed ones as they were yanked away from the jagged hairs on Robbie's cheeks. With the cold tap going again, nine more soft squeezes of the tube of Bacitracin and nine more tiny bandages were needed.

As dawn brought a bright ray of auburn sunlight into the bedroom, Robbie switched off the light and walked to the full-length body mirror behind his door. He gave his back to the mirror and then turned his head around as far as his neck would allow in order to examine the reflection. Whatever was on Robbie's face was beginning to manifest itself onto his back. He saw, in addition to the one follicle that had wounded him, that there were two dozen others of exactly the same size and texture running up and down his back. The only difference with these hairs was that they were more sporadic, growing in about two inches between one another. Then it dawned on him that these hairs looked familiar. It took him several seconds of fixated contemplation before he realized where he'd seen this exact same thing.

"That lady yesterday!" exclaimed Robbie. "That thing sticking out of her neck that I took for a bee's stinger! It wasn't a stinger at all! Whatever is happening to me must also be happening to her!" Robbie remembered the strange foul odor he'd detected on I-95 and then the strange insect he'd noticed on his window upon arriving home last evening. Although he couldn't account for the odor, he made a definite connection between Mrs. Meredith's neck and his own affliction.

It starts in the back of the neck and then travels throughout the rest of the body!

Robbie's fingertips, triaged with dressings, began to throb in syncopation. His body began to convulse as paranoid contemplation of what possibly could be happening to him flooded his brain. In short, Robbie Taylor began to panic, and as he sank into instant despair, his cries reverberated throughout the house.

3

Sitting was no longer an option for Robbie. The outer part and center of his buttocks were also inflicted with hundreds of those same tiny sharp cilia. He considered himself fortunate, in spite of everything happening to him, that he discovered the mysterious follicles on his second trip to the full-body mirror, because sitting down could have proved fatal.

He had stripped naked this time and examined around his erect penis; erect because whenever Robbie fretted over anything, regardless of how trivial or severe, blood would surge into his sexual gland. "Thank God." he whispered as he observed his phallus to be just as it had been prior to this nightmare. It wasn't until he turned around that he saw his ass had been inundated with the menacing hairs.

"GODDAMN IT!" he cried, and retreated back to his bed. He was about to sit down on its edge before remembering what had made him walk away from the mirror in the first place. The last thing he wanted was for these hundreds of ass hairs to press up against his skin.

I could bleed to death if I sat down.

****

Robbie was dressed and out of the house before eight o'clock. As he hit the button on his keyless entry remote, it dawned on him again that he shouldn't try sitting down. He cursed the cilia on his buttocks and withdrew from his car. He slowly stuck one hand down the back of his shorts and carefully felt the center of his ass. The follicles, as before, were not present around his anal cavity.

At least I won't have to worry when I wipe after taking a shit.

He was startled by a thump that came from behind him. It was the sound of his daily paper delivery as it made contact with the bottom front step. The paperboy who had thrown it was already pedaling to the next house with another journal already in hand. Although it was something he'd never taken notice of before, he perceived the boy's own backside was off the narrow bicycle seat. Perhaps it was Robbie's condition that made him observe the paperboy's own ass and how it straddled the seat. Robbie remembered a ten-speed bike he'd bought for himself a few years before after he'd promised a few of the guys on his baseball team that he would take part in a 10K bike ride charity event for the brother of one of the players who had been stricken with pancreatic cancer. The 24-year-old wound up dying two months after the event anyway, so Robbie never felt too guilty about having backed out at the last minute.

"Even if I *had* biked with you guys," Robbie said to another teammate, "it wouldn't have mattered. The guy wound up croaking in the end anyway."

The banishment of the unused ten-speed bike to the dingy garage had a purpose. He had always felt guilty about not supporting his buddy's family, and the bike served as a constant reminder of his unwillingness to get out of bed at 6 AM that Saturday morning to take part in the event.

"A bit of the old *out of sight, out of mind* mentality, isn't that right, Robster?" he chuckled as he threw the bike carelessly into the far right corner of the garage that Sunday after. "I'll just sell it at my next yard sale. Fifteen bucks sounds like a fair price.

Now that he had found some use out of the long-neglected bike, Robbie hastened to dust it off and mount it carefully.

Is this my comeuppance? he thought. *If it is, it's kind of ironic, don't ya think, Robster? I mean, I bought this piece of shit with good intention. Then that good intention flew right the fuck out the window. Now here I am depending on the very bike I wish I'd never bought and all because of these hairs on my ass. It may have taken two years, but I'll say this for Him, God is one patient son of a bitch.*

Robbie swung one leg over the bike and stood on his toes, the bicycle seat just two inches from his bottom. He carefully spread apart his butt cheeks as much as they would go and then slowly sat down. He breathed a sigh of relief as he felt nothing but the seat pressing up against his ass. With his bandaged fingers now gripping the handlebars, Robbie began to pedal down his driveway. As he turned onto the sidewalk, he pulled out the GPS that he had tucked tightly into his armpit and punched in the address he'd taken from the check that Mrs. Meredith had drafted him the day before.

****

Not long after purchasing a much-needed pack of smokes from the corner gas station and lighting up while steering the bike with one wounded hand, Robbie heard a siren blaring shrilly behind him. The front wheel of the police officer's motorcycle approached dangerously close to the back wheel of the ten-speed bike. Robbie looked over his shoulder and saw the motorcycle cop point emphatically to the side of the road.

"You've gotta be kidding me." Robbie said, feeling the sudden urge to finish the newly-lit cigarette in one drag. "First they enforce hands-free cell phones, now I suppose he'll get me for not using a hands-free cigarette."

Robbie pressed the butt of his cigarette between his lips and squeezed the brakes on both handlebars as he slowed to a stop on Constitution Avenue. The cop stopped his bike to where his front tire and Robbie's back tire were practically touching. Robbie thought at first to dismount the bike, but citing the fact that all he had to do was rub his ass the wrong way against the seat to start hemorrhaging, he decided to stay put. His nerves were rattling again, and as he heard the heels of the officer's shiny knee-high black patrol boots click rhythmically on the asphalt, Robbie began to feel nauseous. He kept his hands on the handlebars so as not to give the policeman a reason to draw his weapon. The smoke emanating from the cigarette burned Robbie's eyes and caused him to tear.

If he thinks I'm a cokehead and pats me down looking for my stash, he'll be in for quite a surprise. But would that be considered reverse police brutality? Would you call that civilian *brutality?*

"Good morning, sir." said the cop, removing his sunglasses and hanging them robotically to the breast pocket of his white shirt just above his shield, which indicated the officer's last name: *CARLSON*. Robbie thought it was important to know the name of any police officer that pulled him over in the eventuality that the cop wound up roughing him up. Some cops thrived on bullying, and Robbie never put it past any member of law enforcement.

"Please remove the cigarette from your mouth, sir." ordered the cop in an authoritative, albeit respective tone.

Robbie leaned over the left side of his bike and loosened his lips. The cigarette fell near the toes of the cop. Officer Carlson looked down at the smoking butt, raised his booted toe onto it and crushed it slowly but menacingly hard into the asphalt. This made Robbie think that he'd angered the policeman, and his apprehension was quickly amplified.

"Excuse me, officer," began Robbie nervously, "I meant no disrespect.

The officer replaced his foot to its former position and Robbie could see only a fraction of the pulverized cigarette remaining.

"What seems to be the problem, Officer?" asked Robbie, and he immediately heard his voice shaking. He cleared his throat and added, "I wasn't speeding, was I?" and managed a nervous giggle.

The officer removed his white dome-like helmet and placed it between the crook of his arm and the side of his ribcage. Robbie thought the young officer bore a striking resemblance to a young Jason Priestley from his *Beverly Hills 90210* days. The officer said nothing but managed a slow smile, making Robbie feel uneasy. For a moment, Robbie thought that the young cop would pull back and slug him. He observed the officer's tight leather gloves and thought about how much it would hurt both of them if the officer punched Robbie in the face. It then dawned on Robbie that the policeman must be staring at the embarrassing new hairs on his face. What made the situation even more tense was that the man, whom Robbie was fighting off the temptation to call *Officer Brandon Walsh*, was smiling.

Officer Carlson, thank you very much for finding humor in my misery.

"Have I d-done anything wrong, Officer Carlson?" he asked, sounding even more worried. Robbie had already acknowledged to himself that his own appearance was frightening, but the policeman didn't seem unnerved by it in the least. "If I've done anything wrong, Officer, I wish you'd just tell me what it was so we can get this over with. I was driving *with* traffic, not against. I wasn't on the sidewalk, I didn't come close to hitting any pedestrians, and I signaled when I turned onto Constitution, so…"

Finally the officer broke his long-standing silence. "Don't worry, sir. You didn't commit any *serious* moving violation. But you *are* aware that in the State of Connecticut it is illegal to ride a bicycle without a helmet."

"Oh, shit," began Robbie, "I-I mean, excuse me, Officer, Oh, man. I didn't know that. This is my first time riding. I just got this bike."

The officer paused, looked down and scraped one of his feet against the pavement, grinding the few pebbles that were under his booted foot into the road. "You don't look well, sir. Is everything all right?"

"Yes, Officer. Thank you. I'm just…just…uhm…" Robbie was at a loss, compounded with feeling completely mortified by his ghastly appearance.

"All right, sir. I'm going to give you a break. Since it's your… *first time* on a bike?"

"Uhm, well…"

"Let's just say, Mr. Taylor, that it's your first time riding *in town*."

"Yes." Robbie said with a sigh of relief quickly followed by a chuckle. He expressed his gratitude to the cop by offering him his hand. Carlson didn't accept it, his eyes still fixed on Robbie's. Robbie rescinded the gesture and thought to verbally thank the policeman instead. As he opened his mouth to speak, it registered in his mind that the Officer had addressed him as *Mr. Taylor.*

"How did you know my name?" asked Robbie, quickly thinking to himself if he should have dared to ask.

"Sir?" asked the officer, still grinning.

"You called me *Mr. Taylor.* How did you know my name if I never showed you my driver's license."

The officer put his helmet back on and followed it up with his wide-lens sunglasses. "Take care of yourself, Robbie Taylor." And with that, the officer turned to face his motorcycle. In an instant, Robbie noticed a pointy stinger-like follicle protruding from the officer's neck.

****

Robbie arrived at 87 Edison Court, the residence of Mr. & Mrs. Irvin & Elaine Meredith. As he dismounted the bike, he brushed his right buttock against his seat and reacted instinctively, expecting some consequential pain, but there came none. He breathed a sigh of relief and hastened toward the front door.

"What the hell am I doing here?" he asked himself as he reached for the doorbell with a bandaged index finger. Then he remembered the epiphany he'd had, making the connection between the protruding follicle on Mrs. Meredith's neck and his own sickening collection. Then there was the motorcycle cop who had the same strange hair poking out of *his* neck; the exact same area where Robbie had felt a burning sting on his own neck hours before.

He was just about to ring the bell when he noticed the front door had been left slightly ajar. He stopped and surveyed the narrow crack between the door and the jamb, and attempted to see inside the house.

"Hello?" called Robbie in a timid voice and quickly coughed to clear his throat. "Mrs. Meredith?" His voice was more confident now. "*Mr.* Meredith?"

The house seemed eerily quiet; deserted. Robbie pressed his hand against the red front door and gave one hard push. In an instant he was hit with that same putrid smell he'd sensed yesterday afternoon on the Turnpike. He cautiously covered his nose as he entered, trying not to hit any of his razor-sharp facial hairs.

"It's Robbie Taylor, Mrs. Meredith. Mr. Meredith? You're wife and I were involved in a slight fender bend…" he stopped and wondered if he should be blurting out his relationship with Meredith's wife. He wasn't sure if she had told her husband about the accident. She had been firm about not involving the police or the insurance companies. Perhaps her husband would kill her if he found out she'd rear ended some stranger on the highway.

After calling Mrs. Meredith by name twice more and getting no response, Robbie advanced further into the house. "Something strange is happening to me, Mrs. Meredith. Maybe we can compare notes. I noticed that you had something going on behind your neck and it looked exactly like what I have."

He crossed the foyer and came to the threshold of the living room. To Robbie's amazement, there in the center of the floor and pressed up tightly between the mahogany and glass coffee table and living room sofa was what appeared to be a large gray cocoon, its center split clean down from top to bottom. White smoke emanated slowly from the inside, which suggested that whatever crawled out of there did so not too long before.

Robbie's eyes were suddenly drawn to the grand piano to his left. Under the massive instrument's opened lid, resting on perfectly tuned strings, lay another cocoon, slightly larger and still sealed. The same white smoke, although less intense, slowly escaped from the sides of the pod.

Just then an insect-like leg littered with thousands of jagged cilia grabbed Robbie from behind and wrapped around his torso. Robbie gasped in surprise and followed it up with a scream as the pain registered from the serrated follicles penetrating his shirt and digging into his skin. Despite the tenderness of his new wounds, Robbie managed to turn around to face the monster. He could feel his skin tear as the cilia pulled out of the flesh from which it had taken hold. Before him stood a giant, hideous insect-like being measuring only three inches shorter than he. Robbie stumbled backwards and collided with the empty cocoon. He fell back and into it. The remaining smoke from inside escaped all at once and Robbie now found himself covered in a thick, lumpy, sticky, stinking pink goo that had the look and consistency of human vomit and wreaked of the same odor that Robbie had sensed the day before on I-95; only this time is was ten times more powerful and nauseating.

"JESUS CHRIST!" Robbie cried as he frantically hastened to escape the interior of the cocoon. His violent writhing collapsed the wall of the pod and the remaining goo inside spilled out onto the carpet. Robbie squirmed on his backside, feeling his own cilia pressing up against the skin of his back and ass, but the sharp ends remained pointed outwards. It was like one of those circus freaks who could lie on a bed of nails without registering any pain.

He frantically looked up in an attempt to locate the giant bug that was apparently trying to kill him. It was gone. Robbie got to his feet and immediately slipped on the cocoon's excrement and fell back into the shallow pool of sickening gunk. Some of it splashed onto his face and several slimy drops entered his extended mouth. The foul taste made Robbie gag but it did little good as he wound up swallowing it, resulting in him dry heaving several times. Had it not been for his empty stomach, Robbie would have added his own foul liquid to the alien glop in just one fruitful heave.

The monster that had seemingly absconded released its suction cup-like grip on the living room ceiling on which it had been clinging clandestinely, and landed, two repulsive-looking thin, cilia-littered legs on either side of Robbie's head. It descended its head downward and the spiky proboscis, which protruded out from between its more-than-a dozen lifelessly black eyes would have buried deep into Robbie's head had he not moved out of its way just in time. The sheer momentum of the stinger burying into the floor caused it to become jammed. The alien insect began to squeal acutely and shift violently back and forth in a frantic effort to free itself from the floor, into which nearly a quarter of the proboscis had been submerged.

Thinking quickly, Robbie went to the fireplace and took up an iron poker. Then he ran up behind the struggling creature and shoved the spear through its back. The weapon pierced the beast's heart before exiting through its chest. The creature collapsed dead onto its side and the proboscis snapped in half, leaving roughly two feet of alien snout standing in the center of the Merediths' living room.

About its gray hairy alien neck hung the exact same string of pearls that Robbie had seen on Mrs. Meredith. Suddenly it all came clear to him.

This creature *was* Mrs. Meredith!

4

Christ! Robbie Taylor thought as he shoved the slimy alien carcass into the oversized plastic yard bag he'd taken from the Merediths' garage. *If this thing is what I have to look forward to seeing tomorrow morning in my bathroom mirror, I'll swallow the entire stock of cleaning products the Merediths got underneath their kitchen sink right now!*

He hastened to finish and be out of the house before whatever lay dormant in the piano's cocoon came out. He surmised Mr. Meredith was inside the pod but didn't want to stick around long enough to confirm it. Robbie even joked about it, betting himself ten bucks that it would crawl out of the piano wearing a yarmulke and a men's Rolex watch.

The key to Mrs. Meredith's white Mercedes lay in a large glass bowl on a wooden stand by the front door. Remembering how the sharp cilia on his ass hadn't afflicted him in the least when he'd fallen onto his backside just minutes before, Robbie figured he'd take a chance on driving. Normally he wasn't the *steal the first luxury vehicle that falls into your lap* kinda guy, but the opportunity presented itself in the most convenient way. He didn't think the Merediths' children, if indeed they had any, would make as much a fuss about a missing Mercedes when the living room looked as if an orgy of bulimics had decided to crash for the night.

****

By the time Robbie arrived at the front gate of Yale University, the rank stench of the alien insect corpse had seeped from the trunk into the cabin of the Mercedes. It was all he could do to keep from gasping for air as he rolled down the window to speak to the campus policeman stationed at the entrance. *Another uniformed asshole carrying a pistol*, thought Robbie, and remembered his bizarre encounter with the motorcycle cop. Hoping this exchange would be anything but confrontational, Robbie tightened his hold on the steering wheel as the guard approached. As the unsuspecting man leaned forward toward the opened window of the Mercedes, the odor hit him hard and he withdrew quickly, covering his nose and mouth with the crook of his arm.

"Sorry," said Robbie. "I know it's pretty bad. We tied on one too many last night and a buddy of mine hurled his cookie batter all over my backseat. I tried getting an appointment to have the car detailed, but they said I'd have to wait three days. Something about the right shampoo to clean good quality Mercedes leather not being in stock. Now I ask you, what is the difference between good leather and shitty leather when you're dealing with shampoo? I mean, if you've got leather seats in your Honda, does that mean they use substandard shampoo?"

The guard observed the odd-looking visitor in the fetid Mercedes. As nauseas as the smell made him, he seemed equally repulsed by the black thorn-like hairs sticking out of Robbie's cheeks. Still breathing through his sleeve, the campus policeman threw a guest parking permit decal at the visitor, landing with precision on the edge of his knee. Robbie took it in one hand and waved at the guard with the other as the security swing arm lifted, giving the Mercedes open access to the campus of Yale University.

5

"Holy mother of shit, Robbie!" exclaimed Luther Milton as he helped his friend drag in the large black plastic bag from the parking lot. "I told you to call on me any time you were in trouble, but...*your face*! What the hell happened to it?"

Luther Milton was a friend of Robbie Taylor's as far back as Robbie could remember. Although he always relied on Luther to relate the story of how the two had initially met, it didn't diminish the bond they shared, nor the affection Robbie had for his one and only African-American friend.

Milton was studying Molecular Genetic Pathology at Yale with a keen interest in hematology. To help pay for his Ivy League education, he doubled as part-time assistant to one of the professors within the Department of Sciences, Dr. Helmut Bohe, a German-born geneticist and certifiable misanthrope. Although Bohe treated Luther Milton much like a Neo-Nazi would treat a retarded gay African Jew, Luther knew not to let his anger get the better of him. After all, his future hung in the balance. Luther was basically Bohe's patsy, dropping whatever he was working on, no matter how fragile or important, to run menial errands, ranging from filling Dunkin' Donuts requests to picking up his dry cleaning. He pretended to not understand when Bohe called him a *Schwartze*, although Luther Milton knew the Kraut was essentially calling him a *darkie*. Luther would also turn a blind eye to Bohe's less-than hygienic habits. He'd see the scientist pick his nose and then spread the slimy boogers into Petri dishes for others to find. Usually it would be Luther who'd discover the snotty lumps and swiftly discard them, making sure to use latex gloves as he did so.

In Luther's first semester, Dr. Garret MacDonald, Chair of the Science Department, introduced Luther Milton to Dr. Bohe. The latter held no punches, remarking how minorities were *"taking oaffer all zat vas Iffee Leak!"* and speculated on the inevitable end of a white majority in the student body. Being the prestigious Ph.D of Genetics, having won the Nobel Prize in Biology back in 1993, Yale and its administrators turned a blind eye and a deaf ear to all of Dr. Bohe's disgusting habits and bigoted rants. Even Luther Milton, who resented these high office holders for their tolerance of Bohe, felt equally disappointed in himself for precisely the same thing. He knew what it would take for a man of his background to get to where he wanted to go, and the price was a hell of a lot of ass-kissing.

The whole Science wing of the campus, much like the rest of Yale University, would be deserted for another two weeks, after which the entire student body that was majoring in their respective branches of science would return. Robbie could not have planned the timing any better. With a limited number of campus police about, along with Luther Milton and the occasional janitor skulking around, the place was utterly deserted. Robbie realized this bit of good fortune as the Mercedes made its way down Academic Road.

Guess I don't have to worry about some collegiate fucker poking his nose into the wrong garbage bag, discover what mankind has been surmising for decades, and find himself on David Letterman!

They hoisted the bag onto the table, and, with a scissor that he'd had taken from one of the lab drawers, Luther began slicing open the garbage bag in which lay the remains of the alien. As Luther cut the bag, the resulting gash reminded Robbie of the slit atop the alien cocoon out of which he imagined the insect-like extraterrestrial had crawled, or perhaps leapt.

"What the fuck is this shit?" hissed Luther Milton as the smell hit both men. Robbie backed up, but Luther remained still. Working with cadavers and necrotic organs, Luther was no stranger to foul stenches, and this was no different. "And why is it wearing...*pearls*?" he asked, incredulously.

"I think the cop that pulled me over this morning might be in the same boat." said Robbie, in an attempt to avoid connecting Mrs. Meredith and Officer Carlson to himself. Robbie figured the cop might be closer to turning into one of these beasts than he was, since Carlson had been acting very strangely and had *known* Robbie's name. He wondered if these giant bugs could possibly be mind readers, or at least that their intelligence far exceeded that of a human being. He also presumed that his own transformation might be ahead of Carlson's, as Robbie's change was more apparent. He considered how Carlson knew what he did and at the same time felt a sudden onset of panic not unlike what he'd felt earlier that morning.

"He also had something like what she, well, *it* has all over her, *its* body." explained Robbie to Luther Milton.

"So what are you telling me, Robbie?" asked Luther Milton, angrily. "Are you telling me that this...this...*thing* tried to kill you? You're standing there with your face looking like a porcupine's asshole, telling me that you caught some kinda giant prehistoric Amazon mosquito?"

Robbie approached the table on which the dead thing lay spread out and inert. "Amazon my ass! Look at it, Luther. It's like nothing you or I have ever seen before. Maybe *no one* has ever seen it before. This thing might be from another world!"

Luther dropped the scissors and backed away from both his friend and the corpse. "I refuse to go there, Robbie. In my church, we don't blaspheme and say there are other worlds out there. Because if there *are* other worlds, then what does that say about God? No sir, I ain't going there." Luther Milton hastened toward his friend, a mixture of fear and anger in his eyes. "Why the hell did you bring this in here for anyway?" His voice went down to a whisper. "Why do you need to be coming to me with this shit? If it *is* from another world, you need to forget about it then. Bury it and never talk about it again! Why involve me?"

"Because you're a scientist, Luther," said Robbie, sounding desperate. "Can't you just examine it?"

"And what do you think I'm gonna find?"

Robbie shook his head in confusion. "I thought a scientist would jump at this. It's the opportunity of a lifetime! I figured you'd be thrilled at the chance to perform a real honest to God alien autopsy. It'd validate what all those SETI and Area 51 conspiracy theory junkies have been saying for decades."

"I told you to stop saying that word." hissed Luther.

"What word?"

"*Alien*. We don't know that yet. This might not be anything more than a horsefly on steroids or something. And my area of science is genetics. What made you think I could tell you anything about this shit?"

"I figured science is science." said Robbie in a cynical tone.

"Why aren't you excited about this? Do you think I'm playing some sort of fucked up trick on you? An early Halloween prank? You think I'm waiting to cry *April Fool*? I wish I could take all this back, Luther. I wish I didn't have this crap poking out of my face. I wish I didn't have to worry myself to death that I might be turning into one of those things. I wish I could just go back to yesterday afternoon before any of this shit happened."

Robbie couldn't take it anymore. His face now grimacing and his nasal orifice trembling, he fell back onto a chair and cried, momentarily putting his hands to his face and then recoiling in pain as the sharp cilia dug into his palms, resulting in several new puncture wounds. He got to his feet and went over to the first aid kit and removed a role of gauze.

"Look at me, Luther." pleaded Robbie as he wrapped his hands in the dressing. "I have to know what I'm turning into. I think Mrs. Meredith may have been stung by some creature whose bite transformed her into one of them. Maybe the cop is next, or maybe I am. I dunno. I also felt a pinch behind my neck last night that hurt like a mother. For all I know I could be the next Mrs. Meredith or the next Officer Carlson. I could wake up tomorrow inside a cocoon. OK, if you don't want to believe it's an alien, think then that it may be some new species whose discovery *you* could take credit for! If it makes you feel all warm and tingly inside, just think it's that. But I'll tell you this, I've been trying to make heads or tails of it all since I left Mrs. Meredith's house. It makes sense, Luther! If you think that a bite from some mystery species of insect can cause a person to transform into a human-sized version of the parasite, then it all fits."

Luther stayed quiet for several seconds, and when he finally opened his mouth, Robbie thought his friend was going to say something, but Luther only sighed. Robbie got up and pulled down his shorts and underwear, bent over and showed Luther his backside.

"I normally don't like to moon my friends, Luther, but you leave me very little choice." When Robbie redressed, he turned to face Luther, expecting the man's expression to show more sympathy than repulsion, but Luther just nodded slowly with a look of disgust.

"All right, Robbie," acquiesced Luther, I'll help your pointy white ass."

Both men managed a slight laugh, but neither man was genuine in his cheer. "Leave it here and I'll cut the smelly bitch open and tell you if I find anything that might shed some light on the situation. But you owe me big, buddy. We're talking an extra round at happy hour for the next ten years."

Robbie felt a huge relief in hearing Luther's words. He knew that any discovery Luther made, if any, wouldn't change things for Robbie. But at least Robbie could go to his grave, or his cocoon as it were, knowing more than he did at that very moment in the science wing at Yale University.

****

"WAS IST DAS?" shouted Dr. Helmut Bohe as he entered the deserted lab where Robbie and Luther had been just an hour earlier. The stench of the insect corpse made being in the room unbearable. "MILTON!" cried Dr. Bohe in his heavy German accent. "Vere is zat Schwartze?" Bohe hurried to one of the lab windows and quickly threw open the sash. Then he hastened over to the air conditioning unit in the wall and turned it off. "As hot as it is," he began, "keeping ziss on vill only make zings vorse."

As he turned around, Dr. Bohe noticed the bag on the center table of the lab. He slowly approached it, wheezing and taking out an unused napkin he'd taken from the diner where he'd had his breakfast earlier. He leaned slightly forward, and his gaze met with the hideous face of the giant gray insect. He counted fifteen dime-sized black eyes, which were arranged in three rows of five. In addition to this, he perceived a proboscis of approximately two feet in length whose point appeared to be splintered. Its tiny mouth was partially opened and out of it hung a bright red tongue, thin and flat like that of a serpent, yet its tip was not forked. It had two teeth, one on the top of its mouth and one on the bottom. They were large, white, serrated and triangle-shaped like that of a shark. It had six legs, whose thousands of black hairs lining them appeared coarse and sharp. This was the last thing Dr. Bohe saw. Three seconds later, a large black hand grabbed his face, while the other took hold of the back of his head. Luther Milton, using a fraction of his newfound alien strength, twisted his boss's neck around 180 degrees, killing Bohe instantly.

****

The high-pitched frequency of the language used between Luther Milton and the recipient of his call on the walkie-talkie had the staccato of Morse code and the acute tone of nails racing feverishly up and down a chalkboard. Luther Milton stood over Dr. Bohe's body as he shrieked into the wireless radio he'd purloined from the guard whom he'd killed minutes before at the entrance. The language used was completely understood by Luther's party. Simultaneously, Milton lit a match and threw it into the garbage bag that contained the remains of the alien Mrs. Meredith. The flammable ooze from the insect's body ignited instantly. Within minutes the entire lab was ablaze, but by then Luther Milton had already vanished.

6

On his fourth attempt at calling Luther, Robbie gave up and tossed his cell phone onto the passenger seat of Mrs. Meredith's white Mercedes. He'd been circling for the last few hours, anxiously awaiting word from his intellectual friend, hoping the latter would be able to shed some light on the dead giant insect and perhaps on his own fate.

It was around noon, and staring at himself through the rear-view mirror, he knew his face was getting progressively worse. He glanced left to the driver's side mirror, paranoid that the same motorcycle cop from earlier that morning would pull him over and this time either arrest or shoot him. As he contemplated this, a scarier scenario played itself out in Robbie's mind: Officer Carlson would casually state another fact about him that he shouldn't have known.

Hello, Robbie Taylor, the motorcycle cop would greet him, *I know you jerked off five times last week; once in your shower, three times in your bed and once in your car while eating leftover pizza on your way home from work.*

"Call me back, Luther," Robbie pleaded. "Where in God's name are you? You *always* have your cell phone on you."

Robbie let his imagination get the better of him. He imagined the creature on the examination table somehow coming back to life while Luther had his back to it. Before Luther could turn around, Robbie envisioned the monster pouncing on his friend, much like it had almost pounced on *him*. In his mind's eye he could see the beast grab onto Luther's neck with its sharp incisors and rip open his carotid artery. Robbie's imagination was as vivid as it was paranoid. He could envision his best friend convulsing briefly on the floor as a sea of red pooled outward from his body. This sent Robbie into a panic.

"Jesus!" cried Robbie and frantically tried to make a U-turn to head back to the campus. At first he ventured to make a U-turn in the middle of oncoming traffic like they do on reruns of 80's primetime shows. As he attempted the illegal turn, everything loose in the car's cabin shifted to the right. His wallet, which he had placed beside the gear shift, briefly became airborne and landed in the space between the passenger seat and the door.

"If anything's happened to him I'll never forgive myself," he said, grinding his teeth.

Robbie seized the opportunity to turn into a vacant lot. As he did so, a siren wailed behind him. He hadn't noticed the NO LEFT TURN sign suspended next to the traffic light until after the fact. Robbie squeezed the steering wheel and took a deep breath. He was too scared to look through the rearview mirror, but he assumed the worst when, just like earlier, he heard the sound of boot heels clicking hard on the pavement. And they were getting louder with every step.

Suddenly everything went black. When he awakened, fettered atop a gurney in the middle of a cold dark room four hours later, the left turn he'd made was the first thing Robbie thought about, because it had been the last thing he'd remembered.

7

"Mr. Taylor?" a voice called out politely from behind the darkness. Robbie's eyelids were heavy and his head was swimming as it swayed slowly to and fro. His mind began to clear somewhat and his eyes slowly adjusted to the soft light. He noticed the skin on his face, back and buttocks was now itching. He fidgeted on the table in an attempt to use his weight and the friction from the movement to scratch at it. Due to his dazed state, he didn't much care if this plan would result in his bleeding to death. He convinced himself that an itch that bad and that widespread was worse than the most agonizing pain the human body could ever drum up.

"Mr. Taylor!" the voice called out again, this time more assertively but still not losing its polite cadence. The accent was unquestionably English. For a moment, Robbie thought Colin Firth might have been speaking to him. It dawned on him not too long after things started coming together that he'd somehow lost time between his last memory of turning into the vacant lot and now.

"I've no doubt you can hear me, Mr. Taylor. You need not speak if you feel frightened. Just acknowledge my voice with a nod of your head so that I know you can understand me."

Robbie nodded slowly.

"Excellent, Mr. Taylor." replied the voice as the lights in the room slowly came on. Robbie felt a sharp pain in his temples as the offending brightness quickly caused his pupils to dilate.

"W-where…" began Robbie, weakly; his throat hoarse from dehydration and his stomach burning from malnourishment.

"You aren't far from home, Mr. Taylor."

"Home?" he asked, faintly.

"Yes. Although home as you know it will be utterly unrecognizable to you before too long. Everything you know will be at an end. And with it a new beginning."

Suddenly the portal at the end of the room slid away and in walked Luther Milton, his legs spread abnormally outward as he strode. His posture was crooked as one shoulder was raised, pressing against his ear.

"Luther." Robbie whispered weakly. "Dude. Help m…"

But Robbie was stifled by a sight that would haunt any man for the rest of his days, no matter how brave he claimed to be. His friend began to morph before his very eyes. Morph in the sense that Luther's features were gradually changing. His eyes slowly began to bulge out of their sockets and his left one even turned slightly away as though he were looking in that direction without turning his head. If Luther were white, he might have resembled Marty Feldman in the days when the actor's appearance was almost iconic in American pop culture. The eye sockets were now starting to spew blood and sounded like a tomato being slowly squashed. The force was so great that suddenly a flow of blood spewed onto the opposite wall clear across the room. Robbie's face wasn't spared from being pissed on with Luther's blood either. It looked as if someone had slammed their hand down hard onto a packet of ketchup and Robbie's face just happened to be in the way of the ejecting condiment.

Before he could react, Robbie witnessed Luther's skin become simultaneously inundated with thousands of razor-sharp cilia. From the bridge of his nose Luther's face slowly split in half. It sounded wet and tendon-shredding all at once. What lay under Luther's human skin was something horrifying to Robbie, but expected, nonetheless. It revealed a gray insect-like face that was identical to the giant bug that had been the former Mrs. Meredith. Robbie's first thought was that the insect had come back to life as he'd feared and had done something to Luther that caused him to become one of them.

Luther's human eyes were now melting right out of their detached sockets and his skin dripped off steaming hot like coffee brewing over its pot. His stinger, previously concealed under his human face was now slowly extending outward into a horizontal position.

Robbie's terror got the better of him and he shrieked, frantically trying to pull out of the constraints that kept him immobile on the gurney. "WHAT ARE YOU DOING TO HIM, YOU BASTARDS?" cried Robbie. "WHAT THE FUCK ARE YOU PEOPLE?"

Now completely insect, the being formerly known as Luther Milton approached Robbie. The beast's head was still cocked to one side, but as the rest of Luther's human body had also liquefied away and his clothes with it, Robbie could see that there was nothing left to resemble shoulders. In fact, the entire frame of this being was entirely pest, complete with giant thorax, two antennae reaching three feet past the top of the thing's head, their tips scraping sharply against the ceiling. Robbie counted six slender legs boasting thousands of those same sharp cilia with which he himself was plagued. The sight of this hideous beast terrified Robbie to such an extreme that he lost control of his bowels. Hot, near liquid feces made contact with his skin. The stench of the creature, coupled with his own excrement would have made Robbie puke, had it not been for the fact that his stomach was completely empty. Instead he dry heaved as he had done earlier at the Merediths' residence.

The creature formerly known as Luther Milton leaned down and fixed all fifteen of its alien eyes on Robbie's two human ones. Robbie's horror was at its peak. He felt his heart ready to burst as the diarrhea oozed out of his shorts and fell in drips and drabs to the floor. He tensed his body as much as he could in an attempt to break free of the gurney's restraints. As he did so, the alien being that was once Luther Milton retreated gradually. Its putrid stench subsided somewhat as the creature reached the far corner of the chamber. This afforded Robbie room enough to bring his torso slightly up. As he did so, he caught sight of a figure moving in the doorway.

It was Officer Carlson, the motorcycle cop who'd pulled him over on Constitution Avenue, and again, Robbie now remembered, after he'd made that illegal left turn. The strikingly handsome policeman was still dressed in his uniform, minus the sunglasses and white dome helmet. Carlson's slight smile and casual demeanor greatly alarmed Robbie. The fact that a man in law enforcement could appear to be so unconcerned that a civilian was indubitably being held against his will made Robbie immediately distrust the officer.

"Please do not be afraid, Mr. Taylor", said Officer Carlson in his unfamiliar accent, "I tell you, no one will harm you. Do you believe me? *No one* will harm you."

"Dear God!" cried Robbie. "You're one of them too, aren't you? You're gonna fall apart and out of you is gonna pop one of those goddamn things! Oh, God! MY GOD!"

Officer Carlson guffawed, causing Robbie to once again attempt to break through his restraints.

"Not quite, Mr. Taylor. Although I might seem god-like to you. I *am* beautiful to you and your kind, am I not? You can say it. It wouldn't be the first time I've heard it."

No less tense, but growing curious, Robbie relaxed and fell back on the gurney.

"I-I don't understand." cried Robbie. "I don't know what's going on. What is this all about? What's happening to us?"

Robbie looked over to the creature once known as Luther Milton and called him by name several times as spittle dripped from his quivering lips onto his chin.

Officer Carlson ignored Robbie's babbling and slowly drew closer to him. As he did, his patrol boot heels clicked loudly on the floor, echoing loudly against the naked walls. The beast formerly known as Luther Milton who had initially advanced several paces toward the gurney withdrew once again, this time subserviently, as if bowing before Carlson.

"I'm sure you have many questions, Mr. Taylor. And I shall do my level best to answer them for you. I suppose you've already ascertained from everything you've seen today that neither I, nor Luther, nor your Mrs. Meredith, are what you would call *human*. And that quite soon, you too will join this elite club."

"I figured that out pretty goddamn easily, I suppose." said Robbie bravely, finding courage he didn't know he had. "What the hell are you people? Ha! People! Look who I'm calling *people*! Why don't *you* stink like the others?" He glanced over to the giant insect in the corner and moaned. "And what the fuck did you do to Luther?"

Carlson brought his tight black gloved hand up to Robbie and pressed a single leather-clad digit over Robbie's lips.

"Shhhhh. Quiet down, Mr. Taylor, and I shall reveal all to you."

Robbie had little choice but to do as he was told. Joining both gloved hands behind his back as he paced the floor, Officer Carlson began his story.

8

"I was much like you are now, Mr. Taylor: a young male of his species, decent and congenial, but headstrong and ever so ambitious. Relatively speaking, I was not at all wicked, and there was nothing exceptional about me. But ambition shaped my character and I was always determined to have things my own way."

Carlson paused and looked down at his feet. For a brief moment, Robbie thought that would be the end of the officer's sermon.

"My world was dying, you see. It was only a matter of time before…"

Carlson stopped again, looked away from Robbie and walked toward the portal as though he were going to leave. He stopped short of exiting the room, stayed in place, and continued.

"We weren't a civilization like here on Earth. We were what you'd call *primitive* in terms of technological advancement. We had no machinery and no modern conveniences of any kind. We merely lived off other beings. It was a simple enough existence, feeding on host after host, and they'd go on living as did we. That was the way of things for eons. And slowly, very gradually in fact, we began to evolve, as do all species. Yet our kind evolved in a very special way; a very special way indeed. You see, our biology far exceeded anything found here on earth. We had advanced from minute organisms, much like humans have, into large, powerful beings in a mere one million years. The eldest and wisest among us never knew why, but every generation seemed to improve and grow stronger than the last. Their parents' parents told them of vulnerabilities with which previous generations had been born, and so on. And this was the way of things for ages and ages. Toward the end of my world's existence, my species no longer needed to procreate in the traditional way, as we could make contact with a host and clone ourselves to it. And yet we continued to procreate for obvious reasons."

"What obvious reason?" Robbie said weakly.

"TO CONTINUE TO STRENGTHEN THE SPECIES!" cried Officer Carlson, and to Robbie it sounded like Carlson might be trying to hold back tears. "We had become able to use our stingers to eject our own seed into a host organism." continued Officer Carlson, sounding calmer. He opened a gloved hand and in it sat a tiny gray insect with two large gray eyes and a gray hairy back. It turned its head slightly from left to right until it noticed Robbie lying prostrate on the gurney. Robbie's fear increased dramatically the instant the alien bug fixed its eyes on him. He remembered seeing an insect identical to this one the day before on his car window, the one that seemed to be watching him.

"This organism is injected into the host. It plants deeply into the host's own DNA. It travels the host's entire body, killing off cells and replacing them with our own. Just as it did with Mrs. Meredith, your friend Luther...and *you*, Mr. Taylor.

"Fuck!" cried Robbie.

"You've really got to keep your window screens better sealed, Mr. Taylor. Anything can get into your house, even my little seed." Carlson lifted his hand until the tiny insect was beside his ear.

"This is like some kind of fucking sci-fi horror movie!" cried

Robbie, once again joggling around atop the gurney and grunting angrily.

"I assure you, Mr. Taylor, it was a way of simply controlling nature and our surroundings. In my life, I had never seen any other living organism on my world. By then we had become completely and utterly homogeneous. In fact, it was the generation before that of my great grandparents that eradicated the fireflies. But these weren't what you here on Earth call *lightning bugs*. These fireflies were what caused fire on our world. There were no matches or lighters or the primitive practice of rubbing two sticks together. Our species couldn't create fire. It was an element impossible to create, completely foreign and practically useless to us. And so that element was always left up to the fireflies. At that time, our species could touch, hold, even lick flames that radiated from a blaze if we so wished. My people could not be hurt at all by it as yours could. But as time went on, these fireflies multiplied exponentially and developed into a menace. These pests caused most of our world's vegetation and forests to burn. The very air was becoming toxic to us. In other words, Mr. Taylor, they became a threat to our own existence. So we hunted them. It took eight generations, but they were ultimately eradicated, and, with it, the element of fire became extinct as well. Within a few more generations, my generation that is, the biology of our species evolved to be completely alien to the element. I say, the two became completely incompatible."

Robbie considered what Carlson meant by *incompatible*. As the word left the officer's lips, it resounded over and over in Robbie's head as he once again struggled to break free from the gurney. His throat began to burn as acid from his constricting stomach made its way up his esophagus. It was all Robbie could do to keep from spitting up sour gastric juice. Carlson was growing weary of Robbie's disrespect and lack of attention and so walked over to him and squeezed several of the follicles that littered Robbie's left cheek. Robbie cried in excruciating agony as Carlson pulled at the hairs. Yellow puss began to squirt from beneath the root of the hairs and stained the officer's leather glove.

"You be still, slave." whispered Carlson. "Now then, where was I? Oh, yes. I was at the part where I proved how effective my species was at obliterating other life forms."

He released Robbie's cheek, walked backwards a few steps and continued.

"Because life changed so drastically on my world, it was inevitable that nature began to change. Rain became a thing of the past. Could it have had to do with the extinction of fire? Who could say for certain? We were a faithless race, so the wrath of a vengeful god was never a consideration. Our vegetation soon died out, and I watched as our ocean dried up within a few hundred of your years. And then, as if drought and the loss of our oceans might have caused it to do so, our enormous moon fell from its orbit. I managed to escape from my world before the apocalypse. I don't know if others were as lucky. Maybe some others survived. I don't know and never shall. The universe is infinite.

"As I've mentioned, at the time of the demise of my world, my species was already remarkable. We were able to take to flight fifty generations before, and able to break out of our thick atmosphere and travel into space twenty generations before. And please bear in mind, Mr. Taylor, that a generation among my species is several thousands of your years! I witnessed the destruction of my world as I looked back and saw the moon crash into my planet. Both were obliterated. Everything and everyone I had ever known were gone forever: my friends, my family, *my parents*. And so on my own, alone and frightened, I traveled through the galaxy for hundreds, maybe even a thousand of your years, looking for a new home. I found two worlds before coming here. Within half a millennium, I left them both barren and dead. My thirst for survival became my one abiding concern. And although my species is not reliant on nourishment for an indefinite amount of time, my appetite got the better of me, and I ate my way through those worlds until all life was no more."

"You ate them?" asked Robbie, incredulously. "You ate *every* living thing?"

"As I told you, my appetite got the better of me."

Robbie looked utterly astounded and Carlson knew exactly what the human was thinking.

"Fear not, Mr. Taylor. I eat on a normal basis. And your kind is not in my diet. I admit that if hungry enough, I *would* resort to eating human beings. In fact, as I did on those other worlds, I could eat every living thing on the planet Earth. It might take awhile, but I've done it before, and could certainly do it again! But my appetite was satiated long before I arrived on your planet; wiping out a species for nourishment and survival was no longer a consideration. My purpose for coming here was to find a new home where I could thrive, and where I could reestablish *my* species."

It became clear to Robbie with Carlson's last words what the alien was planning.

"And you will be our glorious leader," stated Robbie evenly.

"Naturally." said Carlson with a grin. "I shall be the benevolent savior who brought his species back from near extinction! I shall be the new god of this world, and all its faiths will merge into one to worship a deity that they can see and hear. I am truly a divine being who has made his children in his own image. You certainly can't dispute that, now can you, Mr. Taylor?"

"Kill me now, then!" spat Robbie. "I'd rather be a rotting corpse in the ground than look like one of those things." He pointed with his chin to the corner of the room where the beast formerly known as Luther Milton was squirming in place.

"You'll feel much differently once you morph out of your human skin," said Carlson calmly. "Just as your Luther and Mrs. Meredith. Once I command you to change into your new state. It will be at my beckoning. In my own good time, not yours. Patience, little creature. Why should you resist? Your life will be endless. You must have surmised by now that I am eternal. Our species evolved into immortals a dozen generations before the destruction of my planet. Age plays no part in our existence! Once I arrived here, I rested. I crash landed into one of your seas and slept for two centuries miles beneath the waves of the Aegean. When I awoke, I made it to land and there, in Athens, did I chose a host. Yes, that is why you see me in this form. I am able to reverse the cloning process and morph into any host. I chose wisely by your standards - this young, handsome, sinewy man by your standards. The only difference is that I shall not age. The way you see me is the way I have been and always shall be while in my human state.

"Of course, I shan't stay in this hideous body much longer.

Mankind's reckoning is close at hand! And there's nothing you can do about it, Mr. Taylor."

Taking the small insect he'd been holding between his thumb and index finger, Officer Carlson brought it up to his right nostril and inhaled deeply through his nose. The insect was instantly sucked up like dust by a vacuum cleaner. Carlson then gave his back to Robbie, and Robbie could hear him begin to heave, making brief, disjointed, acute noises that sounded like subway brakes screeching to a halt.

This sound made Robbie tense his body so severely against the gurney's restraints that the largest and most constraining of the belts finally succumbed. The alien leader was unaware of this as was the alien formerly known as Luther Milton, who had been gawking dutifully at his distressing master.

Without turning to face Robbie, Carlson added, "It's only a matter of time, Mr. Taylor. The metamorphosis has begun. By morning, you will be one of thousands who will have morphed into one of us. It will be a virtual domino effect. By Tuesday there will be thousands more, and by Thursday, perhaps a million. And so on, and on and on..."

Carlson walked slowly out of the room, never once looking back at Robbie, and continuing in a curiously somber voice, "...and on and on and on..."

9

With very little time left, Robbie Taylor knew he had to somehow stop Officer Carlson from taking over the world. The survival of the human race hung in the balance, and he'd been made acutely aware that he was the only person who knew it. With the center strap now loose atop his arms, Robbie could move his hands just enough to undo the second and last strap, which was still holding him down at the pelvis. But he had to be careful, for the creature formerly known as Luther Milton still had all fifteen black eyes fixed on its prisoner.

"Hey, Milton!" Robbie called out playfully. "You know you never looked better? You really should go find a mirror and see the improvement!" The colossal bug cocked his wide head even more than it already had been as if beckoning Robbie to repeat his insult. "Yeah, man," continued Robbie, "your face wasn't too pretty before. You got a cosmetic upgrade, but man, do you stink!" The thing formerly known as Luther Milton slowly drew nearer to Robbie. Its long narrow legs dragged on the floor as it approached and Robbie could detect its foul odor growing stronger. "Come on, big boy! called Robbie. "That's it! Come to daddy!"

The alien reached the side of Robbie's gurney just in time for Robbie to lunge up and heave in the monster's vicinity. Robbie made the alien's stench work in his favor. The odor was so rank and so intense that Robbie's stomach contracted violently, as he knew it would, and spewed several ounces worth of acidic gastric juice right into the beast's fifteen eyes, momentarily blinding it.

The insect screamed in a shrill pitch and withdrew in agony. Robby yanked one arm free of the last strap and untied the other. Then he sat up on the gurney, pulled his right hand back, made a tight fist and delivered as hard a blow as he could to the alien's fifteen eyes, mindful to avoid impacting the menacingly long and powerful proboscis. Two of Robbie's solid knuckles landed with such accuracy into two eyes that the lenses ruptured and spewed black glop into Robbie's face. The animal shrieked again and fell backwards to the floor. Robbie leapt up, stepped onto the gurney and lunged forward, landing both feet firmly on the alien's upper head. The impact instantly crushed the beast's soft skull, pulverizing the brain. As a result, stinking pink goo discharged from the smashed cavity. Luckily for Robbie he landed in a way so that his behind cleared the erect proboscis by mere inches.

With the head alien still at large, Robbie needed to formulate a plan and quickly. His physical body aside, he knew that once his own metamorphosis was at hand, his brain would also morph into mindless capitulation and obedience to Officer Carlson. While he still had all his faculties, he needed to foil Carlson's master plan and defeat him.

He took a quick inventory of the items he had in his shorts pocket. His wallet was gone. Then he remembered it falling out of sight after his failed attempt at a U-turn. He continued digging and pulled out a crushed packet of cigarettes, his lighter and two quarters.

"Damn it!" he exclaimed. "Where's my cell phone?"

He slowly approached the opened portal, stuck his head ever so slightly through it and looked up and down the corridor. His eyes caught sight of something to his left. It looked to be a small mechanical device. It was his cell phone, completely smashed, no doubt having fallen victim to a swift stomp by Officer Carlson's patrol boot.

The floor seemed makeshift, uneven and apparently comprised of various metal parts fused together. Even still, his steps resounded noisily, He removed his sneakers and hung them from two curled fingers. Now in his socks, Robbie felt the lack of traction under his feet working against him. He slid several times on the bumpy metal and wound up falling on his ass. If he were grateful for anything at that moment, it was that his fall was more quiet than noisy.

Tossing both sneakers to the side, Robbie thought it more prudent to crawl through the rest of the space that there was between him and possible freedom. But freedom from this place, whatever it was, meant nothing if he couldn't stop Carlson. Robbie knew it would only be a matter of time before his own eyes turned to liquefying vanilla ice cream and his face split clear down the center. Carlson had to be defeated and time was of the essence. Not just for Robbie, he thought, but for all humanity. It seemed ridiculous to Robbie that he was Man's savior, but it could hardly be disputed. He knew what no other man knew. What's more, he had new knowledge about this menace that he hadn't known before, and he was hoping to exploit it before it was too late for him.

As Robbie reached the end of the corridor, he was startled by a slow muffled clapping sound. He turned around slowly. Standing there was Officer Carlson with a fiendish look on his face. The light from above the corridor illuminated half of Carlson's face at such an angle that it looked like a deliberate pose that a photographer might ask his model to strike during a photo shoot. Although Robbie Taylor hadn't one homosexual bone in his body, he thought that Carlson had perhaps the most handsome, manly face he'd ever seen, even if the creature beneath it was the most hideous thing he'd ever laid eyes on before.

"That was quite a performance in there, Mr. Taylor." Carlson leisurely drew closer to Robbie, and Robbie in turn backed up slowly. "Poor Luther. How could you do that to your best friend?"

"That wasn't my friend. You saw to that yourself."

"You can't stop it, Mr. Taylor. It's spreading like wildfire."

Wildfire.

This word resounded in Robbie's head.

"Right now, people are infected as far west as Kenosha, Wisconsin, as far north as Toronto, Canada, as far south as Taloola, Mississippi, and as far east as Holly, New Hampshire. Just let it happen, Mr. Taylor. Embrace it!"

"NEVER! cried Robbie. "I'll never turn into one of you."

Just then, Robbie's knees began to feel weak and his head began to throb. His face began itching again, more severely than before. He brought his once bandaged fingertips up to his cheeks and felt his skin crawling as the alien follicles began to dance rhythmically back and forth like tentacles on a coral reef.

"W-what's happening to m-me?" cried Robbie.

Carlson grinned. "It's happening."

"What?"

"Your metamorphosis is at hand, Mr. Taylor. It was only a matter of time. And now that time has come. It won't be too long now. You can do it gradually as Mrs. Meredith, spinning a cocoon and going at your leisure, or do as I commanded Luther Milton and forgo the pod.

The latter is much more painful. But as feisty as you are, I believe you'd do better to go the faster, more agonizing route. I think you've earned it."

"No, please!" beckoned Robbie, succumbing to the weakness of his legs and falling to the floor. He felt his back and ass crawl in a synchronized dancing itch. *"I-I give in. I am yours, master. Please! Spare me anymore pain!"*

Carlson appeared satisfied. He slowly approached Robbie until the toes of his boots were touching Robbie's fingertips.

"Let us ascend together then, into immortality...*slave!*"

Before Robbie could answer, Officer Carlson's beautifully virile face contorted in a grotesque manner, as though a hundred tiny balls were swimming around beneath his skin and trying to break through the surface. Carlson's human voice screamed in agony as his eyes instantly melted out of their sockets and a gaping hole opened through the bridge of his nose. Slowly the head alien's long sharp proboscis peered through the hole and the entire human face split clean open down the middle and melted away. The mutant's human frame and police uniform liquefied as it moved calculatingly, almost mechanically toward its slave. Its massive thorax danced musically to its four lower legs as they marched forward. Its proboscis nearing Robbie's face and its giant antennae scraping against the ceiling as it advanced, the alien pointed its two upper legs in Robbie's direction as if to grab him. Perhaps it was an attempt by the alien Carlson to speed up the human's own metamorphosis by tearing off his face with its sharp thousand-talon-clad hand. Ignoring the excruciating pain that was now overtaking his body, Robbie reached into his pocket and pulled out his crushed packet of cigarettes.

"On second thought," said Robbie, "How 'bout a stogie, fuck face?"

The alien stopped and, just as the creature formerly known as Luther Milton had done, cocked his head to one side. With that, Robbie reached up and shoved the pack of cigarettes into the alien's mouth. Then, reaching for his zippo lighter, he popped it open and rolled his thumb over the flint, thus igniting it. The confused alien struggled to free the pack from his mouth with the stubby ends of its two upper legs, after which he would surely intend to destroy Robbie Taylor once and for all. Robbie pulled his arm back and thrust it forward, landing the ignited lighter into the alien's mouth. The soft pink stinking goo that was now dripping from the alien leader's wounded mouth, Robbie remembered, was extremely flammable. He made the connection while strapped to the gurney. Carlson had made a fatal error in confiding in Robbie that his species had eradicated the fireflies of their world and in so doing, evolved into flammable creatures whose bodies developed into combustible organic matter.

"*I say, the two became completely incompatible.*", Robbie had heard Carlson say over and over in his mind.

Immediately, the head alien formerly known as Officer Carlson caught fire and the alien screamed in bitter agony as it struggled to douse the fire now igniting the inside of its throat, traveling down its esophagus and up into its brain. Robbie got up and with the last of his strength kicked the alien over onto its back. It writhed back and forth for several more seconds, making the same high-pitched noises as it did after inhaling the tiny insect seed.

Once the alien leader's body ceased its convulsing, the rest of its body began to ignite. Robbie reached for his sneakers and hastened to put them back on. Now with sufficient traction to run on the metallic floor, he ran down the opposite end of the hallway, which led to an opening. Robbie threw caution to the wind and raced through the crevice without bothering to contemplate where it might lead. He quickly noticed the itching throughout his body had ceased. He touched his face and as his fingertips made contact with the alien follicles they began falling off. He saw dozens of them drop to his feet. He confidently rubbed his face, and, within seconds, his complexion was restored to its former smooth state.

Elated, he turned around to see exactly where he had escaped from. To his surprise, it was a disc-shaped craft about twenty feet long and ten feet high, crudely assembled with what appeared to be mostly automotive parts. He drew closer and noticed, among other things, two particularly interesting characteristics of the craft. One section of black metal boasted an insignia reading *NEW HAVEN POLICE DEPARTMENT*, and another section of white had the Mercedes Benz emblem molded into it. This came as a bittersweet relief to Robbie, who no longer had to worry about getting rid of his stolen automobile.

10

Robbie Taylor considered the smoking wreck for several minutes. It would eventually engulf the entire craft; a fact that somewhat disappointed Robbie. Although he was certainly happy to have escaped his destiny of spending eternity in the body of an enormous insect, not to mention that he singlehandedly saved all humanity, he wished he had taken some sort of proof with him out of the craft. His cell phone had been destroyed, thus making it impossible to snap any photos, and Luther, his only witness, was now gone. Robbie decided then and there never to speak of what had happened to him. He would never mention giant insects, alien pods, stinking flammable goo or saving mankind from an extraterrestrial take over.

Darkness was setting in and finally with the sun going down, so too did the temperature. Robbie could make out a long-awaited, albeit mild, breeze begin to hit his face. It wasn't a cool breeze, but a breeze nonetheless, and it felt quite different than the wind that hit his face as he rode down Constitution Avenue looking like a pin cushion. With the razor-sharp cilia no longer part of his facial makeup, Robbie could feel a breeze on his face that felt complete. He couldn't put it any plainer than that it was just that. *Complete.*

He surveyed his surroundings and noticed he was in a forest. He didn't know yet just how deep into it he was, but he followed the faint rays of the setting sun and by the time twilight had given way to absolute nocturnal obscurity, he had made it out to a stretch of road. According to the direction of the horizon, Robbie ascertained the direction of this road to be northbound and southbound. As New Haven was a shore town, and Officer Carlson's admission that Robbie was close to home, Robbie had to be north of the city.

Uncharacteristic of Robbie Taylor, he stuck a thumb out to every passing car heading southbound. The eighth car, a blue Acura Integra, stopped about thirty feet past Robbie and honked twice. A slender arm stretched out of the driver's side. It was long and feminine. Robbie smiled as he ran up to the vehicle.

"Hey." he said as he opened the door and sat in the passenger seat. "Thanks for stopping. I didn't think anyone would pick up a hitchhiker nowadays. Especially with it getting dark."

The attractive brunette kept her eyes on the road, and once Robbie slammed his door shut, the car slowly began accelerating.

"I'm a little embarrassed." he confessed. "I know I look like crap run over twice, but I've had a very harrowing day. I'd tell you all about it if I didn't think you'd take me for a nut and shove me out of the car without stopping."

She didn't respond.

"I'm Robbie." He extended a hand to the young lady, but she didn't take it. Instead she kept her gaze on the road ahead of her.

"I really appreciate this." he continued, a bit uneasy that she hadn't reciprocated his amiability. "Can you talk? *Parlez-vous anglais?*" laughed Robbie, trying to break the tension. "I was just kidding. I wasn't expecting you to answer in French or anything."

Still the driver said nothing, and her foot steadily pressed harder on the accelerator as the Acura approached a winding curve in the road. Robbie gripped the *oh, shit* bar and let out a nervous "*WHOA!*"

As they cleared the curve, the driver accelerated to 80 miles per hour.

"Believe it or not," started Robbie, "After what I've been through, this doesn't really scare me."

She didn't respond.

"You vying for a spot in the Indie 500?" he paused and observed her lovely profile. "Another joke. Can't you laugh?"

"Laugh?" she asked, evenly, still not making eye contact with Robbie.

"Yeah, you know. Ha-ha-ha. Don't you ever find humor in anything?"

"Humor." she said, void of any emotion. "I'm sorry, Mr. Taylor, but as we evolved, my species lost the ability to find humor in anything. Eight generations before the destruction of my world!"

Robbie's blood ran cold. He froze in fear and couldn't find the strength to even unfasten his seatbelt. And as the car accelerated to beyond 95 miles per hour, Robbie Taylor's heart stopped beating.

When his decaying corpse was found by Connecticut State Troopers three days later, one remarked how nothing on the victim looked out of the ordinary, save for a strange coarse black hair follicle protruding from the back of his neck.

Now, now. Mind that weeping. I have much more to tell and your whimpering may drown out some of my words. And as I've already explained, I need to completely break you. This account occurred several months ago. It is in the form of a journal. As I am ubiquitous, I was there, hovering over the writer's shoulder as he wrote every letter of every word. It's been filed in my memory, and now I have you to tell it to.

For you, I will entitle this...

Cathartic Infliction

May 4, 2012
FROM THE DESK OF J.T. HOLBROOK
Empire University, New York City, NY

So what's there to do? I have the rest of the day to wonder whether or not I'm going to continue on with this charade. I honestly didn't think it through. I mean, mom and dad both believed me when I told them everything was fine. Mom with her usual, *"Have you been eating enough?"*, and dad's weekly, *"Did you see that Nuggets game?"* Dad always forgets that I haven't been into basketball since I was a senior in high school. And mom forgets that the life of a college student is one of eating protein bars and drinking Starbucks from dawn till dusk.

Am I eating? The answer to that question is *yes*, but if she concluded her question with the adverb *well*, then I'd have to hesitate and either lie or come clean that my daily bread is loaded with sugar and caffeine.

Do I like basketball? I suppose I'll always have a soft spot in my heart for it. After all, I did play it throughout high school. We went to States twice, but that was the extent of it. I suppose I would have continued in college had I gotten a scholarship for my athleticism. Not that I needed financial aid or anything like that. Being that dad's an accountant with a Fortune 500 company and mom is chief of neurosurgery at Saint Luke's Medical, coupled with the fact that since I had the brains and the grades to get into any college of my choice, it made for countless applications and college visits. In the end, I decided to go Ivy League, which made me an East-Coast college student. Four years at Empire for my undergrad and another year to complete my Masters *was* the plan. I just never knew my junior year could turn out so bad.

It all comes down to my academics, doesn't it? Like I said, prefacing this journal entry, which will be the first of many, I have to decide if I'm going to continue on with this *charade*.

Mom and dad don't suspect a thing. Thanks to some kind of Privacy Act, a parent is not allowed to know the academic standing of his or her child if the latter is eighteen or older. I'm twenty-one and have never thought of what a good thing this Privacy Act was until I needed to hide a secret, one that was imperative to keep from mom and dad.

May 5, 2012
FROM THE DESK OF J.T. HOLBROOK

Ok, so it's official. I, J.T. Holbrook, only child of Jim Holbrook, CPA, and Karen Holbrook, MD., of Whipping Bloom, Colorado, am dropping out of college. I need this journal for a couple of reasons. One, because I believe writing about one's problems is in and of itself, cathartic. And two, because if I do decide to end it all for myself, this journal will serve to answer the question *why*.

It started back in December of last year. I received a letter from the University shortly after Fall Semester grades were posted online. Mine had gone from straight A's upon my arrival as a first-semester freshman, to three C's, one D and an F some twenty-eight months later. My grade point average plummeted. With a once perfect 4.0 now at a 2.7, the letter basically informed me that any repeat of such poor academic performance in the next semester would not only put me on academic probation, but would surely jeopardize my future prospect as an Ivy League alum. And a trilogy of such lackluster scholastic results would clearly lead to dismissal from the university.

I've heard stories about things like this never happening to students at Harvard. Supposedly, Harvard doesn't want to tarnish its reputation of being the most elite of the Ivy League family, as well as the most prestigious in the country. Harvard intervenes if it is discovered that a student is in danger of failing out of the college and does everything in its power to make sure that doesn't happen.

Empire, Ivy League as it may be, takes a more New York approach to poor performance. Their philosophy is definitely more consistent with every other school on the face of the earth, and doesn't hold back any punches. A typical New York City mentality, if you ask me. My letter pretty much summed up that it was *shape up or ship the fuck out.*

I've decided to ship out. My parents don't know about my decision. Hell, they had no idea that I totally screwed up last semester in all my subjects, that I'm trying to keep my average as far above a 2.0 this semester as I can, and that I'm this close to being thrown out. I can't take another year. I can't handle this. I've already admitted to myself that I'm not as smart as everyone always said I was. President John Adams once told his son, John Quincy, that he (J.Q.) had a *superb mind.* My dad always told me I was smart as a whip. I don't really know if having a superb mind and being smart as a whip are the same thing. Frankly, who knew whips were smart? But I'm sure J.Q. had no trouble at all graduating from Harvard University, and I'm sure he never had to take advantage of its "No Dropout Policy".

Perhaps if I had decided to study law, my situation would've been different. My older cousin, Brad, studied law at Yale. He wasn't exactly the sharpest ax in the toolshed and yet *he* did it, graduating Magna Cum Laude from Yale Law School. This guy failed math in the tenth grade and had to go to summer school for it. I remember his exact words to my aunt were, "I hate logarithms! Who cares if I can do them or not? Is anyone really gonna come up to me on the street and ask me to bust out a logarithmic equation?" But he did it! I, on the other hand, am failing out of college. Me! A smart-as-a-whip student who have always had a passion for math and the sciences and went to the Siemens Competition for Science when I was a senior in high school (I won second place for my idea: a parental masturbator alert monitor). And yet *I* am flunking out of college.

I got a letter in my mailbox today. The RD (that's *Resident Director* to you) on mail duty in my dorm lobby, a dorky little faggot by the name of Roger Hilton, told me that if he were me, he'd wanna check his mailbox for a letter from the Dean of Academics.

I hate that goddamn pillow biter!

Dean Thompson, a black man on a power trip, if you ask me, said that I had to bring my grades up from the Fall Semester if I hoped to continue here at Empire U. I don't know how the hell he knew my final grades for the Spring Semester when I haven't even taken my final exams yet.

I've spent three years in the Biochemistry program. At first, I was able to handle the course workload with no problem. I wasn't one of those minorities, of which there are many here, who need to work in the cafeterias or library to help pay for their tuition (I think it's called a 'work study'). Christ! Sometimes I think these people were accepted merely because they can't blush, don't have freckles and never get sunburn. Anyway, Microbiology kicked my ass. The labs were ridiculous with the amount of work they made me do. And Organic Chem! Now there was the course that pretty much ended it all for me. The proverbial final nail in the proverbial coffin. Organic Chemistry basically robbed me of what precious little there was left of my self-esteem as an intellectual and a student of science. I can't do this shit! It's impossible and I hate it! So much for following in my mother's footsteps. I guess my whip has gone soft.

May 6, 2012
FROM THE DESK OF J.T. HOLBROOK

I've decided to give it one last try. Although I'm in danger of failing Organic Chem and Protein Biochem, which would guarantee my ejection from Empire U., I'm going to give my finals, all my finals for that matter, my best effort. I gave myself a pep talk this morning after reading over last night's entry and thought of how pathetic I sounded. But honestly, (and I have to write this) that if things don't go well, I won't be going back to Colorado. The George Washington Bridge is pretty effective at serving as the stage for a definitive departure from this world. I remember a dude once committing suicide off that very bridge just because his grades had gone south like a December mallard. That's probably what I'll do. I'll stay back in New York until grades are posted. I'll pack up the old suitcase and stay at a hotel. If I can keep my head above water this semester, then I'll be sure to prep for my fall classes during the summer. If it means cramming chapters and chapters of Molecular Genetics and Organic Chem II, then so be it! J.T. Holbrook won't go down without a fight!

May 7, 2012
FROM THE DESK OF J.T. HOLBROOK

I ran into one of my professors, Dr. Gupta. He told me, if I understood his accent correctly, that an *F* in Organic Chemistry will adversely affect my standing in the prestigious Biochemistry Program here at Empire U. If that wasn't bad enough, he said this in earshot of another student, Angela Crawford, who's in the same class. Was it necessary to belittle me in front of a peer, and a fellow classmate at that? That's what I'm talking about when it comes to these intellectual pricks who, as the French say, *"fart higher than their asses"*. Just because they know what they know, that makes it simple. If Organic Chem. is so fucking easy, then why is this bastard just teaching it instead of doing it?

Anyway, back to studying. I wanna ace this asshole's final. I wanna ace all my finals. I wanna prove to the world I'm no idiot. *I wanna show them all!*

May 8, 2012
FROM THE DESK OF J.T. HOLBROOK

I just got back from taking the Organic Chem. final. My hardest exam, and, of course, it was the first one. In other words, less time to study for it. Does anyone up there like me?

May 9, 2012
FROM THE DESK OF J.T. HOLBROOK

After taking my Physical Bio and Physics II finals, which I think I did ok on, I emailed Dr. Gupta about my final exam grade. He hasn't written back yet. It's been an hour, and I'm beginning to think the bastard is ignoring me. Why do I think that? Because I know for a fact he has his email linked to his BlackBerry. I've seen him check it during every class we've had this semester. Not only emailing, but I bet updating his status on Facebook, retweeting irrelevant news out of India and texting Raji and mamaji in Mumbai were all part of his cell phone agenda. Certainly, I could blame my performance in his course on all this constant texting and tweeting and whatnot when he should have been teaching. Perhaps if I failed his exam I could contest my grade because of that. Shit, I wish I'd thought of mentioning his manic mobile device obsession on his course survey he gave out after the final.

May 10, 2012
FROM THE DESK OF J.T. HOLBROOK
<u>I FAILED!</u>

May 11, 2012
FROM THE DESK OF J.T. HOLBROOK
I went to see Dr. Gupta this morning. On the way to his office, I checked my email on my iPhone and saw responses from my Physical Bio and Physics II professors. I passed both, one with a C+ and the other with a C. It doesn't really matter, though. With a failing grade on my Organic Chemistry final, Gupta told me I failed the course and would have to repeat it. I just sat there and stared at him. I was on fire inside. My stomach was burning, as was my throat. I thought I'd spew flames if I even opened my mouth just a centimeter. Words can't express how pissed off I was at that moment, and at the same time I felt so incredibly alone.

In three years, I haven't made any lasting friendships. Leslie Hermann was the only student I ever spoke to outside of my classes, and she and I got together once a week just to study at the library during Freshman year. I mean, I'm a friendly enough guy, but maybe there's something about me that just repels people. I'm being completely honest when I say that I'm not one to put on airs. When I *was* doing well in my classes, I never once boasted about my performance to anyone. High school was pretty much the same. Sure, the guys on the basketball team were cool and we had a good time, but off the court, they'd only acknowledge me in the hall with a nod of their head.

Funny thing, really. Never in my life had I ever felt lonely, although now looking back on it all, I can admit to myself that I've led a pretty solitary existence, socially speaking. I guess I was always OK with it, up until today in Gupta's office that is. Even now, as I'm writing, the void I thought I'd been filling in while writing about my problems in this journal isn't easing the loneliness I feel.

Holy shit! Does it hurt this much to be lonely once the loner has admitted loneliness? I feel like I've been kicked in the gut just after being punched there.

May 12, 2012
FROM THE DESK OF J.T. HOLBROOK

I'm going to inform the University that I won't be back in September. I haven't yet told mom or dad about what's going on. I figure I'll stay back East for the remainder of the spring and figure out what I'm going to do with myself. I doubt if transferring to another university is the right thing. My grades being what they are, Ivy Leaguer or not, I'm looking at wearing a cardboard hat for the rest of my life.

May 13, 2012

FROM THE DESK OF J.T. HOLBROOK

I'm staying at the Potter Hotel down in Chelsea. I like it down here. I find the people are more down to earth in this part of Manhattan, and I will be able to think more clearly, as I won't be in an academic atmosphere. I just have to steer clear of NYU if I decide to move my writing venue from this Starbucks down to Washington Square Park. The summer program will be starting in a few weeks, and, as of now, anything academic is poison to me.

May 14, 2012

FROM THE DESK OF J.T. HOLBROOK

I've spent most of the day in Starbucks, reading *Cujo* by Stephen King. I don't know why I decided to download it onto my e-reader. It was more a random decision. I suppose I wanted to read something connected with death, since I'll probably be dead soon anyway. And besides, I like dogs. Dogs are good company. They're loyal and don't betray you like people are wont to do. I'd get a dog if I thought I'd still be here in a year. The truth is, I don't know if I'll drum up enough courage to do it in a week or even a month. I don't want to leave Manhattan until I make up my mind. The GWB is as good a place as any, 'cause at least I know that it will work.

I ordered an oatmeal and four iced chai lattes. I'm buzzing from the amount of sugar and caffeine I've already consumed and before the day is out I'll probably have at least two more. I don't really feel like leaving here. It's so peaceful, and I haven't heard one mention of school, grades, prerequisites, majors, minors or studies abroad. Frankly, I'm reminded of Empire when I notice Italian tourists, as there are many that visit New York during the summer months. They come in and I hear them speaking Italian. Italy, home of the Roman *Empire*. Or when I see someone reading the *New York Times*. What is New York, but the *Empire* State.

One thing that distracts me a lot from my e-reader is when people come through the door. I always look up to see what comes in. I use the word *what* and not *who* because I'm tired of seeing people as just that: *people*. I'd like to think that I'm beginning to see everything and *everyone* differently. When I see a man and a woman come in holding hands (and this I've seen pathetically often today. Are there no single people in New York City?). I consider that man and woman are not a man and woman, but a *couple*. And when I see a couple come in with their child or children, they are a *family*. And when a policeman comes in, he's no longer a police*man*, but a *cop*.

The same thing applies to this guy who just walked in: Jayson Walker. He lived in my dorm and occupied the room just above mine. I complained to him once, telling him his music was too loud and his incessant pounding on the floor as he walked was distracting me from my studies. Yes, I admit I told him all this to his face, petty as you may think it was to do such a thing. You may think that it'd be foolish to piss off the person who lives above you, as his stomping might turn into juggling bowling balls.

I complained, much to the annoyance of my roommate, Todd O'Brien, who, utterly baffling to me, said I was making an issue out of nothing. I suppose I could have blamed my poor academic performance this year on *Walker The Loud Walker*, with Todd O'Brien as his *O'ccomplice*. But even RD's are pretty ineffective when it comes to responding to dormitory complaints. I told Todd that he didn't mind the noise because he never studied, and I wound up reporting Jayson to faggot RD Roger Hilton the following week, but nothing was ever done. Todd said I was a douche for doing it and told me to lighten up, that this was college and that this was how college life was. He told me I should either attend a suitcase campus college or go back home to Colorado and commute. From March until the end of the semester, Todd and I didn't say one word to each other.

Perhaps I wouldn't have been so hostile about the noise had Jayson considered inviting me up to his place. I wouldn't have minded taking a break from my studies to go have a beer with him. If I had gotten to know the guy, then maybe I wouldn't have thought he was a total dick for keeping me up until two in the morning with his loud, self-involved shit. I should have told Todd that too. Why didn't I put it out there that I really had nothing against Jayson Walker, other than he'd never once tried to get to know me. And that brings me to Todd, who'd been my roommate since the beginning of sophomore year. We got along all right, but he's another one who never once tried to get to know me. I mean, we were always considerate of one another's space and respected each other's privacy, but whenever his friends came to our room, he'd never introduce me to them, never once tried to include me in their conversation, and never invited me to go out drinking with them.

Todd O'Brien joined a fraternity last year: The Beta Kapps. He went from being OK in the fall to being a passive, take-life-the-way-it-is boozing asshole. I stopped complaining in front of him (until the Jayson Walker incident) because nothing, and I mean <u>nothing</u> ever got to this guy. Drunken assholes (both male and female) would hang rowdily outside our window at all hours of the night, mostly on weekends, though I do remember this happening once on a Tuesday or Wednesday. The noise would either not wake him or he'd awaken slightly just to roll over onto his other side.

Seeing Jayson Walker come in to the Starbucks here on West 17th reminds me of Todd O'Brien and his "tolerance of juvenile behavior in American college life". It's funny seeing Jayson Walker holding an iced caramel macchiato in lieu of his usual red plastic cup filled with cheap draft beer (another staple of idiotic American college life).

THE RED PLASTIC CUP OF BEER.

College is full of these idiots like Jayson Walker and Todd O'Brien who always go to parties with earsplitting music, whose lyrics you either can't understand or simply don't mean anything. They chug beer, get stupid, play beer pong with those same red cups full of suds, fuck girls they don't know, then spend the entire following day nursing well-deserved hangovers. And how many of those empty-headed girls that Todd, Jayson and others like them fuck actually get pregnant, only to have abortions? Jesus, is this the future of America? And *I'm* the one who wants to kill himself? If anything, I'm not the fuck-up here. The fuck-ups are your Todd O'Briens and your Jayson Walkers who live to get drunk and act irresponsibly and fuck any and every girl they could. And if they get these dumb bitches pregnant? Oh, well. It's just a simple surgical procedure done thousands of times a day, so long as you have the money to take care of it.

I had thought Jayson Walker was the only one alone here at Starbucks besides me until his bitch walked in. Stacey Miller, another Empire student. Why are they here? The last day of finals was two days ago, and I am pretty sure neither one of them is a New

Yorker. And another thing that boils my milk: if they had removed their heads from their assholes, they'd have noticed me and might have asked what *I* was doing there. But selfish as they and others like them are, they won't see me. They won't notice me. I should use that to my advantage. I'm inconsequential. I can make that work for me some day *if* I decide to spare my life.

I wonder if assholes like Jayson and Stacey ever feel pain? They're like the "popular crowd" in high school. Every minute of every hour and every hour of every day was and still is life with a subtle smile, a sway of the shoulders and a tilt of the head. They flirt their way through life, using their good looks to get them everything from a free caffè latte at Starbucks to people they hardly know holding doors for them and wanting to friend them on Facebook. Nothing bothers these "popular crowd" people. Thousands in this country die every day from disease, injuries from falls or car accidents (from drunk drivers ages 18-21, I might add). Still, these high and mighty dick wads go on and on; *ad infinitum* I believe the Roman's would say.

The Roman *Empire*.

See what I mean about always being reminded of Empire U.? I rant about assholes and it all comes back to Empire U.: land of the red cups of beer and home of the pricks and prick-ettes that drink them.

They'll all read about my death in the Daily News or the New York Post in a week (or a month, but certainly before the end of the year, *if* I decide to do it) and Stacey Miller will say, "Hey! J.T. Holbrook? He went to Empire!" And Jayson Walker will say, "Did you know that loser, Stace?" and she'll reply, "No, but it says it right here: 'EMPIRE UNIVERSITY STUDENT DIES AFTER THROWING SELF OFF GWB'."

So now it's official, I'm the only one in this fucking place that is by himself. Even the homeless-looking guy is sipping on a cup of water with a homeless-looking woman. Even truly pathetic people don't seem to suffer from this affliction:

Loneliness.

May 15, 2012

FROM THE DESK OF J.T. HOLBROOK

I'm at my usual seat here at the Starbucks on West 17th Street in New York City. I've started my day on a bad note. A shitty note, to put it more plainly. As I sit here, the only one alone in a sea of coffee-drinking couples or threesomes, I reflect back on the incident of twenty minutes ago.

I left my hotel room at 7AM and made my way down 8th Avenue. I passed a pet store where some people had stopped to watch a litter of puppies playing in a shredded-paper-filled box in the front window. I stopped as well to get a glimpse. I love dogs. Dogs don't hurt you. Dogs are a comfort and fill a void such as loneliness. Dogs are not at all like people: fake, delusional and self-involved. As I stopped in front of the window, I heard a voice from behind me.

"There's nothing cute about puppy mills!" a woman call out to me. The other people just ignored her. I was the only one to turn around. I couldn't keep quiet. I took her comment to mean that these puppies were not adoptable, just because they came from a puppy mill. So their lives were less important than those of purebred dogs who came from reputable breeders?

"They still need homes." I said to her, and I don't think I sounded angry at all.

"You buy one of these animals," she said, "and you're paying to support inhumane breeders, whose only goal is to make a profit by breeding, breeding, breeding until their bitches drop dead."

"Who are *you* to call anything *inhumane*?" I yelled. "You wanna see *inhumane*, go walk around this town from the tip of Harlem where assholes call themselves Empire elite intellectuals and then continue on to the tip of Battery Park where you'll see tens of thousands of people lining up daily, paying wads of cash to go see that piece of French tin floating in the harbor.

Her look turned sour and she got in my face.

"What's inhumane about that? That's got nothing to do with inhumane. I'm talking about cruelty toward animals!"

People all around us turned and looked at me. I felt like pushing that bitch, but I backed off. I put my hands up and I walked away. How can she not see inhumanity in what I just said? Self-indulgent pretentious college students at a prestigious Ivy League University who only care that their weekends are booked with red cup parties and fuck sessions with strangers! Up at Columbia Presbyterian Hospital you have people of all ages suffering and dying. And people who spend thousands of dollars to come to New York just to see a statue or ascend a skyscraper, money that could be given to charities to save people. But the only thing *they* think about is how close they'll get to the Statue of Liberty or what Manhattan looks like one thousand feet up from the sidewalk.

I hate that anti-puppy mill bitch on the street. I hate Jayson Walker. I hate his perfect body. I hate his perfect face. I hate his perfect bitch, Stacey Miller. I hate their fucking lifestyle of *it's all about me.* I hate Todd O'Brien and his *"hey, that's life, J.T."* attitude. I hate Dr. Gupta, his goddam BlackBerry, his fucking Indian accent and his bullshit Organic Chem course. I hate the Starbucks asshole who served me just now and scoffed and rolled his eyes when I asked him to refill the empty decanter of Half and Half so I could add cream to my coffee. I hate the cocksucker who designed this store with only one bathroom; meanwhile, there are twelve tables in this place and if every chair were occupied with customers with full bladders, you'd have thirty-six people in competition for one toilet. I hate the people in front of the pet store who had enough restraint to avoid getting into an awkward spat with that bitch.

I hate people.

May 16, 2012
FROM THE DESK OF J.T. HOLBROOK

Back here in my usual seat at the Starbucks on West 17th. I got up late. The cleaning lady woke me up with a hard knock at the door. I exploded at her and asked who she thought she was to knock so hard and scare the hell out of me. Her answer was that she had knocked softly twice and was about to enter. It was a good thing she didn't because I would have really let her have it.

I really <u>hate</u> people.

It dawned on me in the shower that I just wasted most of my morning because my wakeup call didn't go through. I remember which desk clerk was responsible for putting it in for me. His name tag read *James Oosten*. I'll give him the business later on. Or I might just go straight to his manager. I could lie and say I missed an important business meeting at Starbucks because of Oosten. I could get him fired. I know I'm only a college student (well, ex-college student), but I could say it was an interview for a summer job. After all, I think I'm smart enough to put one over on a hotel desk clerk.

I'm smart as a whip.

May 17, 2012

FROM THE DESK OF J.T. HOLBROOK

I finished reading *Cujo*. I had to finish it at a table other than the one I'm used to sitting at. I arrived at Starbucks on West 17th a little after eight and there was this gay couple sitting at my usual place. I know it could have very easily been a straight couple that had taken my seat, or two nuns, but because they were gay, I'm gonna be even angrier and just say it.

Fucking faggots.

Anyway, back to *Cujo*. I was especially upset at the end when the protagonist kills the poor St. Bernard. Why did he have to die? I mean, the lady's kid was dying and she felt desperate. Thus her maternal instincts caught up with her. But the kid knew what the score was. He knew he was dehydrating because he hadn't drunk sufficient water. Our bodies, being mostly composed of water, need H2O to survive. It's the most elementary of all biological concepts. But poor Cujo. The dog had no clue what he'd done. He didn't know that the bite he'd gotten from the bat was the reason why he started to lose it. He didn't have the slightest comprehension that what he was doing was wrong. I mean, to *him*, what he was doing was just living…just surviving.

Who are we to determine what is right and wrong anyway? We're told it's wrong to kill yourself. Why? If it's my body and my life and I'm unhappy, then why shouldn't I be able to commit suicide? Because it will cause my family sadness? My family is small. There's just me and my parents. I have no grandparents and only one aunt and three cousins from that singular aunt. My parents have friends, but I doubt if they'd shed a tear for me. So really, would my death be so bad? Who would I really be hurting if I were to kill myself?

Me and that's all.

It would be the right thing to do in killing myself, I think. I can't think of any real reason why I'd want to keep on living. And people kill themselves every day, don't they? I wouldn't be the first or the last. I just wish I had a multitude of friends and family, like Todd O'Brien, Jayson Walker or Stacey Miller. This way I could kill myself and in effect hurt everyone around me. My death would make them miserable.

As it is, my death will only make two people miserable: Mom and Dad.

I wish I could make the world miserable too.

Too bad I'm not famous and beloved.

May 18, 2012

FROM THE DESK OF J.T. HOLBROOK

I, James Thomas Holbrook of 16 Beaver Hollow Court, Whipping Bloom, Colorado, have just had an epiphany. As I opened my eyes from a night of uninterrupted slumber, it dawned on me. It's so clear now. Why had it taken me so long to realize it? I WILL NOT KILL MYSELF.

Killing myself would serve no purpose to anyone. Not to my parents, not to their friends, not to my aunt, not to her husband nor to my cousins. No one. The world would go on (*ad infinitum*) and my death would be front page news, maybe; if nothing else major happened in the Tri-State Area that day, I'll subsequently fade into history as just another sorry son of a bitch who couldn't hack life.

I could even hear those assholes up at Empire having a good laugh at my expense.

"Hey, did you hear J.T. Holbrook jumped off the GWB last night?"

"No."

"Apparently neither did anyone else!"

Then they'd all roar with laughter!

I'll be goddamned if I'm gonna be the butt of anyone's joke. I'd rather make Todd O'Brien, Jayson Walker, Stacey Miller and every other asshole in this world the butt of my own joke.

That's why I've decided I'm not going to kill myself. Doing that, as I've already said, wouldn't hurt anyone. And that is what it should all be about really; just how many of these assholes I can inflict with a pain like no other.

Infliction. Infliction. Infliction.

I'm going to kill people.

As many as I can.

May 19, 2012

FROM THE DESK OF J.T. HOLBROOK

So the question now is *how*? How do I *inflict* this pain and suffering? And *where*? Where would I have access to the most people? And *when*? I have to get ready. And I can only do this once I'm ready. Nothing half-assed.

May 20, 2012

FROM THE DESK OF J.T. HOLBROOK

I have answered one of the three questions from yesterday's entry. *When?* It's going to be July 7th. The date has no significance, other than it's my half birthday. It's also a Saturday, which means there'll be lots of assholes out and about.

Maximum sadness.

Infliction!

May 23, 2012

FROM THE DESK OF J.T. HOLBROOK

I've been incredibly busy the last few days and so haven't had a chance to write a thing. Monday the 21st, I went to The Outdoorsman, a hunting outfit up in Putnam County, New York. I know guns are taboo in the City. Retired NYPD even get hassled trying to keep their own firearms. It's ludicrous. I hear Westchester and Nassau Counties are pretty tough, too. The farther away from the City, the better my chances are of getting what I'll need. I rented a Zipcar and hit the road shortly before 9AM. I still hit a shit load of traffic and didn't get up to Brewster until after ten-thirty.

The guy behind the counter was a ball buster. He told me that I couldn't buy a single handgun until I had a pistol permit.

"What about rifles?" I asked him. He turned around and pointed to the rifles, both hunting and assault that hung on the wall behind the counter.

These could really do some damage. But the problem with rifles is that they're hard if not impossible to conceal. I remember the guys who pulled off Columbine. They used assault rifles and concealed them under trench coats. If I can't get my hands on a couple of handguns, *no problemo*; I'll load up on assault rifles. The gentleman (I use the word *gentleman* here because he gave me insight as to how I could buy a rifle) asked me what I'd be using the gun for. I told him I was from Denver and that carjackings and home invasions were getting more and more common there. "I want to be sure I can protect myself, my family and my possessions." I explained.

"You still reside in Colorado?" he asked, narrowing his eyes at me.

"I do." I told him. "I just study here. Just finished up another year at Empire U."

I immediately realized that mentioning I was Ivy League might jeopardize my chances of scoring a firearm. I expected him to shake his head and mutter, *"Pussy with a gun."*

"If you're not a resident of New York State, that is, you don't have a New York address as your primary residence, and you don't possess a New York State Driver's License, then you can't buy a firearm in this state."

I left the store pretty agitated. The only good thing that prick did was to educate me, elementarily as his info was, about what assault rifles can really do the most damage. I told him that getting off as many rounds in the least amount of time was of the utmost importance. His answer to that was, "Gotta protect that Mercedes!" and offered a slight guffaw.

As I traveled southbound on the Sprain Brook Parkway on my return to NYC, I started thinking of how I could get my hands on an AR-15 assault rifle. I looked up photos of it on my phone. The first showed an army GI holding one while on a tour in Iraq. This fucker looked like he could have taken out an entire village. A bit ambitious, perhaps. My venue will be on a much smaller scale, but one can only dream. The second showed some short dude at a gun show holding one up for the camera. For some reason it didn't look as dangerous as it did in the first photo. I wonder what holding it would be like. Would I resemble a menacing GI or a flaccid wimp with *loser* written clear as day on his forehead?

Anyway, that was Monday.

Yesterday I bought a ticket back to Denver. I slept most of the day. I'm feeling that crappy lonely feeling again, the recycling image of assholes all wrapped up in their own shit once again on my mind. I hear them from my hotel window. I'm on the fourth floor and still I hear the bullshit in the streets.

People laughing.

What can they possibly be laughing about? With all this shit going on in the world...all the misery. People dying at this very moment and yet these egocentric fuckers can laugh? Soon I will be the one laughing...at *their* deaths. The whole world will feel sadness for once.

Frankly the only time I don't feel this crappy lonely feeling is when I'm in my planning stages. I gotta say it's cathartic. Cathartic to plan infliction.

Cathartic Infliction.

I like the sound of that. It sums up my plan nicely.

Cathartic.

Infliction.

May 24, 2012
FROM THE DESK OF J.T. HOLBROOK
Unbeknownst to the folks, I landed in Denver at just past noon.

To whomever reads this, whether it be the FBI, the CIA, the NYPD, the A-fucking-CLU or mom and dad, don't think for one minute that a brilliant, smart-as-a-whip college boy like me would ever be stupid enough to try to board a New York City-bound aircraft with a firearm! That would put an end to my plan of *cathartic infliction* real quick.

No sir! I had reserved a rental car at Denver International Airport. So the plan was to go from the plane to the taxi to the gun dealer, back to the cab, back to the airport, get the car and head back to New York. Needless to say I'm already out of Denver and on my way back to NYC. It'll take a few days, but I have plenty of time. Not only did I buy the AR-15, but I was able to get a handgun as well. Thank God for the NRA and the Republican Party. Up to this point, I'd always fancied myself a Democrat (and a pretty liberal one at that, except on issues of gay marriage and unrestricted immigration), but as I sit here at this rest stop on I-70 in Western Kansas and pen this latest *cathartic* entry, I remind myself why I'm doing all this. There are three reasons, really. There might be more, but as of now I can only think of three. They are the following:

1. People are selfish, cruel and self-indulgent and need to be put down like rabid animals.
2. My own death won't create a great sadness among the masses like my great plan of *cathartic infliction* will.
3. The relief I get from this plan will be even more *cathartic* once I've carried it out.

Just another reminder of why I'm doing this. The lady in line in front of me at the Pollo Loco, where I grabbed dinner here at the rest stop, took her time getting out her wallet, even though she knew she'd eventually have to pay for her order. She knew there was a line forming behind her, but did this speed her up? Nope. And so I add this woman to my list of assholes. Some might argue she was rocking a stroller back and forth and was thus preoccupied. Her little brat was crying so loud, I swear I was ready to go into my trunk, pull out my rifle, load the ammo, come back into the Pollo Loco and just get my *cathartic infliction* taken care of right then and there.

I suppose this evening was a breakthrough for me. Until I found myself in line at the Pollo Loco, I never believed that I could think of hurting just *anyone*. I mean sure, fantasizing about taking out entire families during the crescendo of the symphonic masterpiece known as my *cathartic infliction* is one thing. Yet waiting patiently as sweat poured down my face (because some asshole manager didn't feel the need to crank up the AC), I attentively watched this woman as she dug deeply into her purse for her wallet. Dug for it so late in the game that all the other customers lined up behind me began to fidget and roll their eyes. Her baby was making such a ruckus, as if someone were stabbing him (or her, as I only saw the back of the stroller), I knew right there and then that I could take out this woman and her nipple-sucking offspring without thinking twice.

Do you see, reader? My gripe (up to that point anyway) was with the assholes of the world, basically every adult. That had been my limit. But I never considered children to be part of my *cathartic infliction* plan.

Until now.

I admitted to myself, behind that bitch and her screaming baby, that it would be oh, so *cathartic* to kill them both. Then I wouldn't have to wait for my chicken meal and I wouldn't have to hear anymore crying. And wouldn't that bring sadness to family and friends of this woman? Wouldn't the town from which she hailed join together in grieving unity? Would they not set up makeshift memorials with pictures of her and teddy bears and balloons for the baby?

Now, reader, imagine that on a much larger scale. Imagine fifty or seventy women, and perhaps half of them with their husbands or boyfriends. And imagine that half of those couples have children with them. Throw some senior citizens in there too for good measure and what do you have? A venue for a most *cathartic infliction*. And the outpouring of emotion, grief, confusion, sadness, regret, fear, outrage, anger. Notwithstanding the last two emotions, no one will be able to harm me once it's over! I will be the sole person responsible for this deluge of sentiment and after all is said and done, I'll be safe in a jail cell from the exasperated public. And I don't pretty much care if my name is to be remembered or not. That's not my intent. If someone remembers what J.T. Holbrook did way back on July 7th, 2012, then so be it. I really couldn't care less about fame, glory and immortality, in the infamous sense.

What I care about is stopping the hurting. To do that, I need to do *this*.

Really, reader. You may not see it that way, but it's the truth.

I want the pain to stop.

May 26, 2012
FROM THE DESK OF J.T. HOLBROOK
I'm hauling ass and have crossed through Kansas, Missouri, Illinois, and am now in Indiana. By my calculations, I'll be back in NYC in another fourteen or fifteen hours.

May 28, 2012
FROM THE DESK OF J.T. HOLBROOK

Back in my hotel room in Chelsea. I had a calm, very restful sleep. I ordered room service, very careful to conceal all my weaponry and ammo before my breakfast arrived. The handgun, a .9mm semi (the brand escapes me right now) and the ammo are in the safe, and the AR-15 is propped up in the closet behind a trench coat I purchased at an Army Surplus in Dayton, Ohio. I would have liked to get in some target practice beforehand, but I don't hold a pistol permit in the State of New York, nor do I have a hunting permit. No matter. I have enough ammo on me to get off five hundred rounds. I'll be sure to get at least 250 people.

That is, if I have enough time.

Time. That's the key, isn't it? How many people I can kill greatly depends on how quickly it will take the authorities to respond to the mayhem that will ensue. Another question I have yet to answer is, will I go quietly? Will I surrender or let them take me down? New York State hasn't had the balls or the political unity to send anyone to the electric chair since they reinstated it back in the mid '90's. I guess its recall is more symbolic than anything else. All the better for me. I could get life. And that's what I'll have. *Life*. That will be oh, so much more than I can say for my impending victims.

I can't wait for the *cathartic infliction* to begin!

May 29th, 2012
FROM THE DESK OF J.T. HOLBROOK

These asshole politicians are going at it again with the gun debate on TV. The liberals are crying that there are too many guns in too many hands and that it's far too easy to get a firearm in the United

States. The Republicans say that any new gun legislation making it tougher for gun owners to acquire firearms is a direct infringement of the Second Amendment. These conservatives say gun violence is perpetrated by those of unsound mind and that tougher legislation on the institutionalization of these individuals needs to be implemented. Republicans also claim that "guns don't kill people; people kill people". I believe the Senator from South Carolina said something like, "If these sick gunmen who kill scores of people didn't have guns, they'd find some other means with which to carry out their massacre. Taking guns out of the hands of responsible gun owners is not the answer."

Now I think that JT Holbrook deserves to have his opinion aired. After all, my words in this journal will explain exactly why I decided to kill people and why I used firearms to accomplish it. As I've clearly stated, I am more a liberal thinker. But here is my own view on guns; a man soon to be branded "a sick, murderous gunman".

I choose to use firearms to carry out my *cathartic infliction* because, let's be honest, it's the easiest way to do it. How else *could* I do it? I don't know the first thing about building a bomb. I mean, I'm smart as a whip and therefore am quite sure I can manage to build one. But I couldn't be certain that it would ever go off. I wanna get this right the first time. Think of the Shoe and Underwear Bombers. Think of that Connecticut guy who left his car in Times Square. These guys were working with duds. Guns are much more reliable, and *that*, my Republican friends, is why I choose and why others before me have chosen to use guns. So thank you for making it so easy for us, Party of Lincoln!

So don't kid yourself and say that if guns were outlawed, we gunmen would find different means to achieve the end result. I, soon-to-be the latest gunman in an ever-growing dynasty, am here to tell you that guns are preferred because it's easy to acquire them in the good ol' U.S. of A. and a gun shows no mercy. A bullet knows no age, no race and no sex. And a loaded gun will fire 99 percent of the time.

And remember, I will be using more than one firearm, so there is a 100 percent chance I'll succeed in my quest for *cathartic infliction*!

I hate to say it, but which solution would have saved my impending victims? Discovering who all the mentally ill are and locking them all away? Or removing guns from private hands? Let's put it this way: How would they ever know that I, JT Holbrook, that have never demonstrated the slightest bit of psychotic behavior, would have ever been capable of something like this? People snap. Who's more of a threat? A dribbling, mentally-unstable 63-year old in a wheelchair barely holding on to a half-finished basket he's spent months weaving, or a man who's just had his kids taken away in an ugly custody battle and feels the hatred for his ex-wife swelling in his belly with every passing second? You will never save the world by locking away every last nutcase. And who's to say every whacko would blow away a bunch of people.

Yeah, guns are not the issue...

Sure...

I won't be locked away. Not until after the fact. By then it will be too late. The damage will have already been done. You won't save anyone. You will weep, America. You will mourn. My actions will keep the gun debate hot. The massacre for which I will be responsible will make you question your laws. Your sadness and feeling of helplessness will soon turn to rage and action, and then stall in endless debate. And when the last of my victims is buried, you will have still come no further in your pathetic, endless argument over gun control.

While you go back and forth endlessly, you are wasting precious time. I'm planning to rid the world of many many people while you accomplish nothing! I and my brothers are, at this moment, planning to take your constituents, your loved ones, your children, your teachers, your neighbors, away from you.

Forever.

Can't you see how powerless you are?

June 1st, 2012

FROM THE DESK OF J.T. HOLBROOK

I've answered two more questions. With the *when* out of the way, I was left with the *who* and the *where*. If you are still unclear, reader, as to the *why*, I suggest you go back and reread this journal from page one.

The *who* are the assholes who will be attending a Human Rights seminar at Empire University on July 7th at 10AM, in Auditorium G, also known as room 2102B. The speaker is a Ms. Elizabeth Caswell. She was a reporter for *Time Magazine* and spent two years covering the wars in Iraq and Afghanistan. I read some of her articles. She's one of those bleeding heart liberal journalists who disagrees with the War on Terror. According to most of her articles and lectures, she believes that the War on Terror is American-made and that those responsible for 9-11 were simply responding to America's unshakable alliance with Israel.

The last thing I would ever do would be to agree with some Arab towel head about anything, but I agree that America should abandon this notion of Israel being the above all and beyond. I could give a rat's ass about Israel, or the Jews that live there.

As for Ms. Caswell, she doesn't believe in the War on Terror? What would she say about it if she knew she was going to be a *victim* of terror? I'll be sure one of my bullets finds its way into her head. Now *that* will be a great cover for *Time Magazine*! "Our Journalist Bitch Gets It Between The Eyes" with a close up photo of her lying there with a hole right between the eyebrows!

I heard in Starbucks just yesterday that Jayson Walker and Stacey Miller, Todd O'Brien and little queer Roger Higgins will be there. They're all still here taking summer classes. My luck is the best it's been in months, let me tell you! I overheard Jayson and Stacey yesterday discussing the seminar and the date. This was the exact same day I was planning to take out a crowd of people! This couldn't have worked out any better! It must be divine intervention. Can God truly be with me? Yes! Then I *must* be in the right if I have *Him* on my side! I kind of feel bad about calling myself a non-practicing Episcopalian.

The *where* I already told you will be in an auditorium-size classroom on campus. I hear a few hundred people are expected to attend. If they bring their children, all the better. I pretty much don't care at this point who shows up. Numbers are the most important thing to me right now.

July 7th, 2012, at 10AM, in room 2102B at Empire University.

I'm all set.

They all have a little more than one month left to live.

July 3ʳᵈ, 2012
FROM THE DESK OF J.T. HOLBROOK

I started packing up my room today. My clothes are neatly folded in my suitcase, having just come back from the hotel laundry. I can't even begin to imagine the balance my dad's AMEX is carrying. He's already got such a high balance for credit purposes that he'll never see the additional three or four thousand dollars that I've accumulated on it. I paid for the room, room service, laundry, the plane ticket to Denver, my rental car, gas, tolls, spending money, Starbucks and my guns with it. It's a good thing he and I have the same name. That's what he had said to me when he slipped the card into my wallet as I left for my junior year of college. Thank goodness for parents with means.

July 4ᵗʰ, 2012
FROM THE DESK OF J.T. HOLBROOK

Happy Fourth of July. I'm going to give this country a belated birthday surprise if there ever was one! They'll be talking about it for months!

July 5ᵗʰ, 2012
FROM THE DESK OF J.T. HOLBROOK

Three more days. I'm thinking of leaving the hotel a day early so I can scope out the place where my *cathartic infliction* will take place. My pulse is racing at the thought. I even have a hard on just thinking of it all. I can't believe the notion of killing people makes me hornier than seeing a naked Pamela Anderson licking whipped cream off her tits. I am also shaking a bit. Not out of trepidation, but rather out of sheer ecstasy and happiness. Finally all those mother fuckers whom I've hated throughout college with their Friday night fuck fests, their beer pong matches complete with red cups of piss yellow booze and their Frat House parties will get what's coming to them.

By the way, as I heard myself call out to the porter who brought me my breakfast this morning, I noticed my voice was shaky as well. *Am* I nervous? Not in the least. I expect it's nothing more than excitement and anticipation for my big day set to take place two days from now!

July 6th, 2012
FROM THE DESK OF J.T. HOLBROOK

I left my hotel this morning. I didn't bother to check out. I'll call over the phone and have them close up my account and that will be that. I hopped into a cab, only to realize I had not one single George Washington in my wallet. To my relief I saw the MasterCard, Visa and AMEX logo stickers on the Plexiglas partition that separated me and my expected Pakistani cabby.

I paid with dad's AMEX of course, signed my name and wrote *"In your dreams, asshole"*, on the line marked *TIP*. I threw the receipt and the pen back at him through the opened partition in the Plexiglas and hopped out, suitcase, attaché filled with ammo, and duffle bag where I'd stored my AR-15 and my semi. As I stepped out into the steamy morning air, I could hear the cabby shouting, "VAT YOU TINK YOU ARE?" and then rambled on angrily in Urdu.

I made my way up Broadway and staked out the back entrance to the university. I will spend the night across the street. I'll not bother trying to sleep. I'm way too excited. I'll spend the night at the 24-hour Starbucks around the corner and read. I'll read this entire journal, so that the *why* I am doing this can stay fresh in my mind. I have a feeling re-reading this will only galvanize and make me want to realize my *cathartic infliction* all the more.

July 7ᵗʰ, 2012

FROM THE DESK OF J.T. HOLBROOK

THE DAY HAS ARRIVED! I, J.T. Holbrook, have made it to the day of my emancipation! Freedom from all the assholes of the world! They will no longer have a hold on me once I unleash my *cathartic infliction*!

I entered the campus through the back entrance. I was stopped by a black armed campus police officer. My first reaction was to show him my student ID Card, but that wouldn't have done any good, as it had expired May 31ˢᵗ.

Then I thought to greet him in that *Hey Brutha white boy pretending to be black* fashion, but didn't think I could pull it off. After all, I was so inherently white and didn't have an ounce of black flavor in my vocabulary.

"Hey," I started. "Good morning. I'm here for the Civil Rights seminar going on in Auditorium G."

"That's by invitation only," replied the campus officer. "You need to show the invite to get in." As he said the word *invitation*, he made a gesture with his hand as if holding up an invisible card to me. "Can't get in without it."

So much for using my University ID card anyway. I shuffled slowly toward him and even offered up a smile as idea after idea danced over in my mind. It did make perfect sense not to admit just any ol' Joe Schmo into the seminar; yet, I still hadn't anticipated this snafu. I quickly thought of a response and as I did so, nervously twisted my wrist around, thus causing the duffle bag to hit against the back of my thigh. I looked from the officer down to the bag and considered its contents.

"I'm one of the guest speakers at today's event," I said confidently. "And I seem to have forgotten my invitation on my nightstand."

The officer contemplated me, suspiciously. I pointed inside the one room security house.

"If you go check your guest chart there, you'll see that I *am* in fact on the list. Last name is *Caswell.*"

"Wait here," he said and gave me his back as he went for the guest list that sat atop his messy desk along with a half-consumed cup of Starbucks iced coffee. My cock swelled with blood at the thought that I would soon kill this nigger and that no one could save him or the countless others I would soon take down. I knelt down slowly, fishing for the Remington pistol (I remember the make of the handgun now). My hand rummaged nervously in the bag until I snagged it, almost as if it had been deliberately handed to me. My hand instantly tightened around the grip panel. I brought the pistol from the bag, stood up and walked quickly but calmly into the shack.

"Did you find me?" I said, confidently, and brought the pistol up to the back of his head.

"I see an *Elizabeth Caswell* here." he replied.

I pressed the edge of the pistol to the back of his head. He dropped the clipboard and lowered his head. His palms pressed down onto his desk and his trembling elbow knocked over his coffee. The cool liquid ran around the edges of his fingers but as he was more concerned with my gun's being pressed against his head, wet fingers were the very least of his worries.

It was laughable how easily I got him to capitulate. I ordered him to hand over his keys and instructed him to show me which key would open the back door. He told me in his shaky, almost weeping voice that it was the gold one with the blue tip. I spread apart the other keys from the ring and took the key in question between my thumb and index fingers. Then I reminded him in a very firm tone to not move a muscle as I unfastened the safety strap from his holster and removed his pistol.

"Now you have a choice, my brutha," I said in the most dominant voice I could muster. "I can either cut you down with my pistol or your very own. Which is it to be?"

"P-Please," he pleaded, now unmistakably weeping. "I got a wife and five kids, and another one on the way."

"Six kids then, is it?" I replied. "Big fuckin' surprise, that one is." My anger got the better of me. I closed the door to the shack and squeezed the trigger of my pistol and put a bullet through the guard's head. It traveled out his mouth and shattered the front glass of the guard shack as blood splattered all over. He fell hard onto the desk and my ears began to ring terribly.

My *cathartic infliction* had begun!

I now find myself outside Auditorium G, hiding in a utility closet. I made it into the building easily and as most of the campus security is at the front of the university, it was easier than second grade math to get to where I am now. I only passed three people on my way up here, a freshman and her parents who'd come to the campus to visit one last time before mom and dad dropped her off for good. Maybe they were there sort of as a last-minute assurance that their daughter had made the right decision and wasn't going to find herself regretting it after a month.

It's now 9:55AM and the seminar is set to start in five minutes. I can hear the crowd growing louder by the minute and that tells me the masses are piling in. Will I boast one hundred victims? Two hundred? More?

The sexual arousal I feel is impossible to put into words!

I have with me over five hundred rounds of ammunition (I stole what remained of the black security guard's ammo). Security is present only at the front entrance now. There won't be any guards stationed inside the auditorium. That's common security practice in American universities. Unless it's some high level government official, a liberal celebrity or ex-president coming to speak, security for these gatherings is minimal and very lax.

I'm leaving the closet soon. My AR-15 and Remington semi are now armed and ready to go, as am I. I can't wait for Todd O'Brien, Jayson Walker and the rest of them to see that it is I, J.T. Holbrook, who will end them, causing their deaths, deaths that will afflict their families and friends for the rest of their lives. Even if I have to enjoy this victory from inside a jail cell or from solitary confinement. So long as I get to realize my *cathartic infliction*.

I'm ready, reader. I'm headed out now. But I will set up another four days worth of journal entry pages so as to set a goal for myself. I worry that so much will be going through my mind that I may neglect my journal. With dates specifically set in my book, I will dutifully come back to tell you how it all went.

Here's to *cathartic infliction*!

Christopher D. Roe

July 8th, 2012
FROM THE DESK OF J.T. HOLBROOK

Christopher D. Roe

July 9ᵗʰ, 2012
FROM THE DESK OF J.T. HOLBROOK

Christopher D. Roe

July 10th, 2012
FROM THE DESK OF J.T. HOLBROOK

Christopher D. Roe

July 11ᵗʰ, 2012
FROM THE DESK OF J.T. HOLBROOK

This article, my child, was on the front page of The Sunday Edition of The New York Times dated July 8th, 2012:

LONE GUNMAN SHOT AND KILLED AT EMPIRE UNIVERSITY AFTER KILLING CAMPUS POLICE OFFICER:

A 21 year-old man armed with one assault rifle and a .9mm semi-automatic handgun shot and killed an Empire University policeman Saturday morning before he was shot and killed inside the college. The assailant, Empire University student James Thomas Holbrook of 16 Beaver Hollow Court, Whipping Bloom, Colorado, killed 11-year veteran campus police officer Samuel Smith of Hempstead, Long Island. Shortly after, he was shot approximately 840 times as he entered the auditorium waving the AR-15 assault rifle at the crowd, comprised almost entirely of NYPD officers who'd come out to support a fellow officer who'd been shot in the line of duty just weeks ago.

The event, which included such dignitaries as the Mayor of New York, the Manhattan Borough President and the Police Commissioner, was to commemorate the bravery of NYPD Officer Lee Simons, who was nearly killed two months ago after a perpetrator he'd been chasing shot him in the chest. Simons was on hand, with his wife and two-year-old son at his side, to accept the Award for Bravery on behalf of the citizens of New York City.

It is unclear at this time why the lone gunman entered an auditorium filled almost entirely with armed police officers. Officials speculate that the gunman had intended his target to be the human rights seminar originally planned to take place in said auditorium, but had been moved two days prior to a smaller venue in order to accommodate the nearly 500 participants in the ceremony honoring Police Officer Simons.

Officer Simons was one of the nearly four hundred police officers who drew their weapons and fired at the gunman. It is estimated that over three thousand shots were fired. One eyewitness said it sounded like the finale at a Fourth of July fireworks show.

Ironically, ex-*Time Magazine* contributor, Elizabeth Caswell, who was slated to speak at the human rights seminar, spoke out against the way the NYPD went about taking down the gunman.

"This was overkill in my opinion," said Caswell in an interview with News 3 reporter, Perry Maxwell. "The way the NYPD went about taking down the suspect was excessive and brutal to say the least. This was not a wild animal loose on campus. And even an escaped zoo lion would have been spared such a savage slaughter. I'm sorry to say, police brutality is alive and well in New York City."

When asked if she would have felt differently about Holbrook's death had it been confirmed that she was the intended target, she replied, "Not in the least."

The FBI has taken over this case. Toxicology reports aren't due back for four to six weeks, in which time the Bureau will attempt to piece together the events which led up to this foiled plot. FBI agents will also travel to Colorado where they plan to question the suspect's family, as well as Holbrook's friends both in his hometown and at Empire University.

It was reported that besides a small suitcase and duffle bag, the gunman was in possession of a notebook, with the words *CATHARTIC INFLICTION* on the cover. Although FBI and NYPD officials won't speculate on the contents of this notebook, some believe that it contains vital answers as to why J.T. Holbrook, who came from a wealthy family, could go from an intelligent, out-going Ivy League student with a bright future to a calculating killer.

On an ironic note, Holbrook is the youngest person to be gunned down by the NYPD, and was shot more times than any other assailant, armed or otherwise, in NYPD history.

There now, child. Did you like that story? I thought you might. I saw it all. Ahhhhh-I can feel the fear rising in you. My latest narrative has surely stricken you with a fear unlike any you have ever felt in your life! Your fear has doubled!

The moon! Ahhh, yessssss. The mooooooon. Soon the moon will reach beyond its half phase. My time will be at hand! I still have time to share yet one more tale of terror with you. And you will listen, child. You have no choice but to listen. And I am confident that once it is at an end, so too will be your hope!

Listen...

This story I call...

The Camera

1

Liz Brentwood tore open the top of the cardboard moving box with the blade cutter her father had passed to her. On a sunny hot afternoon in late June, while most girls her age were either out at the mall shopping with their mom's credit card or escaping the post-scholastic heat with a trip to the beach, Liz celebrated her second day of summer vacation helping her family unpack in their new home on 11 Grover Road. She could have very easily phoned one of her girlfriends and sneaked off to the Garden State Plaza, but she was new to New Jersey, and hadn't one friend in the entire Tri-State Area. What's more, her mother, Patricia, had been on her like a hawk lately, and only now seemed to be loosening the leash. Patricia's overbearing maternal instinct kicked in the moment she caught Liz in their bedroom with Liz's boyfriend, Rob Hornsby.

"From this day on, young lady, I am *never* going to let you out of my sight!" shouted Patricia to her eldest child who, up to that point, had been most conscientious and reliable. "I just can't believe you would do this to your father and me!"

Although Liz believed that her father, Paul, had moved the family across the country to get her away from her juvenile delinquent boyfriend, the truth was that Paul had been promoted to Regional Manager of *Tido*, a toy company based in his native California. He started out with the company twelve years ago as part of the design team, charged with coming up with more modern toys for children of the 21st Century who, thanks to the Computer Age, where a physical game of baseball could be replaced by a virtual one through Xbox on an HDTV, were easily uninterested in simple and easy. They wanted complex and involved.

"But I hate New Jersey!" protested Liz, stomping her foot on the recently-scrubbed kitchen linoleum of the family's California home.

"Liz!" scolded Patricia. "Be reasonable. How can you hate it when you've never even been?"

"Everybody hates New Jersey!" retorted Liz. "Even the people that live in New Jersey hate New Jersey!"

Patricia was actually fond of the idea of moving back East. She was a native of Garden City, Long Island, and her roots had been planted there as far back as the late 1800's when her paternal great grandparents emigrated there from Wales. Yet, she was never sure of when her mother's family came to this country. Patricia Blayney's mother always referred to her side of the family, with which she'd cut off all contact when she married Patricia's father, as back road Kentucky hillbilly farmhands. People tend to gravitate more toward one side of their family than the other. For Patricia, it was the Blayney side that won out. For her, there was more of an image telling people her ancestors had come over from Denbigh, Wales, rather than Big Beaver Lick, Kentucky. She'd made that mistake once during a hazing ritual at college. She earned the nickname *Wet Beaver* amongst her sorority sisters and to this day remains the only sister of the *Pi Alpha's* to be branded with a sexually-oriented epithet.

"New Jersey?" Patricia said, gazing starry-eyed at Paul. Up to that point, she'd never thought he'd ever consider leaving the West Coast.

"New Jersey," he replied and briefly flashed her his pearl-white teeth, a testament to never having smoked a day in his life. "They chose me out of a pool of eighty-four employees in my division. I'm their man."

"But, I mean, are you sure you want to move? You told me when we met that you never wanted to move out of Orange County, let alone California."

"I know what I said, but that was before I was offered a thirty percent raise in salary!"

"Thirty percent?" said Patricia, sounding as astonished as Paul had ever heard her.

Before Paul had told her this, she really couldn't trust that he was truly serious about moving back East.

"So this is for real?" she asked, and allowed herself a smile. In her mind's eye, she saw herself sitting with Paul on a plane bound for the East Coast-the whole family in first class with Patricia and Paul sipping champagne while their three children sat fast asleep in the row behind them.

"Oh, yeah. It's for real," he told her.

He picked her up and spun her around and then they both fell back onto their bed. They made love that night and lit up a joint afterwards, taking turns pulling drags. Patricia thought this was the perfect moment to tell Paul what had happened earlier that day.

"What?" said Paul, beginning to pant. "I'll kill the filthy son of a bitch! And Liz! She's grounded until...until..."

To Patricia, Paul appeared to be either unraveling or coming to terms with what their daughter had done. She wasn't sure, so she allowed him a few moments to compose himself and reflect on just what this news meant.

"Then moving is the right thing," he said, finally.

"I wonder," she began, "if it had been *ten* percent, and I hadn't told you about Liz and Rob, would you have turned it down."

"Look, Trish, we both know Rob Hornsby is a loser. He's almost two years older than her, and he dropped out of school this year. He'd been suspended so many times that Liz's Spanish teacher joked that the District was thinking of retiring out-of-school suspension in Rob's honor."

Patricia laughed in spite of herself, at which point she sat up in bed and began gently rubbing her husband's smooth back.

"If we spring this on the kids, Lizzy will think that Rob is the reason we're hauling ass across the country," she said.

"Well, I don't give a damn about what she thinks right now," he replied. "My first concern is my family. Besides, we'll be able to buy another house at a much lower interest rate. The market being the way it is now, real estate's a bargain. What's our current interest rate?"

"Six and a quarter." said Patricia mid-yawn as she lay back down and reached to turn off the lamp on her night table. "What part of New Jersey are we talking about?"

"Regional headquarters are in Weehawken, so, what is that? Northeast I suppose."

Patricia sank her head into her pillow and grinned. She'd have been happy even if Paul had told her South Jersey, but Weehawken, being just across the river from Manhattan, meant that he'd move them no further than a half hour from New York.

"I remember Bergen County being very nice," she said through another yawn. "I have cousins in Englewood. Their house is a stone's throw from Gloria Swanson's mansion. I'll go online in the morning and start pricing homes in the area."

Paul sank into his part of the bed and reached his right arm over Patricia's waist, bringing the small of her back to his belly.

She moaned, pleasantly. "I'm ready for my closeup, Mr. DeMille."

He buried his nose in the nape of her neck and laughed at her Gloria Swanson imitation. She felt his hot breath against her cool skin.

"From Garden City to the Garden State. It's a sign."

"Do you think we have to worry about Rob Hornsby?" he asked.

Patricia moaned softly, finding herself about to drift off, "Not in New Jersey."

2

"Ho-Ho-Kus!" Liz scoffed at her mother as she pulled out the dishes from one of the cardboard moving boxes. "It's the dumbest name for a town I've ever heard in my entire life. Does moving to *Ho-Ho-Kus* have anything to do with me sleeping with Rob? Or is dad just suffering from a Santa complex? And our address: 11 Grover Road. Why not just call it *Sesame Street*?"

Patricia ignored her daughter's sarcasm and continued wiping down the glass windows that adorned the kitchen cabinets. "I think the street might have been named for President Cleveland, sweetie." Patricia told her daughter as she stuck her head inside the oven to assess its cleanliness. "I think he was from Jersey, so it's as likely a possibility as any."

There wasn't any talking to her mother when it came to relocating back East. Liz was well-aware that Patricia's three favorite actors: Anne Hathaway, Meryl Streep and Jack Nicholson, all hailed from The Garden State. Though Patricia's intentions were good, she made the five-day drive, in which she and Paul took turns at the wheel of the moving van, barely tolerable. Patricia would mention famous New Jerseyans: Danny DeVito, Michael Douglas, Bud Abbott and Lou Costello (of Abbott & Costello fame), Alan Alda, Michael Landon... the list went on, increasing a half a page for every thousand miles they traveled. Her efforts were not without reason. She was hoping that she could convince Liz that it was a nice place to live and raise a family and, yet, whether Liz believed what her mother was feeding her was a different matter entirely.

"Honey," Patricia called to her daughter with her head inside the oven on 11 Grover Road, "Do me a favor and remind me to tell your father to look at the stove. None of the burners seem to be working. I can smell gas when I turn the knobs, but the pilot doesn't light. This can be dangerous."

Liz's six-year-old twin brothers, Sean and Jared, could be heard in the dining room playing with their parting gifts given to them by Paul's parents. The boys got Star Wars lightsabers; Jared got the red Sith saber while Sean had to settle for the green Jedi one. At first the boys fought over who would get what, as they both wanted to have the red in order to play the villainous Darth Vader. It was Liz who broke the stalemate and told Sean to remember that good always beat out evil in the end.

"Remember that time we saw 'Watership Down'?" asked Liz. "And you guys were worried the bad bunnies were gonna win. Daddy told us that good always wins over evil in the end."

Once Sean declared he wanted the green, Jared protested, dropped the red one and insisted *he* get the green. It was Paul who, after hearing the whole story, told Jared that the green was Sean's fair and square.

"It doesn't matter," Jared said, indignantly. "Everyone knows Darth Vader is older than Luke Skywalker. That makes him way stronger!"

With the twins fighting over the fate of the galaxy in the still empty dining room and Patricia and Liz busying themselves in the kitchen, Paul, like most husbands, found himself taking charge of things in and around the garage. By no means a jack-of-all-trades, but still able to do small chores around the house like changing locks and unclogging toilets, Paul began emptying the moving van of the items that needed storing. Among them were Liz's ten-speed bike, the twins' bicycle built for two, a garden hose, an eight-step ladder and Paul's untouched tool box he'd gotten from Patricia seven Christmases ago. This latter possession he received after struggling for ten hours to put the twins' crib together.

Stuck to his tool kit was the end of a barely-used roll of masking tape. He called to his wife and daughter. Liz walked through the pantry and stopped at the doorway, which led to the indoor garage.

"Yeah, dad?" she said.

"I need you to put this in the living room closet. I have a feeling we'll be needing it more around the house once I start to paint."

He threw Liz the tape, almost hitting her in the face, but Liz, being the agile teen that she was, managed to move her head in time to catch the roll with one hand.

"Sorry, hon. Do you mind doing that for your old man?"

"Sure, Father Christmas," She said in her best cockney accent and smiled as she left Paul to his work, thus completely forgetting to mention the problem with the stovetop.

Liz made her way past her brothers, who had now moved their intergalactic battle to the living room. As she passed Jared, Liz nearly had an eye put out by an unexpected swing of his lightsaber. Jerking her head to avoid the collision, she suddenly perceived a small door below the staircase, nearly half the size of a standard-size door. She'd never noticed this door before and wondered if her parents ever had, as its outline was fairly camouflaged against the rest of the wall. So much so in fact, that it was hardly a mystery that it had gone unnoticed as long as it had. Liz walked to the tiny entrance and considered it. She assumed that her father meant this closet and not the one in the foyer. She bent down slightly to try and match her own height with that of the door. She slowly twisted the rusty knob, which, like the rest of the house, was old, worn and needed updating. Had the house not been sitting on a lot of a little more than an acre, which was considered large for this area, the house would have been a hard sell. Paul and Patricia agreed that a fixer-upper was in their best interest. Their plan was to enroll the kids in an excellent school district, keep their mortgage payments low and renovate the property over time.

Liz tugged the knob, but the door only half opened and then got stuck just before it could break free of the door jamb. She tugged harder, and this time the knob came off in her tight grip. The door, on the other hand, didn't budge an inch further.

She studied the knob for a moment and allowed herself a slight laugh before skimming the living room for something with which to pry open the door.

Not finding anything at first, she tried inserting her index finger into the hole that the knob had once occupied, but the opening was too narrow, even her pinky was too big. She once again surveyed the room and this time noticed an iron poker, which had belonged to the previous owners, standing beside the fireplace. She hastened toward it, raised it up to her eyes and immediately heard screaming from behind her.

It was Jared and Sean, charging her with their lightsabers swinging high above their heads and seeming ready to attack her.

In a playful gesture, Liz held the poker exactly as the boys were holding their own weapons. She frowned and deepened her voice. "I AM PRINCESS DIANA!" she said, boldly, "AND I AM HERE TO SAVE THE DAY ALONG WITH OBI- ONE!"

"Princess Diana?" said Sean, slowly withdrawing and sounding utterly disappointed.

"Obi-*One*?" said Jared in a shocked tone.

Liz lowered the poker.

"What's the matter?" she asked. "Isn't that right?"

The twins looked at one another, shook their heads in perfect synchronicity and ran back into the empty dining room to resume their combat. Liz anxiously brought the poker to the hole in the closet door. Without assessing what she was about to undertake, she shoved the rod in and brought the handle down carefully so as not to cause the door further damage. Once she determined the poker to be sufficiently wedged, she twisted its handle and pulled.

The door broke free of the door jamb and its hinges creaked loudly. This sound unsettled Liz, as a shiver ran from her shoulder blades down to her tailbone. Immediately, she was hit with the disagreeable smell of old wood, dampness and possible mold.

"Eww!" she bellowed and withdrew a bit, covering her nose with her forearm. She dropped the poker, and it made a loud thud against the aged parquet. "Gross," she murmured, seeing nothing in the darkness below the staircase but occasional glimmers of white that were undoubtedly thick clusters of cobwebs.

I don't think this is the place to be storing anything we plan to use, she thought.

Then she heard a call from the kitchen. It was her mother asking if she'd seen the box marked *drinking glasses*. Liz shouted a distinct *no* over her shoulder and quickly focused all her attention back on the closet. She examined the dark space for a few moments, thinking that it might be cool to see if the couple that had previously lived in this house left anything behind. After all, the door was so wedged and the knob so weak that it probably hadn't been opened in years. As all this passed through her mind, Liz thought it would be a good idea to fetch a flashlight to shine inside the closet. That way she'd be able to see if there was anything worth exploring.

She came back to the closet a minute later with her father's flashlight, which, luckily for Liz, had been unpacked and placed on the utility shelf of the garage just minutes before. She looked down into the flashlight lens as she switched it on with a thrust of her thumb. She briefly blinded herself as its 200 lumens assaulted her retinas and sent a quick, yet dull shooting pain, to her temples.

Keeping her arms steady, she aimed the industrial flashlight into the closet. As it turned out, there was a larger mass of cobwebs than Liz had first assessed, and it had amassed around the entire length and width of the space. Liz was anxious to see if there was anything worth finding in the closet, even if it turned out to be nothing more than a tiny shelf on which to put her father's roll of masking tape. In order to do that, however, she needed to break through the sticky barricade. She knew this wasn't going to be easy as she'd always been absolutely terrified of bugs and spiders. Liz could remember on several occasions walking into a single, nearly invisible string of spider web and feel it stick to her face, wrap around her ears, and even slightly penetrate her mouth. And that was nothing compared to the amount of sticky arachnid mess that now awaited her.

"Fuck." She sighed. "There's no way I'm going in there."

Still crouching, she began to back away and in doing so ran her foot against the edge of the fire poker. Although it held a narrow spike, she thought it would suffice in handling that webby mess. Like Luke Skywalker when he first inherited his lightsaber, she began blindly swinging the poker in random directions in an attempt to create as much of an opening within the web as possible. This would allow her to see through to the other side.

As far as she could make out, Liz saw that she'd broken through nearly the entire barricade of cobweb. She once again switched on the flashlight and peered into the now illuminated space. She could immediately make out several items. The first was a filthy, poorly-wrapped bolt of yellow fabric with a tacky design of sunflowers and watering cans. Then she brought the light over to the right and saw a Raggedy Ann doll that appeared to have doubled as a pin cushion. Liz tried but was unable to count the many pins that had been stuck in the doll's button eyes, triangle nose and pencil-lined smile. She immediately thought of her grandmother's pin cushion that had been made to resemble a tomato. As a small child, Little Elizabeth Brentwood made the mistake of grabbing it as if it was a real fruit and biting into it. Liz smacked her lips a few times and rubbed the tip of her tongue against her palate as the memory of metallic-tasting blood flooded her mouth.

She was ready to throw the tape into the storage space and let it join its filthy veteran *closet mates*, when the light from the flashlight caught something that quickly got Liz's attention. At first it looked like nothing more than a plain orange box. But upon further investigation (for Liz this just meant walking a few paces forward) she noticed that it was adorned with what looked like a black button surrounded by a rigid wheel of the same color. Liz cocked her head a little and saw that there on the wider side of the box, which faced upwards, was another dark round object. She flashed the light onto it.

"A lens," she murmured under her breath and immediately went for it. But just as her brain registered that it was a camera, she felt something tickling at the top of her scalp. She passively brought her free hand up to her hair and latched her fingers onto something that, once in her grip, began to instinctively kick its eight legs in all directions to try to free itself. Liz felt this movement and before she realized what it was, brought her hand to the light emanating from the flashlight and opened her palm. Sitting on it was a large wolf spider whose legs, now still, spanned the entire length of her hand from tip of thumb to wrist to tip of middle finger.

Liz let out a shrill scream and began violently shaking her hand until she was sure her hand was free of the spider. She staggered backwards out of the closet, and then, using the flashlight, frantically scanned the floor inside for any sign of what she deemed to be nothing more than a *disgusting insect*. Thanks to the additional light, she once again happened upon the plastic orange camera. Liz carefully surveyed the floor to make sure the spider wasn't lurking near the treasure. When she was sure it was safe to do so, she thrust one foot forward, leaned down and scooped up the camera along with what seemed to be ten years' worth of caked-on dust and filth. She practically ran out of the closet, scaring herself into thinking that she may have inadvertently scooped up the spider as well. Goosebumps inundated her body from head to toe. She shook off the feeling, thus dropping the flashlight and nearly tripping over the poker.

"Ewww!" she cried, "Goddamn disgusting bug!"

She regained her composure and then looked down at her hand. In her grasp she beheld a Series 120R Vortex 35mm disposable camera that to her looked beyond ancient. She actually laughed out loud at the joke that came into her head.

Instead of 'your mother's so old, Jesus signed her yearbook', a better one would be, 'your mother's so old she got her wedding picture taken with a...'. She stopped and reread the name aloud, "Series 120R Vortex 35mm."

Liz aimed the camera at her face, tilted her head so that her ear was almost pressed up against her shoulder, smiled widely and pushed the shutter. But the button felt like it was stuck; it didn't give at all. Liz brought the camera closer to her and observed the back where there was a series of four dots, followed by the number 15, followed by another series of four dots, and then the number 20. Liz knew this to be the counter's gauge indicating how many pictures had already been taken. But she wasn't quite sure how many pictures this particular camera could take. She flipped the camera upside down, then right-side-up again, looking for something that would indicate if there was any room left on the roll of film for another picture.

Since she had been born in 1996, Liz was too young to remember, or even appreciate, 35mm cameras. She was a child of the all-digital age, where, after you take a picture, you can look at it through the camera's LCD to determine whether or not you want to keep it. Gone were the days of wondering how a picture was going to turn out after you took it. People were glad that technology had brought an end to bringing in their cameras to have the film developed for $15.00, and tossing out half a stack of photos that came out either looking blurry, whitewashed or as if the subject's face had spontaneously started to melt.

On the front of the plastic Vortex, just below the lens, there was small lettering that read '20 EXPOSURES'. Liz swiftly turned the camera back over and checked the gauge.

"18". she whispered, seeing the white arrow pointing to the third dot that came after the number 15.

The frustration that came from not knowing how to solve a problem prompted Liz to tighten her grip along the side of the camera, accidentally pressing the rigid wheel forward, which in turn advanced the film within the camera. She looked down and took her thumb away from the wheel. No longer caring if this would ruin the apparatus, she purposely repeated the action and cranked the wheel forward until it stopped. Then she checked the film counter.

"19," she said, sounding elated. She posed once again, this time with her tongue out and pointed upward, her head back and her eyes narrow. It was as sexy a pose as she could manage without involving other parts of her body. She pressed down on the shutter and heard a soft *click* come from inside the camera. Just then, she felt a sharp pain between her shoulder blades, which quickly traveled down every pain neurotransmitter in her back.

"Ow! Fuck!" she shouted, "Goddamn spiders! That really hurt."

She tried to feel for the bite but worried she'd have to contend with another spider. Deciding not to tempt fate, she rolled her shoulders and pulled away the bottom of her shirt from her waist so whatever was in there would fall out. She didn't feel anything crawling on her and nothing dropped out from inside her shirt. Liz anxiously turned her attention back to the Vortex. She flipped it over and began to crank the film advance wheel. The gauge went to 20, but as the film was finished, the wheel didn't stop. Liz looked the camera over once more, shrugged and finally tossed it onto the couch. She didn't think about the camera again until later that night.

3

Sleep didn't come easily for Liz that night. Although in her own bed, she was now sleeping in a different room in a new house in a strange town thousands of miles from what she considered to be home. She nodded off around one in the morning, at which time she dreamed she was walking through the family's new house on 11 Grover Road in Ho-Ho-Kus, New Jersey. Even though she knew it was supposed to be the house they'd just moved into, the house greatly resembled their previous one back in Pinewood, California. The only difference was that the clean beige walls with crown molding were replaced with the crumbling whitewash of 11 Grover Road. To add to Liz's repulsion of her new home, the hallway in which she found herself walking just outside her bedroom was laden with thick sticky cobwebs.

Calling several times in a timid voice that sounded more like that of a little girl than her own, Liz found herself afraid to move forward. Regardless of how hot her head felt and the beads of sweat dropping down her forehead and temples into her eyes and onto her lips, her arms felt cold and clammy. She crossed her arms and began to slowly rub the cold skin with her hands. She stated out loud how she'd wished she had another poker to get through these particular cobwebs. No sooner did the words pass her lips than she felt something press up against her big toe. She looked down. Although the house was completely dark and devoid of noise, a beam of moonlight shone through a window at the end of the hallway. At her feet Liz saw the exact same poker she'd found in the living room earlier that day.

At first, she was terrified to bend down into the obscurity, worried that another wolf spider was waiting for her to pick it up. But balancing the unlikely event of another spider finding its way onto her exposed skin versus the likelihood of finding out where she was with the help of the poker, Liz chose the latter. She took up the iron spear and began jabbing at the cobwebs. When she had broken through, she saw what at first looked to be an enormous white futon. But as Liz got closer, it quickly became evident that it was a thick and intricate spider web the size of a station wagon. In the center of the impeccably symmetrical weave sat the orange Series 120R Vortex 35mm disposable camera she'd found earlier that day.

Without thinking, Liz stepped barefoot onto the web, which didn't feel sticky on the soles of her feet. In fact, it felt like inflexible twine. She easily advanced toward the camera. When she came to within inches of it, she heard a hissing sound behind her followed by a gust of hot steamy foul air that blew the back of her hair over her shoulders and into her face. She quickly became consumed by a stench not unlike what her brother Jared's pet tarantula tank smelled like after weeks of not cleaning out the dead cricket carcasses.

She began to convulse, imagining a terror behind her that was so great she couldn't fathom what to expect, only that it was worse than her most terrible fear. Again she heard the hissing sound, but this time it was accompanied by a whisper that sounded even more menacing.

"*Good over evil.*" she thought, hearing her father's voice. "*Good over evil. Good over evil. Good always triumphs over evil.*"

"*Feed yourself to me!*" whispered whatever stood behind her.

Liz gasped, jumping forward, twisting her body midair and landing on her ass at the center of the web before peering up to see what it was. There was nothing but darkness. She swept her hands all over for the camera, hoping that its flash might still work. Even if there weren't any more film, she might get the shutter to work and the dimness might trigger the flash. But the camera was no longer there. Suddenly Liz felt the web slowly dip then started to bounce steadily up and down. Out of the gloom she saw a shape slowly coming toward her. In the center of what she saw was a large hairy mass consisting of a single row of a dozen large black eyes and thick long black fangs that seemed to dance rhythmically in the air. Its thin, stubbly-haired, wire-like legs stepped one by one on the web as it advanced toward her, growling, "*Feed yourself to me. Let me spin you up so you can feed yourself to meeeeee!*"

"NO!" shouted Liz, and, feeling something behind her, reached for the camera that had been leaning against the small of her back. She aimed it up at the spider and hit the shutter. The camera clicked and a blinding flash, as bright and as long-lasting as the floodlights at a night game at Angel Stadium, ensued. The beast made a high-pitched shriek and immediately retreated into the shadows as the room once again grew dark. Breathless, Liz sank back into the web and tried to catch her breath, concurrently wiping the dripping sweat from her forehead. She could taste the salty excretion on her lips. As she went to wipe her mouth dry with the short sleeve of her nightshirt, she began to feel a tickling sensation on her legs. The darkness lifted and the entire hallway became bright, as bright as the Vortex's flash had made it just a moment before. The tickling sensation increased and began traveling up her legs to her stomach, then to her neck and finally to her face. With the blinding light making it hard for her to see, Liz squinted as she gazed down at her prostrate body. With one hand she was scratching her body in a futile attempt to relieve herself of the itching sensation that now plagued nearly all of her. She cupped her free hand and pressed the side of it against her forehead to act as a visor. She could see nothing in front of her due to the great white light. But peering down she was able to see very well what had been crawling all over her.

Thousands and thousands of baby wolf spiders.

4

Liz screamed as she thrashed about violently in her bed, kicking her feet and flailing her arms. Jared, who'd been amusing himself by tickling his sister's neck and face, got a punch to the ear while Sean, doing the same at Liz's feet, bit his tongue as her knee collided with his jaw. The two boys drew back from Liz's bed, and began nursing their respective injuries just as Paul and Patricia entered the room.

"WHAT HAPPENED?" shouted Paul.

"WHAT'S GOING ON IN HERE?" added Patricia.

The twins stepped back two paces each and looked at each other, then down at the floor, their faces both racked with guilt while Liz tried to get a handle on the situation. She could hear the sizzling of the radiator pipes behind her headboard as their heat baked her upper body. She assessed her surroundings and swiftly realized she'd just awakened from a frightful nightmare. Liz went to scratch her head and felt her hair scorching. Her scalp felt as if she'd just spent an entire August day at Disney Land.

"OUT!" shouted Paul at the twins. "The two of you OUT…NOW!"

The boys shuffled obediently out of Liz's room in single file. Liz, in turn, kicked off the remaining covers from her bed.

"Little creeps." muttered Liz under her breath but within earshot of her parents. "Sorry if I woke you guys. I just had the worst nightmare of my life."

"We were up already, honey." said Patricia, comfortingly as she sat on the edge of Liz's bed and gently rubbed her daughter's thigh. "Wanna tell mommy about the dream?"

Liz scoffed. "Mother, please. I haven't called you *mommy* since I was ten, and I haven't had to tell you my bad dreams since I was seven. It was just…just a really…bad…"

Liz looked up to see her father tinkering with the thermostat out in the hallway.

"Goddamn piece of shit!" exclaimed Paul. "This house is crumbling around us!"

"Mom, what's dad doing?"

"He's trying to fix the heat," said Patricia, looking over her shoulder at Paul.

"Well that explains why it's so hot in here. For crying out loud, mom, it's gotta be a hundred and one degrees in here. Tell him to turn it off."

"That's just it, sweetie, he can't. The heat kicked on for some reason in the middle of the night. We woke up roasting in *our* bed. We figure the same thing happened to you and the twins when we heard all the commotion out here."

"No, mom. Jared and Sean woke me, *not* the heat."

Liz felt grateful for the malfunctioning thermostat. Had it worked properly, her nightmare would have continued until that army of baby spiders had all but consumed her entire body. And then what would she have dreamed? The very thought was too horrific for Liz to contemplate. And still the idea of sharing her dream with her mother was something Liz grappled with. It might have settled her nerves, but, then again, rehashing it could have caused insomnia. In the end, she decided to keep it to herself, for if she related it to her mother, she might never forget it. And that was all she wanted right now; to forget about cobwebs, giant wolf spiders…and the camera that, until she dreamed of it, Liz had forgotten all about.

****

That morning at breakfast all was subdued. Sean's tongue still throbbed, and he found it difficult to eat, let alone talk. Jared's ear was still tender to the touch, and a black and blue had formed around the cartilage. Neither boy, however, dared to be candid about his injuries. Liz, on the other hand, was suffering from an acute lack of sleep. She, like Patricia, had spent the rest of the night lying in bed, staring up at the ceiling afraid to go back to sleep, albeit for entirely different reasons. Patricia had been worried that the heat might accidentally kick back on again, while Liz had been stirring awake, trying to put her dream out of her mind. Perhaps it was dwelling on the nightmare for the last four hours that caused its images to embed themselves in Liz's consciousness.

"Say, what's this?" Paul called from the living room.

"What's what?" Patricia called back, shouting over Liz and causing the latter to jump slightly.

"It's some beat up old camera."

Liz looked up suddenly, remembering that she had left the Vortex on the sofa. She and Patricia got up from the breakfast table and went into the living room. The twins followed closely behind them.

"Wow!" exclaimed Patricia as she snatched the camera away from Paul. "I haven't seen anything like this in years."

"What is it, mommy?" asked Sean.

"It's a camera, honey," she replied. "But not at all like the kind like you guys are used to seeing."

"Where did it come from?" asked Paul.

"From under the stairs," answered Liz and then felt four pairs of eyes instantly fall on her. She took the camera from her mother, shoved her hands into the pockets of her shorts and shrugged her shoulders. As she did, she felt a dull pain below her nape. She reached to feel for it and remembered the spider bite she'd suffered as she snapped the last exposure of the Vortex. She tried to play off the significance of the camera. Although it was a long shot, as the couple was far too busy with the new house to bother, Liz didn't want her parents to develop the film and see that last exposure. After the "Hornsby Affair", as Paul started calling it, exposure number 20, which showed their daughter striking a provocative pose, would have confirmed his fears that his little girl was growing up too fast.

"It was in that closet under the stairs," she continued. "You know, dad. Where you told me to put the tape?"

Paul looked quizzically at his daughter, and then to Patricia before motioning to the door in the front hallway with his chin. "*That* was the closet I meant, baby doll."

Liz knew there was a closet in the front hallway, but Paul had asked her to put the tape in the *living room closet*.

"Living room closet, front hall closet. Tomato, tom-ah-to. You know what I me..." Paul stopped and looked over his daughter's shoulder towards the door below the staircase. Patricia followed her husband's gaze and set her own eyes on the door that neither of them had noticed before.

"Well I'll be a monkey's uncle." said Paul.

That remark made the twins giggle.

"We didn't see that there before, did we, Paul?"

"Nope. But then again, we came out here on a two-day house hunt and ran pretty fast through 16 open houses in the interest of time. And since we moved in, we've been busying ourselves in every other part of the house *but* the living room. I'm not surprised we missed it."

He started toward the door and noticed that the knob seemed to be hanging loosely from its hole.

"Oh, dad," began Liz, "don't bother with the handle. It's broken."

But Paul tugged on the knob before Liz could finish, and it came off in his hand.

"No shit, Shirl..." said Jared before being stifled with a swift smack to the back of the head by Patricia.

"JARED BENJAMIN BRENTWOOD!" scolded Patricia.

He looked up apologetically at her and she returned his sad puppy eyes with a maternal yet stern look of disapproval, tilting her head and thinning her lips until they completely disappeared.

"Dad," continued Liz, "Here, let me."

She took the poker from beside the fireplace and inserted it into the hole. She gave it a yank, but the door seemed to open much easier this time; so much so that she pulled with more force than was necessary and lost her footing. She fell backward and stumbled into Paul.

"Am I gonna like what I see in there?" said Paul. "Or am I gonna have to add on another two weeks' work and another thousand dollars to the Home Depot charge account?"

Liz could hear Patricia sigh behind her.

"No dad. Really, it's a tiny closet. And I can't imagine you'll ever need to use it. It's kinda gross under there. Honestly, I wouldn't even bother.

Paul looked back at his daughter. "Really?"

Liz smiled and squeezed her father's cheek. "Absolutely. Hey, would I lie to you?"

This comment was all it took to rehash the subject of Liz's no-good boyfriend Rob Hornsby, and how she'd lied about how intimate her relationship had been with him. The rest of the morning was an all-out shouting match with Liz in one corner and her parents in the other; leading the former to ultimately storm out of the house and into the steamy July air. She was almost at the corner of her street when she reached into her pocket to make sure she had her wallet, cell phone and house keys, and in so doing, pulled out the Vortex 35mm disposable camera.

****

Liz arrived a short while later in the downtown area of neighboring Allendale. This *business district* wasn't much more than a single street with ten stores on either side, one of which was Big Jake's Photorama. Most people simply referred to it as *Big Jake's*, despite Big Jake Charpentier, who was as big as his name, succumbing to renal failure a few years before. It was now owned and managed by his pernicious sister, Eugenia, a woman whose nastiness equaled her considerable size. She refused to change the sign above the store for what she called "financial reasons", thus trying through word of mouth to get the townspeople to start calling it *Big Eugenia's Photorama*. She even threatened her three employees with swift and permanent dismissal if she didn't hear them say, '*Have a nice day and thanks for shopping at Big Eugenia's Photorama!*' Needless to say, the new name didn't catch on, and like when they were kids, Eugenia now had to live her life in the posthumous shadow of her older brother.

With her temper still flaring, Liz thought her best bet was to explore the unfamiliar town in which she now found herself wandering, leastwise until she cooled down enough to be able to look her parents in the eye again. Her first thought was to grab an iced coffee; unsweetened with lots of Half and Half was how she liked it. The town's closest thing to a coffeehouse was a Dunkin' Donuts, and she realized this after twice walking up and down the tiny thoroughfare. Disappointed that the nearest Starbucks was three miles north of where she now found herself, and with the heat index already flirting with 100, Liz shrugged her signature shrug and crossed the street toward her backup caffeine supplier.

When she got to the other side of West Allendale Avenue, Liz noticed the weathered pine green sign of Big Jake's Photorama. The word *photo* jumped out at her almost immediately, and her first thought was that she'd be able to develop the film still inside the Vortex. Forgetting all about getting the need for a coffee fix, Liz crossed the street once again, walking with a bit of haste in her stride.

Upon entering Big Jake's Photorama, Liz was shocked to see that it wasn't just a tiny store with an overly-massive photo finishing machine. There were seven aisles filled with the same kind of stock you'd see in a drugstore chain, and at the front of each aisle was an end cap featuring a particular sale of the week. In truth, they were the overstocked items that Eugenia Charpentier tried desperately to move.

Liz walked past the end cap that held the pumpkin spice-scented bath salts that had been marked down twenty percent, and made her way to the photo finishing center, all the while peeking briefly into each aisle to see if there was anything she might need.

Maybe it's a "rama" because it has so much stuff. she thought. *Like what made the Cinerama back home a "rama"? 'Cause it had eight screens. As opposed to the Cinelux, which only had two.*

No one was at the counter, so she cupped her hand and let it fall on the silver bell that sat in front of a small handwritten sign that read, "PLEASE RING FOR SERVICE". The bell produced a loud, unpleasantly acute sound, and Liz was sorry she had hit it as hard as she had. She covered the entire bell with both of her hands until its vibration ceased. Concurrently, one of the employees of Big Jake's Photorama came out from the back room.

He was her age or thereabouts, very thin, taller than her by two inches, had shoulder-length hair and donned a Metallica shirt as well as an oversized cross. Although he was a dark brunet, a large patch of hair just above the center of his forehead was completely white. Liz couldn't help but stare at it. Then as the employee cleared his throat to speak, Liz reacted by making eye contact with him, smiling uneasily as she did so. She knew he must have seen her staring at his hair, because he looked up like he was looking at the ceiling, but kept his head still.

"I know what you're thinking." he started. "*Fashion statement.*"

Liz just shrugged and shook her head a little.

"The truth is, it's a birthmark."

"Really?" said Liz, sounding interested.

"Yup. I got the Michael Jackson disease."

"Michael Jackson?" she replied, not expecting that one.

"Vitiligo. Maybe you've heard of it?"

"I don't think so." said Liz.

"It's a skin disorder," said the employee, as he pointed one of his elbows in her direction. Liz could see very white, almost bleached skin around a sea of pink. "It's when you lose...uhm... pig...pigmen..."

"Pigmentation?" said Liz, tensing up a bit and checking the time on her BlackBerry.

"Yeah!" declared the employee. "That's the word. *Pigmentation*! Anyway, that's the reason why I got these patches of white. If I weren't wearing pants, I'd show you my knee caps."

"Excuse me?" said, Liz, and withdrew a step.

"I didn't mean if I was naked." said the employee and laughed. "I just meant that if I wasn't working, I'd be in shorts and be able to show you my knees. I got vitiligo there too. And even got a touch of it on my left shin. You know what they call me at school?"

He pointed to the patch of white on his head.

Liz thought for a second, and then replied, "Skunk?"

"That's right!" he said and nodded his head several times. "How'd you know?"

"Lucky guess." replied Liz, dully, and offered the employee a false smile. "You know what they call me?"

"No." replied the employee.

"Lucky guesser."

"Ha! Really?"

"Listen," said Liz, placing her palms flat on the counter and leaning back until her elbows locked, "I'd love to stand here all day and shoot the shit, but I need to get some pictures developed."

"Well, you're in the right place! The only place in the Boro of Allendale that has a photo finish."

Liz hummed in agreement. "I'm sure. It's not exactly the Mall of America around here, is it? We just moved here."

"Minnesota!" said the employee, emphatically.

"No." answered Liz. "Not a chance. Not even close."

"New Hampshire? I got an uncle that lives in Holly."

"California," said Liz. "*SoCal* to be precise."

"I was closer when I said Minnesota."

Liz pointed to the photo finishing sign in an attempt to get the conversation back on track, but the employee interrupted her before she could speak.

"Well," he continued, "New Jersey's not so bad. We got lots of people that come over from New York State to do their shopping."

"Somehow I doubt that." Liz said, very matter-of-fact.

"No, honest. Our sales tax here is only seven percent. And there's no tax on clothing, footwear or any other essentials." He looked Liz over a bit more carefully, staring down at her exposed belly button, which was pierced and boasted a large cubic zirconia. "Where's home for you now? Your folks buy in Allendale?"

Liz scoffed and shook her head. "No. Ho-Ho-Kus. But it's just temporary. I'll be moving back to California real soon."

Liz looked briefly away, trying to make it seem like she was interested in the current issue of *Here & Now* magazine on the rack beside her whose headline read "10 WAYS TO TRIM WINTER FAT FOR THE SUMMER". She wasn't very good at lying, even when she had been telling her mom that there was nothing going on between her and Rob Hornsby.

Her eyes caught sight of a basket in front of the counter that held different kinds of disposable cameras. She knelt down and rummaged through the assortment. They were mostly water cameras; plastic ones like her Vortex but that had been reinforced with a thick clear plastic covering. The employee leaned forward and watched Liz poke through the stock.

"Not much call for disposables anymore. I'd say almost one hundred percent of the photos we develop now are digital." He pointed to the solitary self-serve photo kiosk. "Since we got that gizmo in, it's been doing all the hard work, pretty much. Customers choose the pics they want to print, adjust the color, crop, rotate. Really cuts out the middle man. All I do is go into the computer, see what's queued for printing and…

"Why do you sell disposables then?" she asked, still looking through the basket of disposables.

"Those ones *do* sell. The waterproof ones, I mean. Kids still like to take pics under the water. Can't do that with digital cameras or cell phones, so…Are you looking for a disposable camera?"

Liz ignored the question. She was expecting to find a Vortex camera similar to the one, if not the same one, that she had on her. The last thing she wanted was for this Alice Cooper knockoff to poke fun at her for trying to develop such a relic.

She stood up abruptly and startled the employee, who jerked back.

"How much does it cost to develop these kinds of cameras?" she asked, pointing to the basket of disposables.

"Oh, depends." he said, pulling back his shoulders and sounding like he was holding his breath and about to stretch. "I'm the only one here today so I can give you a discount."

"A discount?" asked Liz.

"Sure. Let's say, I'll develop anything you have and you and I go grab some sushi or something later on."

"Sushi?" replied Liz, curling her upper lip in repulsion. "Should I puke on the counter or the floor?"

Liz noticed a skateboard leaning up against the photo machine and surmised that it belonged to him.

"How much for twenty exposures?" she asked. Her voice clearly sounded frustrated and impatient, but this just went over the employee's head. She found him annoying, yet fairly handsome, and although she'd been a California cheerleader who presumably would be apt to date preppy jocks, Rob Hornsby was a Goth-type who also wore all black and had a mutual affinity for skateboarding.

"How 'bout Sunday? We're closed Sundays."

"HOW-MUCH?" repeated Liz, sounding final as she leaned closer to him.

The employee, still thinking he might have a chance, also leaned in closer as if prepared to kiss her. "I told you." he said, beaming at her.

"Right. Dinner…with *you*."

Liz paused and nodded slowly, thinking of a comeback that would make this Neanderthal get it once and for all.

"OK." said Liz.

"R-Really?" said the employee, blinking several times.

"Yeah, sure. Oh, by the way. Do you sell shampoo for lice?"

Liz wished she had more film in the Vortex so she could snap a shot of the employee at the very moment she asked him that question. It would have all been worth it to remember how stupid he looked when she uttered the word *lice*.

"Why do you need that? Does your little sister got lice or somethin'?" he said, and managed a nervous chuckle.

"No, I don't have any sisters."

"No sisters," said the employee, belting out a louder but no less nervous laugh.

"I have twin brothers."

"Twin brothers," repeated the employee.

"Yeah, and they're always playing in public sandboxes. They had lice twice just this past school year."

"Oh, and you need it for them?"

"Not exactly. I said they *had* lice. *I'm* the one who needs the shampoo."

Liz cocked her head back slightly and swayed her head from left to right, showing off her long, healthy, chestnut-colored hair to the employee in an almost flirtatious manner.

"But I don't have it on my head," she said, smiling.

"Not on your head?" laughed the employee. "Where else can you get...?" he stopped as Liz peered down at her crotch. "You're kidding, right?"

"Hey, it's hair, isn't it? But I'm really excited for our little date on...what day did you say was good for you again?"

The employee backed up, nearly tripping over a box of frames he had yet to open.

"Uhm..." he began, "I actually have two jobs and I forgot I... uhm...I'm working...uh, did you say you wanna develop some...?"

Liz pulled the Series 120R Vortex 35mm disposable camera from her pocket and handed it to the employee.

"It's kinda old," said Liz.

"It sure is." said the employee, his tone sounding more like it had been at the commencement of their encounter. "But it should still develop. If the film hasn't been compromised."

"Compromised, like how?"

"Like, was the camera dropped in water?"

"Not that I know." said Liz, and then wondered if the former owners of 11 Grover Road ever tried to take pictures under water with the wrong camera.

The employee closely examined the Vortex.

"Its seal doesn't seem to have been opened." he said. "Nope, I'd say it was O.K., but we won't know for sure until I develop them.

"How long will it take?"

"Well, we're not busy, so about twenty minutes ought to do it. It'd be sooner if they were digital, but there's a whole 'nother process involved with 35mm film. In fact, make it a half hour just to play it safe.

"And how much is it? The *price* to develop them this time, please."

"Is this color film?" He examined the camera's casing again.

"I have no idea."

"Black and white's more expensive to develop. It should be about twelve dollars for color and about eighteen for black and white."

Both prices seemed excessive for Liz, who only had an Andrew Jackson in her *Taylor Swift L.A. Concert 2012* wallet, but was really intrigued to find out what was in that Vortex.

Liz looked at her watch. It was one-fifteen.

"Ok, I'll be back at a quarter-to-two."

****

Liz was back in the store at exactly one-forty-four. She wasn't sure if the photos were ready yet but didn't mind if she'd have to wait another five or ten minutes in Big Jake's Photorama. The employee had offered to call her on her cell phone the minute the photos were ready, but saying she was nervous about giving him her number was severely understating her reluctance. Liz was certainly bursting at the seams to see what was on the camera, but knowing she would be walking out of Big Jake's Photorama once and for all, never to see Ozzy Osbourne, Jr. again, added to her eagerness.

She rang the bell on the counter of the photo finishing station much gentler than before. The sound that came out seemed tinny. She thought to hit it again, a bit harder this time, but before she could, the employee emerged from the back room door.

"Ah, you're back," he said, checking his cell phone, an older model, flip phone. "And right on time!"

"Did they come out ok?" asked Liz, anticipation evident in her voice.

"Uh...that they did," said the employee, mumbling as he took a sip of soda from a can with a long green straw. "And good news!"

"Huh?" asked Liz.

"They were color photos, so the damage comes to..." he paused and checked the receipt that Liz saw had been taped to the envelope; the one in which were some stranger's photos that she was paying to have developed. "$11.88."

"Oh, well that's not so bad I guess."

"Yeah. It would've been cheaper if…"

"I know, I know. If they'd been digital prints. Next time I'll be sure to bring in my memory card and you can develop my photos from camp last summer.

He only grinned, sort of insincere, knowing she was being equally disingenuous. As he took her money and was making change, Liz glared down at the red envelope that held the photos. She wanted to grab the packet and tear it open. She couldn't wait to see what the camera had been hiding. Did it simply contain photos of some kid's party? Of Christmas? Of Thanksgiving dinner at a relative's? Of the previous owner and his wife having mad, passionate sex? She *had* to find out.

She received her change but didn't bother counting it. She snatched the red envelope from the counter, ignored the employee's *"Have a nice day"* and was out of Big Jake's Photorama in a matter of seconds.

She ran across the street and sat on a bench, on which hung a shiny brown plaque with yellow lettering. PLEASE GIVE UP THIS SEAT FOR OUR ELDERLY AND HANDICAPPED. Liz leaned back, completely covering the message. She ripped open the envelope and looked at the first print. Her mouth dropped open as her eyes skimmed the photo.

5

At 5:15, shortly after Patricia asked Paul for the third time if they should call the police, Liz walked through the front door. She kept her head down and made a beeline for the staircase. Halfway up, her mother's voice made her stop.

"Where have you been, young lady?" asked Patricia, sounding like she'd been crying. "I thought we were going to have to call the police."

"For what?" Liz asked, annoyed. She didn't like talking back to her mother, but ever since Rob Hornsby, insolence came easy to her. "I was fine, mother. A girl can't get into much trouble around here."

"You can't just leave this house and not tell us where you're going," rebuked Patricia. "It's still a strange new place and you could get lost, not to mention there are brown bears all around this time of year."

Patricia knew this was more an empty threat to keep her daughter in line, and her hopes weren't high that it would work.

"Bears? Oh, mother, please."

"I saw a deer outside our window last night," said Jared.

"I'm going up to my room to take a nap," said Liz, faking a yawn. "Can we finish this later?"

"You better believe we will, missy. Your father just went out to the garage, no doubt to cry his eyes out," imparted Patricia in yet another ploy to solicit remorse from her daughter. "You worried the bejesus out of us!"

"Ok, mom," said Liz. "Anything you say. Call me when dinner's ready, will you?"

She closed the door to her bedroom and plopped down on the bed in a position that suggested she was prepared to nap on her stomach. She immediately felt pressure in her upper thighs next to her crotch. She turned onto her back and emptied her pockets. Out came her cell phone, her girly Taylor Swift wallet and the change she'd been tendered by the employee at Big Jake's Photorama. In her other pocket had been the set of twenty photos that were shoved inside right after checking out the first picture. She looked at the initial photo once more, shaking her head and sneering at it.

"Twelve bucks. A big waste of money, this was. What was I thinking?"

The image was clearly that of the kitchen on 11 Grover Road, although the walls were the shade of urine yellow. She'd seen that color on a wall once in her Aunt Delilah's living room. Her father had called it *Post-psychedelic piss.*

This rather ordinary photo disappointed Liz, and she didn't see the point in checking out the rest. She carelessly tossed the pile onto her nightstand, but the kitchen photo stayed at her side where she'd left it. She turned onto her side, tucking her arm behind her ear and then leaned into her elbow. Just then Liz noticed the first photo laying beside her and held it more closely to examine it again, this time trying to keep an open mind. She rubbed the tip of her index finger gently against the edge of the glossy photo. Doing this felt cathartic. Her eyes began to glaze over as she looked to that very edge and inspected the refrigerator just above her thumb. It was littered with all kinds of papers. Although it was too difficult to make out any of the items, Liz assumed they were coupons, report cards, Christmas photos of someone's kids, and possibly a recipe or two.

Maybe the people who sold mom and dad this house didn't have any kids, thought Liz and replaced the idea of report cards with adoption rejection letters.

As she made this mental correction, Liz noticed something strange outside the window above the kitchen sink. It was a silhouette of some kind, rather small, somewhat round and transparent. This might have been why she hadn't seen it before. Liz brought the picture closer and squinted so hard that she felt a muscle spasm under her left eye. No sooner did she take the picture away from her face than she managed to make a clearer determination of what the figure was. She looked at it again and it finally registered.

The figure in the kitchen window had two smaller circles for eyes within the disk-shaped silhouette. Below these two shapes Liz could make out a horizontal line bent around the center. If she hadn't known better, she'd have sworn she was looking at a face.

"It's just smudges," she told herself. "Steam from the sink must have fogged up the window and then someone must've drawn on it."

But that wasn't right. Part of this *face* overlapped the window pane, so it couldn't have just been on the glass. She rolled it over and over in her mind until she met with sleep twenty minutes later. She didn't think of the photo again when she awoke to her mother calling her down to dinner, neither did she consider it as she ate supper with her family. It didn't dawn on Liz to do any further investigating until she awoke from another nightmare later that night.

****

Liz came downstairs at 2:56 in the morning to get some warm milk. She'd always heard that was the trick to get to sleep when sleep was the last thing you thought you could do. She shuffled blindly into the kitchen, having knocked into several pieces of furniture, not from any semi-somnambulant stumbling, but because she still wasn't used to where all the furnishings were. Any nocturnal fatigue she'd still had disappeared once her knee collided with the sofa table and knocked over her mother's favorite snow globe. It made a loud lump against the floorboards, but luckily for Liz, it didn't so much as suffer a chip.

She restored the globe to its rightful place and continued slowly to the kitchen. Once there, she reached into the refrigerator for the milk, but the only things she found in there were a bag of peeled, pre-washed baby carrots, half a head of iceberg lettuce, two tomatoes, a rather nasty looking avocado that looked like it had been ripe four months ago, and an unsealed bottle of Poland Spring.

"Shit!" exclaimed Liz and slammed the door shut. She turned around and pressed her backside up against the fridge. She felt thirsty and thought it may have been for the best that she didn't have the warm milk after all. She wanted something cool to quench the thirst that she was beginning to feel. She considered taking the opened bottle of water but remembered her brother Sean had drunk from it at dinner, and she was all too aware of how her baby brothers always backwashed. She went beside the sink, opened the dishwasher that indicated *cycle finished* on its dial and removed a squeaky clean drinking glass. She ran the tap for a few seconds first.

As she brought the water to her lips and began to drink, Liz raised her eyes to the window above the sink. Instantly something jumped out of the darkness and hit against the pane. She gasped, nearly inhaling the contents of the glass. This caused her to cough hard in order to expel what water she could. The rest went down her throat and the aftertaste made for an unpleasant first encounter with New Jersey tap water. Her nerves now on edge, Liz needed time to steal herself. She held her throat until the coughing sensation subsided. She straightened up and peered bravely out the window. It turned out to be nothing more than a wayward branch from the spruce just beyond the exterior of the kitchen. She reflected on what she'd seen in the same window in that first of the 20 exposures.

Once back in her room, she sat on her bed and put her pillow on her thighs. She tilted her body slightly toward the lamp on her night table and began thumbing through the rest of the prints. The second photo was also a shot of the kitchen, although this one had been taken from the stove and faced out into the dining room. Liz shrugged and went to the next, frowning at the thought that this was how she was going to spend her night: unable to sleep from nightmares, resigned to looking at crummy photos taken by people she didn't know, and forced to live in a place she didn't care to.

"Now if Justin Bieber were visiting when they…" started Liz, and then dismissed the outlandish thought. "Nah. Mom said the Vortex was extinct by the early 90's. My Justin didn't come along until a few years later."

The third photo was taken in the dining room, and, although the chandelier above the table was illuminated, the flash had apparently gone off. She could tell because the extreme right of the photo showed part of the dining room window where some of the glare from the flash had hit the glass. Liz noticed another figure, similar to the previous one, in that very window. She felt like her heart had just skipped a beat. Unlike the previous shape in the kitchen window, this one seemed to have actual mass, as it was solid.

"What the…?" she said under her breath. She glanced up for a moment or two to think what it could mean. Relief set in once she realized that this reflection was that of a man. She continued to study the figure a bit more. She could make out the following: he had sideburns, a thick mustache and was holding something. "The guy who sold dad the house," she said at last. "Mr. Rempley. Only a lot younger. He's holding a camera. He took the picture and as the flash went off, it caught his reflection in the window."

Feeling utterly stupid, Liz moved her thumb away so as to continue on to the next photo. When she did this, she uncovered a shape within the flash, not far from where the former owner of 11 Grover Road had been standing. It looked similar to what she'd seen in the first photo, but slightly more visible. It definitely looked like the composition of a face, although not that of a man. She dismissed it as a trick of the light and went on to the fourth photo. This one, Liz determined, was taken from the same vantage point as the window where she'd seen the reflection of the younger Mr. Rempley. The photo showed the kitchen in the distance, but seemed to focus on the window above the sink.

"What the hell were these people up to?"

In this photo Liz looked briefly to see if that same facial image was still present on the kitchen window, but the shot had been snapped from too far away and the image of the window was tiny.

The fifth photo showed the dining room from the living room. Liz immediately noticed that the door to the small closet under the stairs was wide open. She looked in vain to see whether or not there was anything remotely different or interesting about the inside of the closet. The one wall that she could see within looked cleaner, and the inside of the door was a bright white, but that was all. Liz realized there was no flash in the photo, and the room had been considerably darker than the dining room, which, with its large window, had a profusion of light.

In the sixth photo, Liz could make out her living room with its whitewashed fireplace and an excess of what she considered to be outdated furniture. Standing to the right of the hearth was, she assumed, Mrs. Rempley with a look half of concern, half of alarm. Above the woman, Liz could see part of what looked like a blade and the external motor casing of a ceiling fan. She took the photo with her downstairs, switched on the lights which, ironically, came from the very thing she had gone down to see.

"Yup." she said. "Same ol' ceiling fan. It looks like they fixed it up good as new."

She began to piece together what the previous owners might have been doing.

"So the Rempleys were taking pictures of the whole house from any angle they could get. Why? So they could show their family and friends just how tacky they were? To prove to their interior decorator just how badly they needed her?"

She went back to her room and this time crawled into bed, twisted her hair up into a ball, held it together with a scrunchie and propped the pillow up against the nape of her neck.

"Or, Mr. Rempley took these shots to show Mrs. Rempley just how much she needed to clean." Liz surmised, laughing at the thought and imitated Mr. Rempley. *"Edna! Look at the friggin' mantle in this photo! You're not dusting every inch of the house like I told you! No bridge for you Thursday! You can tell those crusty bitches you always have here that they can go to hell. Although being in Jersey, they might tell you they're already there!"*

Laughter came easily to Liz when there was something worth laughing at. These scenarios she had created could keep her up the whole night. She had to cover her mouth to keep her laughter from waking her family. She noticed that she had even started tearing. Her sides were starting to ache and she had managed to dribble onto her chin. She reached to wipe it off with the hand that had been holding photo number six and in so doing moved the thumb that had been covering something that quickly halted her amusement.

What she saw in the photo made Liz Brentwood's heart feel like it had suddenly leapt into her throat.

6

Without giving any word to her parents as to where she was headed, Liz left the house at half past eight the next morning. No breakfast and very little sleep wouldn't be a concern to her so early in the day. She promised herself she'd eat as soon as she returned home and would take an extended nap between lunch and dinner.

"I know he did something to these," she growled. "I know it. And he'd better come clean or losing his job won't be the worst thing that happens to him today."

She walked with such haste in her step that she made it to Allendale by foot within a quarter of an hour, and arrived at Big Jake's Photorama a few minutes after that. She entered the store and was about to turn to walk toward the photo finishing area when she heard a deep voice call from the front counter.

"Can I help you, miss?"

The owner of the voice was a husky woman in her mid fifties holding a cigarette carton in each arm. Her hair was nearly all gray, very short and slicked back with gel. She boasted an underbite that caused her chin to protrude worse than any caricature Liz had ever seen.

"Yes," began Liz. "I was here yesterday and got some film developed. I don't remember his name, but he was the only employee working then. It was around one o'clock."

"That'd be Kyle Harris," said Eugenia Charpentier as she pointed her elbows outward, letting the cigarette cartons fall onto the counter.

"I used to schedule the pipsqueak to work the evening shift, but he'd always come in stoned. I figure no one smokes up before lunch, so I gave him the day shift. Something wrong with your photos, hon?"

Liz hated it when people called her *hon*. It was what her Aunt Delilah always used, and it had been somewhat tolerable for awhile, but after Delilah had told Liz that her pink lipstick made her look like a cheap slut, that sealed the deal for what she thought of her aunt from then on.

"No, sir."

As soon as the word *sir* left her lips, Liz reacted with an instant look of surprise and put one hand over her mouth.

"I'm sorry. I mean '*ma'am*.'"

Eugenia Charpentier narrowed her eyes at Liz and grinded her protruding jaw back and forth. For a second, Liz thought the woman was going to spit out chewing tobacco-colored spit.

"HARRIS!" shouted Eugenia, and then giving her back to Liz, the proprietor of Big Jake's Photorama went back to stocking the cigarette wall. Within moments, Kyle emerged from the back room door.

"Yeah, Miss C.?" he called, looking to Eugenia, and then frowned once he noticed Liz standing in the middle of the store.

"Oh." he started. "Hi. I didn't expect to see you again so soon."

"Oh, really?" asked Liz and she crossed her arms and tilted her head slightly. "After what you pulled?"

"This is a store, Harris," croaked Eugenia, "not an after-school hang out. If this is a social call, tell your little friend she can buy something now and talk to you later."

Thinking quickly, Liz grabbed a bag of Cool Ranch Doritos and tossed it onto the counter.

"I'll take this, please." announced Liz to the owner.

Eugenia looked over her shoulder, considered the purchase, shook her head and went back to her work.

"We really need to talk." said Liz angrily to Kyle.

A snort escaped Eugenia's nose.

"Did I do something wrong?" asked Kyle.

"You know perfectly well what I'm talking about."

"Got photos developed," grunted Eugenia. "That's a good one, missy. D'you knock up your little girlfriend, Harris? I didn't think you could get that little worm of yours through anything other than a sheet of paper with a pushpin hole in it!" Then she looked at Liz. "Does he got the Irish curse, hon?"

"Excuse me?" asked Liz, sounding irritated.

"C'mon, Miss C," protested Kyle, though his tone was still respectable.

"You know. Does he need to shove three fingers into you at the same time to compensate for his lack of...?"

"Miss C., please!" begged Kyle.

Liz thought Kyle sounded pathetic. Boss or no boss, Liz would never let anyone talk to her like that.

"Oh, come off it, Harris!" said Eugenia. "You know you Irish are all the same."

"And I suppose *you* know firsthand which guys have the biggest dicks?" said Liz boldly to Eugenia.

Kyle looked wide-eyed from Liz to Eugenia.

"WHAT DID YOU SAY TO ME?" shouted Eugenia.

"'Cause I gotta tell ya," continued Liz, "I've seen less testosterone on the field at an Army-Navy football game."

Eugenia growled something under her breath and took a step toward Liz and Kyle. She didn't see the mound of empty cigarette cartons that had accumulated at her feet and she tripped, thus falling headlong over them. She quickly disappeared behind the counter and Kyle ran over, cleared the counter with one jump (a sight that made Liz grin in spite of herself) and quickly disappeared as well.

"Uuuuhhhhh." Liz could hear the woman's manly voice groan from behind the front counter. "Goddamn!"

"You ok, Miss C.?" said Kyle as the two of them slowly emerged. Kyle struggling to hold up Eugenia's weight.

"GET OFF ME, PENCIL DICK!" shouted Eugenia and pulled her arm from Kyle's grasp. She honed in on Liz and sneered. "Take your slut outta here before I forget to be nice and shove a pink slip up that pasty white ass of yours. You'll be the youngest prick ever to hit the unemployment line in Hackensack."

"I'm not his…" started Liz, and then considered how little good it would do to try to explain anything to this woman. As Kyle walked back over to her, Liz locked her arm in his. "Shall we, baby?"

Kyle was speechless, but decided to play along as best he could.

"C-could I take my five, Miss C.?"

Now at the refrigerator section of the store, Eugenia Charpentier took a bottle of water from one of the shelves and pressed it against her forehead where a bump was starting to form.

"Take your *fifteen*, Harris. I don't wanna see you till this starts workin'!" And with that, Eugenia popped open a small brown bottle she'd taken from the breast pocket of her men's short sleeve dress shirt and shoved two Xanax into her mouth. Then, taking the cold bottle from her head, she unscrewed the cap, took a long swig of water, replaced the cap and pressed it hard back on her sore head, thus making her grunt unpleasantly.

****

"Ok, *Kyle*," started Liz. "What gives?"

"S-Sorry?" he replied.

The two walked from the front of Big Jake's Photorama down to the train station two blocks down. On the way, Liz tried to get Kyle to admit the prank she thought he'd played on her without her having to come right out and accuse him. She needed patience, mostly because she hadn't a clue of how to say it bluntly; *it* being what she'd seen in the next few photos.

"I don't wanna take up all of your break time," said Liz.

"Aw, that's ok. I'll take my lunch now. That'll give me time to catch a few smokes. Miss C. won't know if I extend my break. Those pills she sucked down are pretty legit. She's probably already made her way up to the manager's office where she'll conk out for an hour or two. She's done it lots of times before. It's become sort of protocol."

"What about the store? Who'll watch it?"

"Like always, she'll have the place locked up good and tight till I come back from break. I got my own key."

Liz removed the crumpled set of glossy four by six photos from her shorts pocket, removed the rubber band that held them together and began showing Kyle the first five photos.

"What do you see in this picture?" she asked him. "More specifically, do you see anything in the window?"

Kyle took the photo and studied the window. He bent the photo in the direction of the sun to get a better look. After several moments he shook his head and frowned.

"Nope. I don't see a thing, except for a tree or two outside."

Liz looked suspiciously at him and tapped her chin several times. She continued on to the next several snapshots and then stopped just after the one taken of the ceiling and part of the ceiling fan.

"And you mean to tell me that when you checked all these over, you didn't notice anything strange?" said Liz.

Kyle turned away, putting a Parliament menthol cigarette in his mouth and lighting it with a Zippo that had an inscription that read "*allergic to the law*" on it. He took a long drag, cocked his head away from Liz and exhaled the smoke into the humid July morning air. Then he faced her, sniffed loudly through his nose and cleared his throat. This all made Liz assume he was buying time so he could come up with some lie to tell her.

"Uhm, I have a confession," he began.

"I knew it!" declared Liz.

"No, no. Listen. I lied when I told you I thought they all came out great. The truth is I never looked at 'em. I mean, I *meant* to look at them. I'm supposed to. You know, pull out any that show overexposure, or ones that are blurry. That kinda thing."

"Then what *were* you doing?" snapped Liz, sounding like a district attorney cross-examining a witness for the Defense.

"I'm sorry. W-What's your name? asked Kyle, sounding slightly intimidated as he leaned back away from her."

Liz looked down and remarked at how she was leaning so far forward that it looked like she was either ready to jump Kyle or put him in a headlock. She sat back and took a deep breath.

"I'm Liz."

"Ok, *Liz*," began Kyle, "I sometimes like to go out behind the store and smoke a joint. And I can only do it when my boss isn't in the store. I had the place all to myself for two whole hours. So after you left I set your film up in the machine and, well…"

Liz considered Kyle's answer, and for a long time she didn't say anything. It actually did make sense that Kyle was telling the truth for several reasons: first, photos one through five were all fairly normal, except for the strange image which, frankly, was quite inconspicuous. And if Kyle were planning to scare her, he'd have messed with all the photos and made the prank easier to spot; Second, Miss Charpentier had confirmed that Kyle was a pothead. Liz had a hard time thinking of how someone as dimwitted as Kyle seemed to be could do to the pictures what she had seen in them. She had surmised that a person who knew how to develop film somehow knew how to compromise their results. But now she wasn't so sure Kyle Harris was that person.

They heard the distant sound of a horn blowing, and soon after they saw an NJ Transit train approaching. Liz surveyed the platform, expecting to see at least a few people waiting for the southbound commuter train. But as it was already just after nine in the morning, local commuters were already at work.

Liz flipped to photo number six and practically threw it at Kyle. He caught it and peered down at it as he took another drag of his cigarette. Liz kept her eyes on Kyle to see if his reaction would be genuine. She had a sinking feeling he would react the same way she did. This didn't sit well with Liz. If Kyle had nothing to do with this, then something had been seriously wrong at 11 Grover Road back when the Rempleys owned the property. This prospect frightened Liz.

Kyle mulled over the photo for what seemed to be an eternity for Liz. She watched as each of the ten cars of the commuter train roared past them, thus unnerving an already irritable Liz. She checked the time on her cell phone twice then stood up and began pacing. But she allowed Kyle the time he needed because she believed his opinion would be indispensable.

"I don't get it," he said at length. "Is this some kind of joke?"

Liz stared at him. "Is it?" she said, locking her gaze with his.

"Why would I wanna do something like this?"

Liz considered his question all the while knowing that she'd given Kyle plenty of ammunition to want to get even with her after the way she'd acted the day before in Big Jake's Photorama.

"Ok, Kyle. So if you didn't do this, who did?"

She wasn't ready to accept that the photos were authentic. To acknowledge so would mean admitting that terrifying things existed in this world.

"What makes you so sure that someone *has* to be behind this? It could be original."

"Original," echoed Liz.

"Yeah, as in *part* of the picture."

She snatched the photo back from him and started to the exit ramp but stopped short.

"Because if I allow myself to believe that as a possibility, then I'm accepting that something terrible might be living in my house."

Liz came back to the bench and collapsed next to Kyle as though her legs had given out on her. He was about to speak when she abruptly grabbed photo number six from the pile and went to tear it.

"NO!" shouted Kyle and snatched it from Liz's clutches. He pressed the photo tightly to his chest and began to flatten out the creases she'd put in it. "Are you insane? This could be something big!"

"Kyle, you haven't seen the others."

He paused.

"Others? You mean it showed up again? How many times?"

"I'll show you. But before I do, you've gotta promise me something."

"Sure." said Kyle, acting like a salivating dog waiting for a juicy bone. "Anything."

"You can't tell anyone about this. Not your parents, your friends, your boss, no one."

"No problemo!"

She put her hand out and Kyle knew she meant to have photo number six back. He gave it, reluctantly, hoping this wasn't just a ploy so she could destroy it.

"Make a mental note of this," she pointed at photo number six. More specifically, she pointed at the abnormality in the photo.

"Yeah, I know. I don't think I'm gonna forget it anytime soon."

"I'm just saying you'll want to remember it so when I show you the next three you'll have a better grip on what we're dealing with."

"We?" asked Kyle, grinning.

"Don't get any ideas," said Liz, tilting her head a little so her hair could hide her smile.

"Ok, first the mundane. We've got a living room," narrated Kyle. "By the way, just out of curiosity, you were just kidding when you said you had crabs, right?

Liz lowered her head and giggled.

"Of course," she said. "What girl would openly admit that?"

"Ok. Just checking. Now then, back to the photo."

Kyle looked back down at photo number six.

"We've got a fireplace with no mantle."

"No," interrupted Liz, "there *is* a mantle, but they painted the entire thing, hearth, facade, mantle, completely white so you can't see it. It's kinda hidden."

"Like camouflage, right?" joked Kyle.

Liz laughed. "Yeah. It's really hideous."

"Alright," continued Kyle, "we've got one ugly-ass fireplace, part of an outdated ceiling fan, a really cheesy imitation Thomas Kincaid print in a bland gold trim frame…"

"Kyle!" chortled Liz. "Come on, be serious. This is no joke."

He cleared his throat and winked at her.

"Ok. Now I see what looks to be the arm of a banister at the bottom of the pic, so I assume this was taken from your staircase?"

"You'd assume right," replied Liz. "Go on."

"Now for the…*supernatural.*"

Suddenly Liz grabbed for Kyle's crotch. This made him jump, thinking she was going to punch him in his balls, but she only reached for his packet of cigarettes. She removed one so fast from the pack that it broke in the middle. She was about to light it when she realized what she'd done. She scoffed at it, threw it to the ground and then leaned forward. She placed her elbows on her knees and began to rock back and forth.

"Should I go on?" asked Kyle, softly.

"Yes. Don't stop."

"We've got a woman standing to the right of the ugly fireplace. She looks worried. And next to her...to the right of *her*, we have... we have a...a..."

"Go 'head," pleaded Liz. "Say it."

"We have what looks to be the face of some creature. No body, just a face. It's parallel to the woman's face. It's slightly larger than hers, and the eyes are solid. Not sure what the exact color is, though. Dark, definitely. Maybe black? Dark gray perhaps? It's got a long nose...no, it's more like a snout. It looks like this *snout* has rings around it. The mouth is slightly open and from what I can make out, it looks like there are two teeth; sharp pointed teeth that are showing."

He stopped and looked in Liz's direction, "Is that right? Did I get it all?"

"That's right. You did." She sat up and fished for photo number seven. "Tell me what you see in this one."

She passed it to him. Their fingers touched briefly. Kyle left his hand there, hoping Liz would reciprocate, but she didn't. Liz fretted over hearing Kyle recount what he'd seen in this photo. It took him longer than photo number six had. It was all Liz could do to keep from *freaking the fuck out*, as she would later put it. She put her feet up on the bench and squatted.

"Kyle, please say something."

"I…," he started, then, unable to find words, just gasped.

"JUST TELL ME WHAT YOU SEE THIS TIME!" she shouted at him.

He shrank back a little. Liz put her hand on his shoulder and apologized. He smiled and put his hand on hers. This time she didn't pull away.

Going back to the photo, Kyle spoke confidently, as though touching Liz had galvanized his courage.

"I see the same vantage point. We got a guy standing where the lady once was."

"Mr. Rempley," said Liz, sounding like she was correcting Kyle.

"Ok, Mr. Rempley standing where his…*wife*…?"

Liz nodded.

"…where his wife had been in the previous shot. And…and…," Again he looked in Liz's direction. "And we've got the same…*entity;* its mouth wider…more of its teeth…uhm…very sharp teeth, I count three of them. And even though there's no *body* visible, I can see a… well it's not a hand. I'd call it a…uhm…a *claw*…which looks like it has four thick fingers, each with its own long and thick sharp nail. The claw is just below its face, a bit to the left and it looks like it's…"

"Like it's about to tear something apart, right?" Liz finished.

"Right," Kyle agreed. "Whatever it is, it's not friendly."

"Nothing that looks like that could ever be friendly," she said.

Liz leaned over again, flipped her hair over her face and Kyle could hear her start to cry. He put his arm on the small of her back and rubbed it.

"I'm sorry." he said. "I didn't mean that. We don't know what happened. And this was a long time ago, right? For all we know, the Rempleys had the place exorcised."

"I've only heard of exorcisms for people," said Liz, and sucked dripping snot through her nose.

"I don't think this is the right time to debate the issue," said Kyle, lightheartedly. "I think I wanna take a look at the rest of the pics."

"Shouldn't you be getting back to work?"

"We've got loads of time. Two hour Xanax-induced nap, remember? Besides, this beats vacuuming and putting price tags on bottles of Milk of Magnesia."

He nudged the side of Liz's knee with his own and offered her a smile. She peered through her long thick hair and saw he gave her another wink. She brushed her hair away from her face, feeling tempted to wink back.

"There's something else in this photo that's different." she said. "Can you tell?"

Kyle looked carefully at the seventh photo and shook his head.

"I don't." he said. "Unless you mean Mr. Rempley's demeanor. It's very…I don't know…unworried. Not at all like Mrs…"

"No," interrupted Liz, "I don't mean anything like that. Look at the demon."

"Liz, we don't know if that's what…"

"What else could it be? Whatever it is, Kyle, it's not human. And never was," She thought for a second, facing the sky. "Christ, what if it's still in my house?"

Kyle didn't reply.

"I mean this was what, fifteen or twenty years ago?" she asked. "What if the Rempleys did nothing about it? I mean, they never even developed the film, so how do we know they ever found out what was going on?"

"Liz." said Kyle as he rose from the bench and knelt down in front of her. He tenderly gripped her arms and met her gaze. "Listen to me. There's no way they did *nothing* about it. There's no way these guys could live in a house with some strange shit going on for twenty years. Could *you* imagine living like that?"

"I dunno. These people were strange. My dad even said he felt uneasy about buying the house from them because they seemed so eccentric and even anxious about closing the deal."

"Maybe living with a…I mean…after *having lived* with a demon, it made them that way."

She thanked Kyle for his thoughtfulness and shook her head.

"You need to see the rest of the photos. But first tell me what's different about the demon. You still haven't told me if you see it."

Kyle studied the image and then gasped.

"Oh, shit! It's…it's…

"It's more visible this time," Liz concluded. "Easier to see. Like it's becoming more…*real*."

****

The arrival of the next train unnerved both teens. They agreed to leave the train station, even though it had afforded them total privacy, as they were still the only ones who had been present on the platform, and no one had gotten off either of the two trains. They retraced their steps two blocks back to the main downtown strip and entered the Allendale Diner, which was situated directly across the street from Big Jake's Photorama.

"What if your boss saw us come in here?" asked Liz, concerned. "It's been more than a half an hour."

"Believe me," said Kyle, "the sign on the door said *closed*. I told you she would close up. No doubt that Xanax will make her take the afternoon off."

Liz chuckled as the two took the first booth by the entrance.

"I think you need to look at these last three," she said, and Kyle heard Liz's voice trembling a bit.

"*Last three*?" he repeated. "Liz, there were twenty exposures in total. What about the rest? Are they that bad?"

"Kyle," started Liz, and stopped as the waitress approached their booth and offered them each a menu.

"You kids wanna start off with something to drink?" she asked.

"Two coffees and lots of privacy, please," Kyle said politely, but sounding firm and final.

He held up the menus to the aging waitress without looking in her direction. She shoved her pad into her apron, snatched the menus and walked away, mumbling something that sounded to Kyle and Liz like, "*Goddamn rotten no good son of a...*"

Although she hadn't been keeping track of all the things Kyle did in the past hour that endeared him more to her, she was thinking of starting now.

"So what about the rest, Liz?" asked Kyle. "Am I gonna see them?"

"Just look at the last three and we'll go from there."

She reached into her pocket and pulled out the bundle of prints. She fanned through them until she reached number eight.

"Tell me what you see." said Liz.

"I see...Oh, Christ!"

The waitress returned with a glass coffee pot with a brown plastic top. Liz flipped over the two inverted cups that had already been on their table and held them up. Meanwhile, Kyle continued his observation of the eighth photo. Liz could see both worry and uncertainty on his brow. Kyle waited for the waitress to leave before he spoke.

"I see the entire staircase. This was taken from the foot of the stairs, I guess."

"You'd be guessing right," confirmed Liz, thoughtlessly adding a third teaspoon of sugar to her coffee, an act that was testament to her deep obsession with the photos, as she had never liked sugar in her coffee before.

Kyle breathed deeply and drummed the tips of his fingers against the back of the photo. "It looks like our demon is anything but camera shy," he said.

"Right." Liz agreed.

"He's...*It's*...definitely more pronounced here. But not really more solid. It's more...I guess the word would be...complete?"

"Yup."

"He's...*It's*..."

"Yeah. *It.*"

"I see more of its outline. It's got a neck now. Thick and...I think it's got scales? There's another hand...claw, also in the same position as the other one. The mouth is showing four very large and sharp teeth. He...*It*...is standing on the...one, two, three, four, *fifth* stair. Jesus, he's close to the camera this time. He looks so much..."

"Bigger," finished Liz. "Now look at this one."

She passed Kyle the ninth photo. Without looking at it, he took a sip of his coffee, winced at its acrid taste and anxiously reached for the sugar. Liz took his cup and offered him hers, explaining her mistake with the sugar. He added some cream and stirred before taking the cup to his mouth and downing the whole thing in one gulp.

He studied the ninth photo, which showed one of the upstairs bathrooms. The demon was present in front of the toilet bowl. Its transparency hadn't filled out from the last two photos, but its silhouette was more complete. Kyle could see protruding lines coming out of its now visible chest and arms. He told Liz that he thought they might be thick, stubbly hair. The mere thought made Liz cringe.

The tenth photo was the most disturbing of them all. The shot was from the vantage point of the same bathroom into one of the bedrooms. The beast was standing on the far side of the bed. Its outline was almost complete, although, because of the bed, its legs were not visible.

"That's my bedroom, Kyle," whispered Liz. Kyle could see her trembling.

"Yours?" he replied.

"Yeah. And what creeps me out almost as much as seeing this thing in my own room is that my bed is in the exact same position as that one!"

"Damn."

"You don't get it. Think of what it was like for me. I was looking through these pictures alone, in the middle of the night, in that same room, on my bed. It was bad enough seeing this...this...*thing* outside my kitchen window. Then in my living room. It was like it kept coming closer to where I was. Next it was on the staircase, then in the bathroom next to my room, and then *in* my room! I threw the pictures, envelope and all, off my bed and ran downstairs. I took my blankets and slept in the our new BMW. People say that new-car smell is the best smell you could ever imagine. But the way I felt last night, it just nauseated me. Whatever sleep I got wasn't worth it, 'cause I just had another nightmare. In fact, I haven't slept well at all since we got here. Christ, it was so hard going into that house this morning. But I did. I waited until everyone was up before I went into my room. I had thrown the photos over the left side of my bed, exactly where he...*it* had been standing. When I cleared that side of the bed..."

"Yeah?" asked Kyle, sounding anxious.

"The photos were all there, just where I had thrown them. But..."

"But what?"

Just then the waitress returned.

"Warm your coffee, sir and madam?" she asked in a patronizing tone.

The two leaned back and let her fill their cups.

"Thank you," said Liz.

"Yeah," agreed Kyle. "Thanks."

"Yup," answered the waitress, indifferently. The sound of the waitress's shoes shuffling across the floor agitated Liz.

"Go on, Liz. You were saying? About the photos on the floor next to your bed?"

"Yeah," she replied, "right. Well, they were all there, but they weren't scattered."

"What do you mean?"

"Kyle." she said, whispering as she leaned over the table. "They were stacked back up, neatly. And in *order.*"

"You mean...?"

"The first photo was first. The second one was second, and so on. In the exact same order you gave them to me yesterday!"

"Holy shit!"

Liz nodded. "Crazy, I know.

She paused and leaned into the table.

"Kyle, I realize that photo was taken a long time ago. But just seeing their bed in the same spot where my bed is now, and the thing standing exactly where I had thrown the pictures. It scared the hell out of me."

"What about the others?" he asked.

Liz scoffed.

"After I saw that little surprise waiting for me behind my bed, I just snatched them up and left the house to look for you."

"You mean to tell me that even after all you've seen, you *still* suspected *me*? What did you think, that I waited till I scared you out of your room and then sneaked through your window and neatly put them back in order and sneaked back out again?"

Liz could hear anger in Kyle's voice, and briefly thought he was going to get up and leave."

"It freaked me out, ok?" she spat at him defensively. "Then I thought my brothers might have done it. I tried to rationalize everything. I wanted to believe there was some other explanation. I dunno."

She turned away from Kyle's gaze, then met it again and put her hand on his. This time it was he who pulled away.

"I'm sorry I accused you." she said at last. "I just had to be sure."

"Yeah. I get it."

"Good over evil," muttered Liz.

"Huh?"

"Nothing. It's just something my father once told us. I've caught myself saying it a lot lately."

Kyle checked his watch.

"I should be getting back."

"What about the two-hour Xanax nap?"

Kyle sighed.

"Let me see the others."

Liz shrank back.

"You *do* have them, don't you? Are they just as bad? Worse?

"I don't know," she confessed.

"What do you mean you don't know?"

"I never looked at the rest!"

"Why not?"

"Are you kidding, Kyle? After I saw that thing in my room I didn't wanna see anymore. Call me a chicken shit if you want. I don't care. I just wanted to forget it. But I can't."

"Liz, please tell me you didn't throw the rest of the photos out."

"No. They're in my pocket."

"Let's take a break then, for sanity's sake. We can look at the rest if you like once I get out of work. I work till four. That is, if you need someone with you."

"Yeah, I do. Thanks."

Kyle fished for his wallet. He pulled out a five dollar bill and left it on the table. They got up and left the diner before the waitress noticed her generous tip.

"One thing I don't get, Liz," said Kyle as they arrived at the door of Big Jake's Photorama. "Why would these people take all these pictures and then not develop them?"

"I dunno. I thought of that too after looking at the seventh photo. I guess only the Rempleys can answer that."

"Alright, we'll look at the rest of the photos and then we can decide what to do next."

As Kyle turned to enter the store, Liz called his name. He looked over his shoulder and raised his eyebrows at her. "Thanks," she said. "It's nice to know I have a friend."

7

The afternoon wore on, but ever since Liz had come home from her meeting with Kyle Harris, she found it difficult to tear herself away from monitoring the clock in the kitchen. Kyle said he'd be working until four, and that gave Liz a little over six hours to play the waiting game. She decided to go into the living room and give the family DVD player a little workout. As she sifted through her parents' collection of pre-1990 movies, she remembered Mrs. Rempley in that very room, standing beside the fireplace with a look of concern and the image of the demon beside her.

Perhaps she could watch the DVD from the stairs. That way she wouldn't necessarily be *in* the living room, and with dad out front doing some much-needed landscaping and mom and brothers upstairs, she'd be surrounded by a sense of security. But Liz remembered the photo of the spirit standing on the fifth stair, and put that idea out to pasture as well.

Is there no place in this house I could feel safe? The bathroom? My own bedroom?

Liz agonized over what the other photos would reveal.

God, what if that thing shows up in bed with the Rempleys? I'll never sleep in this house again!

She joined her father outside, sitting at the bottom step armed with a pad and pencil. She began writing down things she thought were important, like: *Why did the silhouette of the demon grow more distinct with each photo? Why was the demon becoming clearer and more visible with each photo? Did the Rempleys ultimately leave because of this entity? Why did they take these pictures and then never develop the negatives? Were they aware that something supernatural was going on? Did they ultimately do anything about it?*

She circled these last four questions and drew a star next to them. Then she wrote down a "TO DO" list.

1. Finish "TO DO" list.
2. Meet Kyle at Big Jake's Photorama at four o'clock.
3. Go over the second half of prints with Kyle.
4. If they're more of the same, go to 4a. If they're bad…really bad, go to 4b.

> 4a. Find the Rempleys and talk to them.
>
> 4b. Find the Rempleys, tell mom and dad and find a priest. If a priest refuses to help or says there's nothing he can do, go to 4c.
>
> 4c. Move the hell back to California.

Liz took a moment to read over what she'd written, in which time her father came over to grab the hedge clippers that lay at Liz's feet.

"Whatcha doin', sport?" asked Paul, playfully.

"Uh, nothin'," replied Liz, hurrying to hide the list. She tore it from the pad and crumpled it up. "Trying to come up with a list of things I need to do, but the trouble is, I don't wanna do any of them all by myself."

"I know, sweets," he replied, frowning. "Your mom and I thought it was best to move now so you guys would have the whole summer to adjust and meet new people before the new school year. But I guess we should have waited and let you have one last summer with your friends back home. Not much chance of you making new girlfriends *outside* of school, huh?"

Yeah, thought Liz, *maybe if you didn't rush into buying a house, you might have found one that needed less work and didn't have a monster living in it.*

"True that, dad," replied Liz, and faked a wide grin.

He mussed her hair and went to the edge of the property to start in on the hedges. Her eyes followed him as she slowly reached for the "TO DO" list that she'd jammed into the last pages of the tablet and wondered if there was anything else that might need to be added to it.

She thought of one last thing.

5.   When this is all over, Kiss Kyle Harris….*on the lips.*

****

As agreed, Kyle and Liz met up in front of Big Jake's Photorama at 4 PM sharp. Instinctively, Liz gave Kyle a hug, fairly tight for someone she'd only known for a day. He reciprocated, wrapping one arm around her shoulder blades and squeezing.

"Ow!" she gasped, pulling away from Kyle and quickly sucking air in through her teeth.

"Sorry," he said, offering her a double shoulder rub instead.

"Oh, it's just a spider bite I got on my back. I didn't think it would still hurt this much.

"He must've been some spider! How's it going otherwise?"

"Like the twelfth hour of a migraine." she replied.

"Uh-oh," said Kyle, looking over Liz's shoulder. "Here comes Mustache Marge."

"Who?" she asked, confused.

Liz looked behind her and saw a wide-hipped, middle-aged woman with wide calves bulging through white knee-high tennis socks. Her thighs were so sizable that it must have required great strength and force to shove them into her Daisy Duke Denim shorts. Equally massive were those two pale arms that swung wildly back and forth in perfectly opposite synchronicity as she strutted.

"Hey, there, Marge!" said Kyle, cheerfully.

Marge managed a soft grunt and frowned when she saw Liz.

"Liz," continued Kyle, "this is Marge *Soarbutch*."

"It's *Zorbitz*, little dick!" Marge growled.

Liz sniggered and immediately faked a cough. She buried her nose and mouth in the crook of her arm.

"Where's Eugenia?" snapped Marge.

It was right there that Liz was close enough to Marge to perceive that the woman had a subtle black mustache, which greatly contrasted her curly short salt and pepper hair. Mustache Marge hooked her sausage-like fingers onto the door's handle and, showing very little exertion, over swung it, causing the door to slam hard against the side window panel.

"Catch you later, *Mustache*!" said Kyle once the door shut, and then turned to Liz. "I guess you kinda figured out…"

"Uh, *Mr.* C.," joked Liz.

The two laughed as they crossed the street and reentered the Allendale Diner. To their dismay, the same server greeted them.

"Ah," she began, "the coffee brigade is back. Lemme guess. A private booth and a pot of coffee?"

This time Kyle and Liz took the very last booth at the end. Liz dug anxiously into her two front pockets and produced twin piles of prints. Out of her left pocket came the ten they'd already seen, while the right produced the pile they had yet to go through. Kyle observed this new pile and inhaled deeply, and then Liz did the same. Just then, Liz felt a vibration coming from her pocket. She pulled out her cell phone and saw that she'd received a text message from her best friend, Samantha, back in California.

"*Hey, girl!*" read the text. "*Miss you! Meet any hot Jersey boys yet?*"

Kyle watched as Liz's thumbs texted feverishly.

"*Hey, Sam. Can't talk now. Call you later. And yes, with a real cute guy now. Details to follow.*"

Liz switched her phone to silent and shoved it back into her pocket.

"Sorry," she said.

"So," said Kyle, "these are the next ones."

"Yeah." answered Liz. "You want a swig of coffee first?"

"I wish I could light up in here. Damn anti-smoking laws."

The waitress soon arrived carrying that same glass coffee pot with the brown plastic top. This time it was Kyle who held up the two thick ceramic cups.

Liz didn't wait for the waitress to leave. She looked down to catch a glimpse of the eleventh, but she only saw the white backing of the initial photo with *Big Jake's Photorama* and the previous day's date stamped in the center. In a way she was relieved to see that the pile had been unconsciously turned upside down. She pushed them all over to Kyle and shook her hands at him.

"You look at them first now," she said. "Then I'll look them over and tell you what *I* see."

"Alright," he agreed, turning the pile over and bringing it closer to him.

Liz drummed her fingernails loudly on the table, causing the old couple across from them to look over in disapproval. Without looking away from the eleventh print, Kyle slowly brought his hand over to hers and pressed down on it gently but firmly. She stopped and they both left their hands there until Kyle was finished with the photo.

"Alright," said Kyle, calmly. "I'm done."

He passed her the photo, upside down. She considered it for several seconds. The white back with *Big Jake's Photorama* and yesterday's date stamped in black stared menacingly back up at her. She tried to read Kyle's expression to give her some idea of what to expect, but his countenance was bland. She breathed in deeply, held it for several moments, pinched the photo between her thumb and index finger tips and slowly turned it over. She couldn't speak at first, instead managing a weak gasp and covering her mouth.

"Are you ok?" he asked her.

She nodded, the rest of her body inert.

"Tell me what you see." he said.

****

"What's the story with those two?" asked Mustache Marge as her lover closed up the till and ran the credit card machine. "Who's the chick?"

"I think Harris got his bitch knocked up," answered Eugenia.

"No shit! Harris?"

Eugenia went to the window beside Marge and spied out through the partially opened Venetian blind that gave them a clear view of the Allendale Diner's window, through which they could see the two kids. Liz was visibly upset, and the two women could make out Kyle patting her forearm, and at one point taking her hand and caressing it.

"Oh, yeah," said Mustache Marge, snorting her laugh in a devious and apathetic way. "She's knocked up alright! Friggin' straight people and their carelessness. No better in my opinion than friggin' gay dudes down the village spreadin' their AIDS around all over the place like it's…"

"Say, Marge," interrupted Eugenia. "Wanna go out on a little adventure tonight?"

"How's that?"

"I mean that little slut's gotta tell her mom and dad sooner or later. I gotta feeling it's gonna be soon, like tonight. And needle dick'll be telling his drunken Mick folks the same thing. What say we get ourselves some front row seats?"

Marge understood her partner perfectly. The two had always thought on the same scheming wavelength. They greatly abhorred people, as they'd been treated like pariahs most of their lives. Now older and wiser, they were committed to spending their remaining days seeking pleasure and amusement at the expense of others.

"I like the idea, Euge," Replied Mustache Marge, licking her lips. "I like it *a lot*!"

****

"Tell me what you see." repeated Kyle.

"I…I see a yard," began Liz, "a green lawn with two trees in the back. There's a lawn swing with a canopy over it. Next to it, there's a lawn gnome wearing a pointy red cap." She looked up at Kyle. "No demon." she said.

"Right." he agreed.

Liz looked back down at the photo in an effort to be sure.

"It makes sense," said Kyle. "The thing is only *in* the house."

Liz looked away, frowning and seeming to be deep in thought.

So what's the answer? she thought. *Do I just camp out in the yard every night for the rest of my adolescent life?*

"What about the first image?" she asked, sounding concerned. "*Was* it outside the window? It looked like it was in front of the window. On the *inside*. But I can't be sure."

"What if it couldn't have been *outside*?"

"What do you mean?"

"Liz, its face was so transparent that it was barely visible. I don't think it was outside at all. It was probably…I dunno…hovering over the sink."

Liz grinned.

"Yeah," she began, "it probably can't leave the house!"

"Ha!" exclaimed Kyle, sounding as triumphant as if he and Liz had just solved a cold case.

"So if it's still around, and we don't know that it is, but *if* it's still around, it can't leave my house."

"That's a pretty safe assumption to make," smiled Kyle as he looked down at photo twelve.

His smile faded almost immediately. Liz grabbed his free hand and asked what was wrong. Kyle's and Liz's eyes met and Liz could read his terror in them.

"Not good," he said. "Not good at all."

She snatched the photo from him and stared at it.

"Tell me what you see," Kyle instructed Liz.

Liz covered her mouth and began crying.

"I see…I see…the back of the house from the vantage point of the…I-I guess it's the swing. Standing on the patio stairs, there's the thing. I can see his legs now. Scaly legs and feet…no, they look more like blocks than feet. They're sort of square and it looks like there are thick claws on the end of its toes. Both hands are raised up and look clutched. They have sharp nails on all the fingers."

She considered all this for a moment and then Kyle spoke.

"So much for my hypothesis of a strictly domestic demon. It's following them around the house, apparently. Even coming outside with them. And it's getting more pronounced in the photos. So what does that mean? What happens once the film in the camera finishes?"

"*What happened*, you mean," she said, "once the film was finished. Don't forget I found the roll all used up."

Liz was deliberately lying to Kyle, remembering that she'd used the last exposure on herself. Too afraid to contemplate the resulting photo, she figured she'd come clean once they reached the end of the photos.

"Right," answered Kyle. This already happened. A pretty long time ago."

"Kyle, I've been thinking this over. I think we should tell someone. Someone older."

"No. Not yet. Remember how long it took for me to believe this?"

"Not *that* long."

"But even still. Grownups are harder to convince. Even when the proof is right in front of them; they always seem to find another answer, even if it's bullshit and they know it's bullshit. No, Liz. I think we need to figure this out on our own. I don't mean we can't ask questions, like finding the Rempleys. I like that idea. But the less we tell them the better. Unless we have to, that is."

She nodded and they went to the thirteenth print, this time looking on together.

Unlucky thirteen turned out to be just the opposite. It was the most normal of all the photos. It showed a group of people in a restaurant. Among them were Mr. and Mrs. Rempley, and they were seated at a large table in the company of four other couples. The most remarkable thing that could be said about this photo was that the demon was not present. The flash of the camera reflected in the lenses of Mr. Rempley's glasses.

8

When the waitress came by to heat the couple's coffee, Kyle asked if she could lend them a pencil. She pulled one out from behind her hair and dropped it on the table without saying a word and filled their cups to the rim with piping hot Joe. Liz took a napkin and began making notes. She jotted down information on each photo, beginning with the first and continuing until they got to number fourteen.

"You ready for the next one?" asked Kyle.

"I'm ready," replied Liz.

As Kyle went to flip to number fourteen, Liz arrested his hand with hers.

"Kyle, we need to find the Rempleys. No matter what, we...*I* need to find out what happened."

"I know," agreed Kyle. "We'll find them." He dropped the pile and gripped her hands tightly with his. "I promise we will."

Good over evil, Liz reminded herself.

****

After they had looked at the remaining photos, Liz took up the pencil in her trembling hand and began writing. She wrote:

Photo #14 – The basement at 11 Grover Road. Photo focuses on a corner where there's a mousetrap. Its hammer and holding bar are still engaged but no cheese is on the catch. There are mouse droppings all around the trap. In the background there is the bottom left side of the oil tank (also present in photo #15). One of the demon's large scaly feet can be partially seen. It's standing in front of this part of the oil tank. From what can be seen of the demon, its form is well-defined and its color is apparent. Its scales are a greenish gray and the single visible thick talon is yellow.

Photo #15 – The basement at 11 Grover Road. Photo shows full image of the oil tank. Tank looks rusty. There are four horizontal lines, like gashes across the tank. Kyle reminds me the hands of the demon each had four digits. This photo is dim. There is light emanating from above the shot. Apparently, it had been taken below a light fixture. No demon seen in the photo.

Photo #16 – The smaller bedroom…my bedroom. Photo most likely taken by Mr. Rempley. Mrs. Rempley is holding up one of the pillows. It's been ripped open and the stuffing is seeping out. The photo appears very dim. As Mrs. Rempley's chin can only be seen, her reaction can only be inferred. The demon cannot be seen in the photo.

Photo #17 – Dining room at 11 Grover Road. Mrs. Rempley's holding up a glass of white wine. She's seated at one end of the table, her back is to the kitchen. She's smiling, but it's a sad smile, like she's forcing herself to. Behind her is the demon. His claws are clutched high over her head. He is no longer transparent. He is as full and as clear as Mrs. Rempley herself. His eyes are fixed on her and they look angry.

Photo #18 – Dining room at 11 Grover Road. The chandelier once hanging over the Rempleys is now a broken twisted mess on the table. Neither of the Rempleys is in this shot. The demon is also not present here.

Photo #19 – This photo shows Mrs. Rempley showing her arm to the camera. The sleeve of her shirt is torn open and there's a bloody gash down her arm. The demon is not present in this photo.

"Wait a second," said Kyle, "Mrs. Rempley."

"Yeah," agreed Liz, "she…"

"Yup," said Kyle. "She's changed. She's aged twenty or thirty years."

They looked at one another for a long time before Kyle broke the silence.

"Her hair's gone completely white!"

****

"Kyle," began Liz, "where's the last photo?"

"You're asking *me*?"

"Kyle, this is no time to be fooling around. That last shot was of me."

The two sat quietly and thought. Kyle squeezed his knuckles until Liz heard them crack. Then he pushed the heel of his hand into his chin, cocked his head slightly and cracked his neck. Liz, on the other hand, straightened up in her seat and pinched her shoulder blades together in an attempt to get her back to crack. This caused a knee-jerk reaction, and right away she felt the spider bite that still hurt. It worried her that a sensation of pain was even radiating down the center of her back.

"What did you do with the negatives?" he asked.

"What negatives?" she snapped in a frustrated tone.

"Liz, the film from the camera. I put them in the envelope with the prints after I finished developing them. They were tucked into the back of the red envelope I handed to you."

"Oh, shit!" she yelled, and the elderly couple looked over at them again. This time the old lady closed her eyes and slowly shook her head.

"Young ladies don't act at all like young ladies nowadays." she snapped.

"Now, now, Gertrude," said the old man. "Finish your fries."

Kyle apologized with a smile and pointed at the lady's plate, "Those sure look good!"

The two teens paid with another five that Kyle had taken from his own funds, and they left the Allendale Diner in a hurry. Once outside, Kyle grabbed on to Liz's arm. Still spying on the two teenagers from inside Big Jake's Photorama, Eugenia Charpentier and Mustache Marge Zorbitz began to cackle loudly, leaning their considerable weight against one another and sucking on beef jerky sticks just as if they were lollipops.

"They're on the move, Euge!" croaked Mustache Marge, smacking her lips around the jerky.

"C'mon, Marge," said Eugenia. "Let's follow the little twerps. They might be going to tell her parents she's preg-o. This we gotta see!"

****

The Brentwood house was subdued. The BMW was gone from the driveway, and, to Liz, the house seemed lifeless. This was the first time she'd been alone in her new residence. When she and Kyle entered the house, the home alarm system sounded. She entered the code while Kyle considerately looked away. He invited himself into the living room and nodded slowly as he took in the space that he knew so well without ever having been in it before.

"Better taste than the Rempleys's, I can tell you!" he said.

"Thanks," laughed Liz and offered her guest a cold drink.

They entered the kitchen where Liz found a note on the counter by the refrigerator.

"Who leaves notes anymore?" asked Kyle.

"Shit," gasped Liz and checked her cell phone, which she'd set to *silence* at the diner.

Four missed calls, one voicemail and two text messages.

Kyle picked up the note and read it out loud.

"*Liz, check your cell phone! - Mom*"

Liz read the first and second texts together. They were both from Patricia.

Text message 1: *Pick up your phone!*

Text message 2: *Liz! Pick up!*

Voicemail: *Liz, it's mom. Where are you? Why aren't you answering? We had a little accident. We're off to the emergency room. Nothing serious. The twins were wrestling at the top of the stairs and Jared fell. He said Sean had pushed him. Dad thinks Jared's arm is broken. Please call me when you get this. Love you.*

"Double shit!" yelled Liz.

"What did she say?" asked Kyle.

"My brother's in the hospital. His arm might be broken. Let me call my mom."

"Poor kid," said Kyle. "Ok, in the meantime, I'll look for the envelope. Where are your trash cans?"

"In the garage. Go out this door."

Liz pointed to the pantry door and within a few seconds, Kyle was out of sight. Even though she was worried about Jared, Liz fretted more that the garbage might have already been picked up. She prayed that Kyle wouldn't be too long. It scared her being in the house by herself.

****

Kyle emerged from the garage just as Liz was about to text her mother.

"Nothing," said Kyle, sounding out of breath. "I think they picked up your trash this morning."

"Triple shit!" growled Liz.

"There's a simple solution," replied Kyle.

"What?"

Kyle took his cell phone from the clip that was attached to his belt and held it up.

"Modern technology." he said. "We've been so stuck in the 80's with that damn Vortex that we forgot we can take photos whenever and wherever we want. And who needs a photo finishing center!"

"Kyle, you're a genius!" said Liz, and landed her hands hard on his shoulders. "I could kiss you!"

Kyle looked down at her hands and grinning, looked back up to Liz.

"Kiss me when this is all over."

She backed off a little, cleared her throat and pushed back her hair.

"Right," agreed Liz. "First thing's first!"

Kyle paused, considered his cell phone and then dropped his hand at his side.

"Right," he said.

"Right," she repeated.

"Yup."

"Kyle, what is it?"

"Nothing. It's just…well…which one of us wants to be in the pic?"

Liz hadn't thought of what being in the shot actually meant. Did either one of them want to see a demon standing next to them, possibly about to strike? And if the demon were so clearly visible in 198-, then how would he look in June of 2012?

"Ok," Kyle said, finally. "I'll be in it. Here."

He hit the camera button on his keypad and handed the cell phone to Liz. She closed her eyes slowly and took a deep breath. Her hand shook badly as she aimed the phone up at Kyle and grabbed her wrist with her other hand.

"WAIT!" yelled Kyle and Liz jumped a little.

He walked over to her, put his arm about her waist and landed a kiss on her trembling lips. They held it there for several seconds, after which Kyle slowly pulled away and tilted his head.

"There!" he said. "To hell with waiting till this is all over. I've been wanting to do that all day."

Liz smiled, "I'm glad you did."

Kyle sucked a full lung's worth of air through his mouth and instructed Liz to take the shot before he lost what nerve he had.

The phone's shutter sound effect clicked. Liz, still looking forward in Kyle's direction, handed the phone to him. He took it and checked the screen. He saw the living room floor and part of his Nike sneakers. The photo had already been stored in his photo album, and the phone's camera was standing by ready to take another shot. Kyle hissed a *shit* under his breath and wondered if the last of his courage had left him.

"You know," started Kyle, his hand trembling badly as he used his thumb to tap through to his photo album, "m-my cousin over in Waldwick once took a pic in the nude with his phone. Then he got his cell stolen the next day and a week later that pic was all over his high school. My cousin couldn't show his face for..."

Kyle stopped. Liz came close to him but refused to look down at the phone's LCD. Kyle gave what sounded like a sigh of relief. Liz grabbed the phone and studied the screen. There was Kyle standing before the brightness illuminating through the bay window.

No demon.

Liz anxiously took another shot of Kyle before he was even ready to pose. She quickly checked it.

No demon.

Then she handed Kyle the phone and instructed him to take a photo of her.

"Would you like flash or no flash, miss?" he joked in a British accent.

"It doesn't matter. Just take it before I lose my nerve."

The shutter clicked and Kyle checked it first. He observed Liz in the photo standing in front of a potted floor plant and a framed impressionist painting of a basket of fruit hanging on the wall behind her. The brightness from the bay window behind Kyle made the photo come out decently.

No demon.

They went back and forth, in all parts of the house, taking photo after photo of one another and every time the frightful entity that had reared its grotesque head in the photos taken with the Vortex was nowhere to be seen. To make sure, Kyle used the zoom in feature of his phone to scan every inch of each picture.

Still no demon.

"What if he only appears on 35mm film and not on digital shots?" asked Liz, as she poured Kyle another glass of lemonade.

"Liz, you saw yourself that nothing was there. We took twenty-three pics. Not one showed anything but you and me."

"Still. I'd feel a lot better if we…" she stopped.

"If we went to see the Rempleys?" he finished.

"Well, maybe they got a priest after all. Maybe after the chandelier incident, Mr. Rempley decided he'd had enough and did something about it."

"Ok, Liz. Do you know where they moved to?"

"I'm pretty sure my dad has their contact info on his rolodex."

She got up and went into the den. Kyle gulped down the rest of his lemonade and began to draw a figure eight on the table with the wet bottom of his empty glass.

Liz came back in the room with something jotted down on a post-it note.

"*Mr. & Mrs. William Rempley. 232 Willow Lane Hoboken, New Jersey 07030.*" Liz looked up at Kyle. "Is Hoboken far?"

"We can take NJ Transit. We can be there in less than an hour."

"So, you really wanna do this?" she smiled.

"Yeah, Liz," he smiled back. "Let's go see the Rempleys."

She planted a soft kiss on his cheek as the two walked out of 11 Grover Road.

9

"*HOBOKEN!*" shouted a voice over the loudspeaker as the train pulled into the station. Kyle and Liz stepped off and walked to Washington Street where they succeeded in hailing a cab. Kyle gave the cabbie the Rempleys' address and within two minutes they arrived at 232 Willow Lane.

Liz liked that this town had more of a city feel to it. Hoboken's cosmopolitan flare and panoramic view of the Manhattan skyline gave her hope that there were exciting places not too far from Ho-Ho-Kus. Yet no one could argue that she was living through plenty of action without any need for visiting a city like Hoboken.

They stepped up to the front door of 232 Willow Lane, and Kyle rang the bell. The curtain behind the door's glass window moved and an eye emerged. It narrowed un-welcomingly at the sight of the visitors and Liz's first thought was that the Rempleys, whom she'd only briefly met the morning she and her family had moved into 11 Grover Road, would turn them away without a word.

An elderly woman opened the door. Her hair was helmet-like but no longer white. Considering her advanced age, Liz assumed it to be salon-dyed. The old woman was none other than Mrs. Rempley, and she smiled pleasantly but also appeared perplexed.

"Yes?" she said as the door creaked open. "Can I help you?"

"Hello, Mrs. Rempley," said Liz. "I don't know if you remember me. I'm Elizabeth Brentwood."

"Brentwood?" repeated Lorraine Rempley. "Oh, you're Paul and Patricia's girl."

"Yes," answered Liz, faking a laugh. "I am. This is my friend, Kyle."

"Kyle," said Lorraine Rempley, sounding friendly and tilting her head forward.

A few moments of awkward silence ensued, at which point Kyle cleared his throat and asked if they might come in.

"Oh," said Mrs. Rempley, now sounding hesitant, "certainly."

She tugged the door wide open and stepped to the side to let the teens enter. She led them to the living room and asked if they'd like something cold to drink. Liz politely said no, but Kyle asked for a glass of water. Mrs. Rempley mentioned that she had been about to make some iced coffee. She went into the kitchen, leaving Liz and Kyle alone in the living room. They heard her talking to someone, though what was said was unintelligible. The two kids looked around the room. It resembled Liz's own house in that there were half-empty moving boxes all over the place.

Within moments Mr. Rempley entered with his wife, and he greeted Liz amicably. In her mind, Liz compared the much younger Mr. Rempley she'd seen in the photos with this senior version. Although she'd previously met the Rempleys, seeing them as young as they were in the photos made Liz expect them to still be as young as they had been back in 198-.

"I hope you're not here to tell us something's wrong with the house!" said Bill Rempley, and burst out in a guffaw that echoed off the bare walls.

"No, no," said Liz, quickly, and added her own laugh. "Nothing like that."

"Well, actually," interrupted Kyle, raising an index finger as he accepted the glass of water from Lorraine Rempley, "There *is* one problem we needed to ask you about."

Liz elbowed Kyle and he grunted.

"Well," answered Lorraine Rempley, condescendingly, "what exactly would that be, dear?"

Bill Rempley got up and tended to a moving box that had been propped up on one of the end tables.

"Was there anything..." began Kyle, "*funny* going on in the house, your old house, that is? I mean, back in the 80's?"

The Rempleys exchanged glances and that put Kyle and Liz on edge.

"Well," began Bill, "let me see." No, I don't..." He rubbed his chin and then tapped it as he returned to his wife's side. "No, I don't think so." He turned to Mrs. Remply. "How 'bout you, Lorraine? Do you remember anything *funny* back at Grover Road?"

Lorraine offered the teens a slight chuckle. "Well," she began, "I gotta tell you. There was a bit of a scandal involving that senile old Mrs. Gillespie back in 1989. Remember that, Bill?"

"Oh!" he exclaimed. "I sure do!"

"I'm sorry." interjected Liz, shaking her head slightly. "Mrs. who?"

"Mrs. Gillespie, dear," answered Lorraine Rempley, evenly. "She's dead now, but toward the end, she..."

"She used to come out of her house and accuse Lorraine and me of spying on her," interjected Bill Rempley. "But not just spying.

She actually said we were undercover CIA agents that had infiltrated the neighborhood to monitor her hanging her bloomers on the line out back and fixing her blue hair in her bathroom mirror. All wild accusations of course. What's more, our house on Grover Road had been built on a fairly sizable lot and was surrounded by trees and shrubbery. This made it impossible for us to see into anyone's house and impossible for any of our neighbors to see what we were doing in our own! She even said we'd been taking pictures of her and secretly sending them to Washington. Have you even heard such a thing?"

Liz nudged Kyle.

"Uhm," said Kyle, "pictures, you say? You know, speaking of pictures, Mr. Rempley, we actually found a camera the other day that might belong to you and your wife."

Liz studied the Rempleys, awaiting a reaction. At first, they seemed oblivious to what Kyle was talking about. But once Kyle mentioned the orange Vortex that Liz had found in the small closet under the stairs, Bill and Lorraine shied away.

"Oh," answered Bill, extending his hand out to Kyle. "And you came all the way down here just to give it back? That was grand of you two!"

"Uhm," Liz cut in, "No, we don't have it *with* us. Actually, we just wanted to know…"

She looked to Kyle for guidance. He clued in immediately and continued.

"We wanted to know if it was important to you. I mean, if it had any pictures in it that you considered important."

"And you came all this way just to *ask* us if we wanted the camera? You didn't bother to bring it?" asked Lorraine Rempley, somewhat annoyed.

"You say you found it in the small closet under the staircase?" said Bill.

"That's right, Mr. Rempley." replied Liz.

"Bill!" scolded Lorraine Rempley. "That's neither here nor there. We tried looking for that camera and were very upset when it didn't turn up. So if you two don't mind, I would appreciate it if you would return it to us as soon as possible. It's got…"

Liz and Kyle simultaneously leaned forward anticipating Mrs. Rempley's next words, causing the elderly couple to recoil concurrently.

"It's got our vacation photos from Hawaii on it," lied Mrs. Rempley. "Fond memories that we, up until now, thought were lost… except for what we remember."

As Lorraine Rempley brought her arms up, Liz perceived a long scar down her right arm.

"Right," said Bill Rempley. "So if you could just send that back, I'll be more than happy to reimburse you the postage." He pulled a twenty from his wallet and offered it to Kyle. "I think this will more than cover the expense. And the rest is for both your train fares back to Ho-Ho-Kus."

Kyle didn't accept the money and looked over instead to Liz. She whispered something in his ear and motioned to the scar on Lorraine's arm.

"Oh," began Kyle, pointing to the scar, "I'm sorry. Did you have an accident?"

"This?" asked Lorraine apprehensively as she also pointed to her arm. "Oh, Bill, remember? It was, ehm…"

"It was a long time ago," said Rempley, "but I seem to recall the…well, the accident with the chandelier. Remember, hon?"

Lorraine didn't reply.

"Yes," said Bill, nervously, "yes. The craziest thing, really. Lorraine and I were in the middle of dinner and the chandelier just fell from the ceiling. Part of it clipped her arm and, well you should've seen the blood! She refused to get it stitched up. It took *forever* to stop the bleeding." He paused, turned his head to Lorraine and said under his breath, "Yes sir, that was a crazy week."

****

After the two teenagers left the Rempley residence, Lorraine turned to her husband.

"They know something, Bill. They must."

He nodded, "Do you think they developed the film?"

"That damned camera," she hissed. "What those children must think of me!"

"Now, now, Lorraine. Don't jump to conclusions. They left seeming satisfied with our explanation of things. I think we've seen the last of those two."

At that moment, Kyle's and Liz's heads emerged from the open living room window and Kyle spoke firmly.

"I think you two owe us an explanation."

10

"It was back in the summer of '86 when we bought that orange throwaway camera, wasn't it, Lorraine?" said Bill to his wife as she poured Liz and Kyle the fresh coffee she'd been brewing into ice-filled glasses. Several pieces of ice snapped and cracked as the hot liquid began to instantly melt it.

"Yes, I believe so," she answered in almost a whisper.

"We'd only been in the house less than a year when strange things began happening," continued Bill."

"What kind of things?" asked Liz, imagining she already knew the answer.

"The curtain rods would collapse," he replied. "The furnace would shut off for no reason. There'd be banging noises on the walls coming from *inside* the room. Whatever happened, at least one of us was always right there to witness these...*occurrences*. We just learned to put up with it. But nothing had ever hurt us up to that point, mind you. There were just things around *us* that were going, *haywire*, I guess you'd call it. But it really started getting more serious in late June of 1986. We'd only been in the place about nine or ten months. Our son Miles was graduating from high school, and my brother Cole and his wife came over from New Rochelle, New York. That evening, before we left for the ceremony, I asked Lorraine, my sister-in-law and my brother, who was Miles's godfather, to pose in a photo with our son. I didn't have a camera of my own, so I borrowed Cole's."

Kyle and Liz both nodded, and Bill and Lorraine remarked later in private just how interested the two teenagers were in Bill's story.

"Well, anyway, I took Cole's camera and snapped a shot. I then realized, as did Cole, that I had forgotten to hit the flash button. Cole took the camera and did some poking and prodding and had me try it again. They all said 'cheese' and *click*, I snapped what I thought would have turned out to be a great shot. But no sooner did I snap that shot, I could've sworn I'd seen someone, or at least, *something* else appear in the viewfinder; a yellowish outline. I wasn't sure at first what it was. You know how your eyes tend to play tricks on you sometimes? Well, the flash went off and I thought I saw another figure standing next to Lorraine.

"Like I said, I couldn't make out anymore than the frame of some*one* or some*thing*. I paid it no mind and I told the four of them to stand over by the staircase-Miles on the first step, Lorraine on the second, Cole on the third and Linda, that's Cole's wife, on the fourth. I took another shot, and, as the flash went off, again I saw the fleeting yellow outline of a figure, this time standing on the fifth step, right next to Linda!

"I cringed and dropped the camera. I think I even allowed myself a little squeal. Cole pushed past Lorraine and Miles and ran for his camera. He cursed me and, surveying the damaged goods, found that the lens had cracked. I wound up paying for the repairs. I don't really remember how much it cost; but then, the price for a new camera lens on that old Kodak 35mm isn't why the two of you are here, is it?"

Liz and Kyle remained silent and waited for Bill to continue his story.

"I didn't tell anyone what I had seen. Not even my wife," Bill looked at Lorraine and added, "Well, not at first, anyway." And then stroked her dark brown hair.

"I lay in bed that night, staring up at the ceiling and reflecting on what I'd seen. I may not have been sure of what I'd seen the first time when I noticed it next to Lorraine; I say *it*, mind you, because up to that point I didn't know what it was. But when I saw that figure standing on that next step beside Cole's wife, I was sure something was there. Something *was* among us.

"I went to Big Jake's Photorama the next day up in Allendale and bought a disposable camera. This one was a yellow...Xerin, I think it was. It was one of those *emergency quickie* cameras that came with only ten exposures. When I got home, I decided to test it out on my own before letting Lorraine in on what I was up to. I wanted to be sure, you understand. I didn't see any point in alarming her unless there was something to alarm her about.

"As I readied myself for the first shot, I looked around for something to capture. Then I realized it didn't really matter. So ultimately I decided that a shot of the living room bay window would suffice. I didn't use the tiny viewfinder this time. I looked at the window with my naked eye and hit the shutter. *Click.*

"Nothing. So I cranked the wheel to advance the film and went for the bust of Beethoven on the piano. *Click.*

"Still nothing. So I backed up and tried it again. And again, nothing. No strange shape appeared whatsoever. I was beginning to think I'd imagined the whole damn thing. Then it dawned on me that the figure appeared for a split second when the flash had gone off. It seemed pretty logical that if my eyes were playing tricks on me with the flash...well, you can see where I'm going with all this. So I pushed the little flash button that indicated *on* and tried Beethoven once more.

"The flash lit up the room, and as sure as it had happened with Cole's camera, I saw the figure! I was able to make out its form a little better than before. It was as if it got easier to see each time. Up to that point I had thought it was simply because I hadn't been looking for it.

"I told Lorraine what I had seen, both with Cole's camera and now with the yellow disposable Xerin. I remember how you looked at me when I told you, honey. You looked at me like I had escargots coming out of my nose.

"Anyway, I walked over to the piano and asked her to take a photo of me. She protested at first, calling the whole thing sophomoric or some kind of good SAT word like that, I don't really remember. I told her to just do it. She brought the camera up to her eye, aimed and...*click*.

"'There,' she said. 'Nothing. I didn't see a thing.' But I had forgotten to instruct her to switch on the flash. In the interest of time, I flicked it on for her and walked back to the piano. She closed one eye and went for the shot. '*No*', I hollered and told her to keep both eyes open and the camera away from her face. Again she protested but I waved my hands up at her and demanded she take the damn picture. *Click*.

"The flash momentarily blinded me, but in that split second that I squeezed my eyes shut and saw a bunch of purple dots in a sea of black, Lorraine let out a scream and dropped the camera. I went over and picked it up. It appeared sound, but then again it was plastic. I asked Lorraine if she was alright but quickly noticed she was trembling.

"Five exposures had been taken and five were left. Lorraine wouldn't describe what she'd seen at first and insisted I throw the camera away. She told me to not even think of developing the negatives. I ignored her and used up the last five photos, wasting the sixth exposure because the damn flash button defaulted to *off* after every shot. I suppose that's to conserve the battery, although I don't know how much battery ten lousy pictures could use up.

"So now I had four exposures left. I made sure I engaged that flash button each time, and even though Lorraine seemed terrified about the whole affair, she still followed me. She held onto my shoulders with each of the last four shots I took. I could tell that she, like I, was holding her breath every time I clicked on the shutter.

"The rest of the shots were in the dining room. The first of these five produced the same figure I had seen before, but this time it was a bit clearer. It seemed to be getting clearer with every shot I snapped, but was still only a faint figure. The fact that it was becoming more visible was a bit unsettling, I must admit. Still, I was determined to see this thing through. So I snapped another picture while standing in the same place and this time we could have sworn we saw the figure's eyes, which now seemed to take on a more dark gray or blackish hue than its former yellow. More importantly, we saw what we assumed to be one of its hands reach for the chandelier. On the second to last photo, Lorraine begged me to stop. I could tell she was really scared. I backed up into the living room, switched on the flash and aimed into the dining room. She latched on to my shirt from behind and, with both of us holding our breath, I clicked on the shutter.

"This time, we saw the figure, vague as its form was, move its arm. See, up to this point, the apparition appeared to be immobile during that split second when the flash appeared. But this time...this time both Lorraine and I saw its arm move. It advanced toward the chandelier! I couldn't wait another moment. Without the slightest hesitation I approached the threshold to the dining room. Lorraine grabbed my waist and told me '*no*', so I stopped just short of entering, aimed the camera and was about to hit the shutter when Lorraine hissed, 'The flash! Don't forget the flash!' I was grateful to her for that. Had I ruined our last exposure, we might have missed what ensued. I switched the flash button to *on* and hit the shutter. *Click*.

"And just as sure as you two kids are sitting there, the chandelier moved. That is to say, it was struck! The flash lit up the room and that...that *creature*, we saw it swing its arm and...*swatted* the chandelier! I don't know what frightened Lorraine and me more, the brisk movement of that...*thing*, or the fact that he was able to move an object.

"I tried to get the flash to go off again, but I guess it was disabled since there was no more film. I ran out of the house with one thing on my mind. I had to get another camera. Lorraine ran out after me. I don't even think she bothered to lock the door did you honey? We got in the car and headed for Big Jake's."

Liz leaned forward and almost raised her hand like a student in a classroom asking her teacher a question.

"Did you develop the pictures?" asked Liz, feeling very uneasy.

Kyle sucked his teeth, "Liz, let the man finish."

Bill Rempley nodded, "No questions till the end, boys and girls," he joked, although no one felt like laughing.

Rempley continued.

"So, we got to Big Jake's Photorama and he, that would be Big Jake himself, told us he was sold out of the Xerin disposables, but that he had another. I'm pretty sure the name was *Xerin* because you can still find them if you look in the mom and pop photo stores like Big Jake's. But I think the brand that you two found, well hell, I haven't seen those in years. The name escapes me. You mentioned it before, didn't you?"

"It's a Series 120R Vortex 35mm disposable camera," recited Liz.

"Right," agreed Bill. "Big Jake recommended I buy the Vortex and even took one from its packaging to show me. He informed me that the Vortex had twice the amount of exposures and cost only three dollars more than the Xerin. I think I would have bought it even if it had cost ten times more. We were in need of a camera and the Vortex was the only disposable he had. I think he really wanted to make a sale. That store never did much business back in those days."

It was all Kyle could do to keep from snickering.

"As Big Jake rang me up for the Vortex, he asked about my Xerin. 'Don't ya wanna develop those?' he asked and pointed a stubby finger at the yellow disposable. Lorraine and I briefly glanced at one another. She thinned her lips and nodded her head. I set the Xerin on the counter and pushed it in Big Jake's direction. I think that was when I was the most nervous, seeing him put it in a cardboard envelope, tear off the perforated receipt and throw it in the bin labeled 'IN BOX'.

"Lorraine and I decided not to use the Vortex until we saw what came out of the Xerin. I asked Big Jake if he could put a rush on our camera. He told me he'd do it right away. The concept of one-hour photo was still pretty new back then, and I wasn't exactly sure if he'd get it done that day. We stayed close to the store all the while Big Jake was developing the pictures from the Xerin. I kept poking my head through the glass to check up on his progress. I couldn't really see more than him standing behind the photo counter, but that was enough to tell me he was on the job.

"About twenty minutes later I looked through the window again and saw Big Jake had moved to the front counter. Lorraine and I entered the store and he immediately called out to me. 'Got your photos for you.' he said, 'Don't think you're gonna like what you see.' Lorraine grabbed my hand and squeezed it. I tell you, I don't think my heart pounded as hard when I saw that chandelier move. 'Half your photos came out too dark,' he said. I swatted my hand at him and told him it was fine. I added that Lorraine and I had been toying with the idea of taking a film class and wanted to test our skills before committing time and money. 'I'd say that you two could sure use a class after seeing *these* photos.' he said, jovially. Honestly, when you come right down to it, Big Jake was a tell-it-like-it-is kinda guy and didn't see anything wrong with snooping around in other people's business. I think he liked developing people's photos because it was a fool-proof way of spying because he could never get caught. His sister was the same way. Always poked *her* nose where it didn't belong. But that's neither here nor there. I'm getting away from the story.

"We left the store and made our way back to the car. Before I could start the engine, Lorraine hurried me to open the envelope and look at the photos. And…"

Rempley paused and Liz and Kyle leaned forward again. Kyle

began moving his hands in a circular manner as if to tell Rempley to get on with it.

"There was nothing in the photos," said Lorraine Rempley. "That is, nothing unusual."

"No dem…" started Liz, and then caught herself before she could say the word that seemed easier to say now than it did a day ago. "I mean, there was no phantom figure, or outline, whatever it was that you saw with the flash?"

"Precisely, dear," answered Mrs. Rempley. They were just pictures of the images we had captured with the camera. The chandelier, of course, came out a bit blurred, being that it moved just as the flash went off."

Kyle interjected.

"So did you two come to any conclusion?"

"Well," began Rempley, rubbing his thighs, "this, *phenomena* as I like to call it, seemed to only take form when we took a photo."

"With a flash," added Mrs. Rempley.

Liz put a shaking hand on Kyle's knee.

"Are you thinking what I'm thinking?" she whispered to him.

"Yeah," he replied. "The pics we took with my cell phone didn't prove anything. We didn't use a flash for any of them."

"Do you want more coffee, kids?" asked Mrs. Rempley.

They shook their heads. Finding that she needed to do something to keep herself calm, Mrs. Rempley refilled her own glass. The heat from the coffee steamed her glass as her ice had already fully melted from the coffee that was already in there.

"Mr. Rempley," said Liz, "the Vortex camera you bought. The

one I found. I know you took more photos. I found it at nineteen exposures used. We…we developed them."

Mrs. Rempley gasped as she dropped the pot she'd been holding. Hot liquid spilled all over the coffee table. Liz and Kyle got up and helped Bill Rempley sop up the mess. Lorraine Rempley just stood erect, completely catatonic before her husband and their guests.

"I'm sorry, Mrs. Rempley," said Liz, "I didn't mean to upset you."

"If you didn't want to upset me, then why did you come here?" shouted Lorraine Rempley at Liz and Kyle. "That experience traumatized me. I wasn't right for months after. It was a great relief not finding the orange camera. Things got worse when we took pictures with that one. I was convinced, even when Bill said otherwise, that there might have been something on the photos from the Vortex. That…damned monster…it got so clear in person; I thought it was inevitable that it would show up in the new photos. But Bill talked all the worry out of me. After awhile, I convinced myself it had all been our imagination."

"We're real sorry, Mrs…" began Liz.

"Why did you come here?" snapped Mrs. Remply. "You still haven't said. You must've had a reason to come all the way down here. Why?"

Liz and Kyle told the Rempleys about the photos from the orange Vortex. All the while, Bill Rempley held his wife tightly. Liz felt badly that Mrs. Rempley had started to cry.

"So you see, Mr. and Mrs. Rempley," said Kyle, "the demon started coming out *in* the photos. We just need to know if he…I mean *it*…is the reason why you finally sold the house."

"We sold it because my wife was tired of being terrified of her own home," snapped Rempley. "She said she'd *convinced* herself it was nothing, but she didn't really believe it. I know you didn't, Lorraine. I couldn't bear to see you jump every time there was a flash of lightning. The way you looked around as if that thing were going to appear. And your hair…"

Lorraine Rempley smacked her husband's chest. Rempley paused and cleared his throat.

"After we took the last picture with the Vortex and that…*demon*, as you call it, pulled the chandelier down almost killing my wife, I decided enough was enough. In a rage, I took the camera and threw it out of the dining room. I didn't see exactly where it went. At that time, it was usual for us to keep that small door under the stairs open from time to time. I suppose it must have been open when I threw the camera and that explains why we couldn't find it afterwards. We *did* look for it for a spell, mind you. Apparently by the time we initiated our search, one of us must have already closed that tiny closet door. I remember Lorraine saying it was a blessing that we never recovered it. She said it was for the better. After all, everything started with taking pictures. We never bought another camera, and things were quiet from then on. Sure, there were the occasional footsteps coming from other parts of the house when no one else besides us was home. Sometimes we saw things like the contents in our medicine cabinet inexplicably rearranged, or the mop somehow transplanted from the broom closet to the center of the kitchen. But that was as bad as it got once we stopped taking pictures." Bill Rempley looked at Liz. "It left us alone, Liz," he said. "I promise you that. I think just so long as you don't…"

"…take any photo flashes." finished Liz.

Rempley paused.

"That's right," he said, solemnly, and then added, sounding more cheerful. "After all, a deal's a deal in the real estate business!"

"You mean everything went back to, kind of normal?" asked Kyle, sounding incredulous. "Nothing but strange sounds here and there? Nothing...terrible or frightening?"

"Nothing," replied Rempley.

"I think," began Liz, "if I were alone and I heard footsteps coming from somewhere else inside the house, that would freak the shit of me. I wouldn't exactly call that *nothing.*"

"Lorraine and I agreed to never again take any pictures in that house. And I suggest that you do the same, miss," Rempley pointed a scolding finger at Liz. "Especially since this...*thing* was taking on a more physical shape with every photo we took. When you consider all the facts, you can come to the conclusion that it seemed...well, to be getting stronger. What I mean is, it seemed to become more prevalent in our own world. As if the flash acted as some sort of gateway, bringing it more and more into our own time and space... our *dimension*, I suppose." Liz sighed nervously. "It's all speculation, mind you." added Rempley. But it's as good an answer as any."

"But if we stop taking *flash* photos," began Kyle, "then it should be ok?"

"Logic would say that's true, young man," said Rempley. "It seemed to be pretty strong back in 1986 when it ripped the chandelier out of the ceiling. I'm sure you saw that in the photos from the Vortex. That was the last photo we ever took in that house. I'm sure you and your family haven't had the opportunity to take any flash photos yet, Liz. Am I right?"

Liz shook her head and almost said *no*, then remembered that she had used the last exposure of the Vortex, snapping a photo of herself. She was about to speak when Kyle suddenly cleared his throat, tapped Liz's thigh twice and got up.

"Thank you, Mr. and Mrs. Rempley," said Kyle. You've been really helpful. And I'm sorry if our visit upset you, Mrs. R."

"Throw those photos away, will you?" said Mrs. Rempley. "I don't want to see them. I don't even want to know they exist. Better yet, burn them. That's what I would've done with that damn camera. I'd have burnt it."

****

The two kids left the Rempley residence for the second time and walked to the sidewalk. Immediately Liz was overcome by the heat of the afternoon and reached to take off her long sleeved shirt, under which was a lighter, spaghetti-strap shirt.

"Liz," began Kyle, "that last photo you took on the Vortex. Was it a flash pic?"

Before she could respond, Kyle gasped. Liz pulling off her shirt had caused the lighter shirt beneath to ride up, exposing nearly her entire back to him.

"What the hell happened to you?" he asked, a deep air of concern now in his voice.

"What do you mean?" Oh, you mean this?"

Liz touched just below her nape and felt the scab. "I told you a spider bit me, just after I took that last photo with the Vortex."

Kyle brought the tip of his finger up to where Liz's finger was and slowly followed it down her back. She winced and pulled away.

"Ow!" she exclaimed.

"Liz, that's no spider bite." said Kyle, worriedly. "You have four deep scratches down your back!"

11

The medicine cabinet of the bathroom outside Liz's bedroom was well-stocked. In it Kyle found everything he needed: Bacitracin, cotton swabs and plenty of gauze. The Brentwoods kept a veritable hospital in their lavatories, and, barring the need for stitches or major surgery, Kyle could count on anything ranging from dental floss to thermal heat patches. After attending to Liz's wounds, Kyle and his patient sat down on her bed to think of the next course of action. She tried first to call her mother, but neither Patricia nor Paul answered their cell phones.

"Hospital," said Kyle as he wrapped up the left over gauze. "No cell phones allowed."

"Shit," hissed Liz and quickly began typing a text message into her phone. "They'll get this then as soon as they turn them back on."

With her two thumbs moving at lightning speed and near perfect accuracy, Kyle joked that West Coast girls, along with being known for their swimsuit bodies, should also be known for the speed of their thumbs. He moved closer to Liz on the bed and brought his leg up onto the mattress, but kept his foot hanging off the side. His shin was now touching the side of her thigh, and he was sure she felt his jeans on her soft California-tanned skin. He liked it that she didn't move away. He felt close to her, and somehow he knew she felt likewise about him. He took the same finger he'd traced over the wounds on her back and pretended to write his name on her thigh. He always enjoyed the way it tickled when he did it to himself in the same place, but he had never been close enough to a girl to do it to her. No girl he'd ever known would have ever allowed him to touch her the way that Liz was letting him now.

"What are you doing?" smiled Liz, still flipping through her cell phone.

"Nothing," replied Kyle and quickly stopped. "What are *you* doing?" he asked and moved even closer to her. He moved her hair away from the side of her face and set his chin on her shoulder.

"There's nothing on the Internet that says there's any connection between flashes from cameras and spirits or demons," she said.

She scrolled down one page and then the next on her phone's web browser, but the further she delved, the less in common the hits had with her initial search. Before she finally gave up, the seventh and final page had websites for FLASH FRIDAY HAPPY HOUR AT HOOLIGAN'S IN CLIFTON and DR. CARLO DEMONE OF DEMONE SURGICAL CENTER IN WANNAQUE - REMOVE SPIDER VEINS IN A FLASH!

"Nothing," she sighed, and dropped her phone onto her bed.

"You know we can set my phone or yours to *flash* and try again."

Liz inhaled deeply.

"Not after what the Rempleys told us," she said. "That clinched it for me. I don't wanna take another photo in this house. *Ever.*"

"Not even to be sure?"

"Look at my back, Kyle. Doesn't that pretty much sum up the experiment? Besides, I think taking another flash photo might be inviting trouble. Maybe Rempley was right. It's getting stronger. The chandelier and Mrs. Rempley's arm, then my back. I think we need a priest."

"What we need is to find those negatives," said Kyle, taking his chin off Liz's shoulder and planting a soft kiss on it.

She looked at him with no expression. He thought she'd be angry and kick him off her bed and then out of her house. Instead, she leaned forward and kissed him on his upper lip. He reciprocated, taking his lower lip and briefly sucking hers. Before he knew it, she had already wrapped her arms around his neck and pushed him back onto her bed. Kyle was battling two instincts, his own carnal lust that told him to go as far as he could with this beautiful girl who he'd imagined fucking as many times as humanly possible, or stay focused and get back to finding a way out of the potential terror that now surrounded both of them. Liz didn't give him much time to think it over. She grabbed him and turned onto her back, the bacitracin and gauze having done their job at relieving most of the discomfort. In the heat of the moment, Liz misjudged how much room she and Kyle had on the bed, and they fell onto the floor.

Liz landed on Kyle as they hit with a loud thud. Kyle touched the back of his head and felt it was sore. Liz asked if he was ok and went to feel if he had a bump. As she brought her hand up from her side, it moved over something just under her bed. She grabbed it and held it above Kyle's chest. She released part of it and it opened. It was a series of plastic sleeves and in each row there held a strip of four negatives.

"Oh, my God!" shouted Liz.

"Are those the..." began Kyle.

"They were here the whole time!" she said, and then jumped up, nearly kneeing Kyle in his testicles and held up the first row of negatives to the light of her lamp.

"What do you see?" he asked, fixing his shirt as he got up from the floor.

"These are all the…kitchen…dining room…living room…these were all the ones we saw."

"Well go to the last one." urged Kyle.

Liz did just that, but narrowed her eyes and brought the negative closer to the light.

"I can't really make it out. I see me. That's it."

"Come on." said Kyle.

"Where are we going?"

"To Big Jake's," he said. "We've gotta get that last negative developed."

****

They arrived in downtown Allendale just after seven. The store had been closed up since four and there weren't many people out on the street due to the excessive heat of the day. Liz glanced across the street and saw that every booth inside the Allendale Diner had been occupied. She knew that more than herself, Kyle had to be particularly careful. If Eugenia Charpentier and Mustache Marge saw Kyle enter the store after closing, especially with a girl they assumed to be his pregnant whore, they would hang him twenty feet by his nuts before flipping a coin to see who would get the privilege of cutting them off.

"Hurry, Kyle," urged Liz as she looked left then right.

"I am," he said, jingling the keys on his ring and searching frantically for the one to the front door of Big Jake's Photorama.

"Why can't we just go in from the back? It's gotta be safer."

"Because I don't have the backdoor key. But we can leave through the back when we're done. Just remind me to lock up this door before we go."

"With everything going on, you think I'm gonna remember that?"

"Voilà!" he said, triumphantly and showed Liz the key, dangling it two inches from her nose.

She arched her back and pushed the key back toward him.

"Great," she said. "Now get us in. And hurry up. I think I see someone coming."

"Did your mom text you back yet?"

"No. And I'm really worried. How far is the hospital?"

"Depends. There's Valley Hospital in Ridgewood, or they may have gone to Hackensack University Medical Center.

"Great. I don't even know where my family is right now. We can't even get in touch with them if we need them. If anything happens…"

Just then, there was a click in the door followed by another series of frantic jingles from Kyle's keys. He pulled the door open and entered. Liz followed closely at his heels. Regardless of how much sunlight was still outside, the store's blinds were all drawn, making the place almost entirely dark.

"Any chance in hitting the lights?" asked Liz, playfully.

"Are you crazy?" whispered Kyle. "And lower your voice. If that dyke finds us in here, we're fucked."

"Oh, please, I'm not afraid of her. You, she could fire. But I'm no one to her. What do you think she'd do? Come on to me?"

"That'd be punishment enough, trust me," said Kyle.

Liz didn't have time to laugh. They got to the photo finishing counter and Kyle turned Liz around and unzipped the small pocket of the knapsack she had strapped to her back. He removed a manila envelope, inside which was the single plastic sleeve that contained the last four negatives of the Vortex. He then hit a black switch on top of the machine. This produced a soft wheeze coming from inside the massive mechanism and a few *chugga chugga* sounds from the finishing tray.

It took several minutes for the machine to reach *Ready* status, during which time Kyle and Liz just stood there, holding each other. Kyle released Liz and took the last of the Vortex's four negatives and slipped them into the feeder cartridge. He then placed it slowly on the machine and pushed it down until he heard it lock into place with a loud snap. The noise made Liz flinch and she considered just how on edge she was. She watched as Kyle programmed something on the digital keypad of the massive machine and then with a flick of his wrist, his middle finger struck hard on the last of the keys.

The machine came to life, sounding like a plane about to take off. The cartridge that Kyle had placed in the machine soon disappeared. He backed up slowly and felt for Liz's hand. He found it just in time for the first of the four prints to shoot onto the finishing tray. As Kyle had retreated to where Liz was standing, he was no longer able to see the top of the machine, and so couldn't tell which of the photos it was. Suddenly another photo spit out, and then another, and finally the last one. Kyle went for the pile of prints, and Liz followed fast at his heels. He took them in his hands before quickly bringing them to his breast and then looked to Liz for instructions.

"What do you want to do?" he asked. "Do you want me to look at them first?"

"No," she replied, her breath short. "No, I want us *both* to look. *Together.*"

"Alright," replied Kyle, tipping his head.

He brought the photos face-up, and they peered down at the top print.

Liz shied away almost immediately.

"Damn it," she said.

It was photo #17, showing a smiling, yet visibly uneasy-looking, white-haired Mrs. Rempley holding her white wine up while seated at one end of the dining room table. Behind her was the demon, its claws clutched over her head and appearing ready to strike.

Kyle flipped to the next photo, #18, showing the mangled chandelier on the dining room table. He turned to the next one, #19, which showed the long flesh wound on Mrs. Rempley's arm. As Kyle pushed his thumb against the edge of the photo to reveal #20, Liz grabbed his hand and squeezed it.

"Not here," she said.

"What?" asked Kyle, thinking he'd misunderstood her.

"It's dark and creepy in here. If that photo shows us bad news…"

"You mean like the bad news on your back?"

She paused.

"Kyle, I think we both know what's in the photo. It's almost like before when I first looked at these and accused you. I didn't think it was likely that you went so out of your way just to scare a total stranger. But there was that little shred of doubt that it might have still been a trick. This is kind of the same. Seeing that…*thing* will be enough to convince me for sure."

"Alright," he said.

****

Soon after, Liz and Kyle exited the store from the back. Liz had not forgotten to remind Kyle to lock up the front after all. They returned to the front of Big Jake's Photorama and then crossed the street, stopping in Coleman's Drug Store so Kyle could buy another pack of smokes. Two pairs of eyes watched the teenagers from a 2003 Chevy Cavalier.

"What did I tell ya, Marge?" said Eugenia as she slapped her partner's wide thigh and spit out the pit of a prune she'd been sucking on. "This just keeps gettin' better and better. Holy shit! We're like friggin' Cagney and Lacey! Following those two twerps all the way down to Hoboken. You almost gave us away on the train, though!"

"I told you I wanted to get something from the dining car," argued Mustache Marge.

"Yeah, well you should've thought of getting something to eat at the station before we boarded."

"Well, how was I supposed to know Harris's car was between the dining car and our own?"

"Next time we go on an adventure, do me a favor and pack some Twinkies, will you, Chris?"

"Ok, Mary Beth." replied Mustache Marge as she shoved her ninth prune into her stubbly orifice. "Say, I never figured that Harris for a thief."

"I'll nail the son of a bitch!" said Eugenia, clutching the steering wheel tightly and speaking through a mouthful of prunes. "When I get done with old pencil prick, *Breaking and Entering* will have a new meaning for him. I'll make sure they send him up the river for at least a year. He'll come out so fucked he won't even be able to sit down on a toilet seat."

Mustache Marge laughed so hard, she belched and farted at the same time. Part of the skin of one of the prunes she'd been munching on was now hanging off the corner of her mouth. Eugenia gave her partner a disapproving look.

"Lay off my prunes, dude," said Eugenia. "You'll get the shits. And don't even think I don't know what you're planning. If you think you're gonna blow up my bathroom again, you can think again. I'll send your stinky ass down to the Shell station. Let them fuckin' Arabs smell your bomb. They won't think of messing with America after they get a load of what you can cook up in a crapper. I tell you, we could win the War on Terror with just one ounce of your shit for ammo!"

"Hey," whispered Mustache Marge, as if someone might be listening, "what did you think of all that malarkey about cameras and monsters back there?"

"I'm glad you asked that," said Marge as she spit out two prune pits into her hand and then dumped them into an empty Styrofoam coffee cup. "I think Harris and his bitch are high as kites. What's more, she needs an abortion and is afraid to tell her parents. He needs to fund his addiction and keep her high too. Why else would she be with him? You'd have to smoke some prit-tee strong shit to wanna stay with a fuck up like Harris. And Harris's white trash family ain't got a pot to piss their rented beer in, so this is his way. Extortion."

"Still, Eugenia, you didn't find all that camera business a bit... *creepy*? And that man was confirming what the kids were saying."

"Harris concocted this whole plan to get money."

"How do you mean?" asked Mustache Marge.

"His girlfriend feeds him the story about scary pictures belonging to the people who'd sold her family the house. He figures they'll want the pictures back and hauls his ass and hers down to Hoboken to shake down those Rempleys. But I'm one step ahead of him and his piece of snatch."

"But Harris and the girl didn't bring the pictures with them," said Mustache Marge.

"Huh?" replied Eugenia, confused.

"That's what they told the Rempleys. And Harris never mentioned money."

Eugenia thought for a moment, then shook her head impatiently and shoved Mustache Marge to get out of the car.

"*What-are-you-doing*?" protested Mustache Marge as she now found herself pressed up against the passenger-side door.

"I got an idea. I'm gonna go get some stuff in my store. I also wanna see if Harris managed to open the safe and, if so, I gotta see how much he took. I'll go in through the back entrance. Don't wait for me. When those two punks leave the drug store, take my Chevy and follow them. Make sure you find out where they're going. I'm hoping it'll be back to her house. In fact, I'm almost positive that's where they're headed. Then come back and get me. Got it, Chris?"

Mustache Marge grinned fiendishly at her partner, "Got it, Mary Beth!

12

11 Grover Road was as deserted as before when Liz and Kyle came up the path to the house. The family's new BMW was still absent from the driveway, and Liz had a sinking feeling she might be spending the entire evening alone in that house.

"I'm gonna try my mom again," she said, swinging the knapsack around and yanking her cell phone out of it. She hit her mother's missed call on the screen and brought the device up to her ear. Immediately she heard her mother's voice say *hello*.

"Mom? Mom. It's me. Thank Go…" Liz stopped and listened as her mother's voice continued.

"You've reached Patricia Brentwood. I'm sorry I can't answer the phone right now. If this is an emergency, I can be reached at seven one four, five five…"

Liz hit the *end* button on her phone and threw it back in her sack.

"Shit." she said. "Her phone is still off."

"Try your dad." said Kyle.

"No. If her phone is off then his will be too. You said so yourself. Hospital policy. I just hope everything's alright."

"I'm sure it is," reassured Kyle. "So what do you wanna do?"

"Let's go in the house. Even though I'd rather sleep in a bed infested with potato bugs."

The door creaked loudly as Liz and Kyle entered. The house was stuffy, and, right away, Liz went over to the thermostat on the living room wall. It had been set to 78, but it felt more like 88.

"We've been having trouble with the central air," she told Kyle, as he made himself comfortable on her couch.

After fiddling with the thermostat controls for about a minute and getting no results, she whacked the mechanism with the heel of her hand and joined Kyle on the sofa. He fetched the knapsack, which lay at his feet. He removed the photos, and Liz jumped up and began turning on as many lights as she could, not stopping until she was in the kitchen, illuminating that room as well. She saw the silver tea kettle on the stove and thought a little more iced coffee was in order. She called to Kyle, asking if he wanted any. He said yes, and so she filled the kettle, set it on one of the four burners and flicked the switch. The burner clicked; however, it produced no flame. Liz waited patiently, and even began to smell a hint of gas. Before she could remember her mother mentioning that the burners were broken, Kyle's voice distracted her.

"Liz!' he called. "Hurry it up, will you? I'm getting antsy."

It was dusk now, almost full dark, and, for Liz, the house had a lugubrious feel to it. Now consumed by goose bumps, she hurried out of the kitchen, turning off the light before leaving, but the burner still clicked.

She rejoined Kyle on the sofa and he put his leg over her thighs. She put one firm hand on his knee and another around his ankle.

"You ready?" he asked.

"I don't really know what I'm supposed to be ready for," she replied. "All I know is…I'm scared to death, Kyle."

He leaned over and planted another kiss on her quivering lips. She looked up at his vitiligo birthmark and ran her fingers through the spot of white hair.

"Is that genetic?" asked Liz, wondrously.

"Huh?"

"Will your kids have that too?"

He chuckled and shrugged.

"My doctor said it was, but no one else in my family has it. My sister once found a gray hair on her head a few years ago and freaked out. Everyone thought it was the beginning of the end for her. It turned out to be…just a gray hair."

Liz laughed, and they kissed again.

A brisk movement by one of the curtains on the bay window caused Liz to shriek, startling Kyle. She placed her hand on her fluttering heart in an attempt to steel herself as she felt a subtle evening breeze hit her warm body.

"Did you open the window, Kyle?" she asked.

"No," he replied. "I never went near it.

She quickly shook it off and assumed it'd been accidentally left open as her parents rushed out of the house with the twins, bound for the hospital. But the house *had been* stuffy when she and Kyle entered.

It was hot today, she thought. *And the window being open made the house hot and stuffy.*

After convincing herself she was letting her imagination get the best of her, she edged closer to Kyle and patted his ankle.

"Go 'head," she said. "Let's see that last photo and get this over with."

Kyle slowly flipped to the last picture. The image they beheld hit them hard. Liz gasped and Kyle whispered a *Jesus H. Christ* under his breath. The photo showed a slightly crooked shot of Liz, beaming unnaturally with her head tilted, her tongue out and pointed upward, her head back and her eyes narrow. To her right, just above her shoulder, was the demonic visage in all its horrific grotesqueness. Its color was even richer and fuller than it had been in photo #17, which had been, up to this point, the last photo taken of it. Its mouth, now wide open, exposed its four rows of sharp fang-like teeth and a short, fat tongue with fork-like pincers at its tip. One four-clawed hand was clutched just above Liz's shoulder. Its eyes, wide and angry, were fully opaque, yet the flash had created a bright artificial pupil in its right eye.

Before either of the teenagers could speak, the room lit up brightly, as though a flash of lightning had just struck outside. Kyle immediately felt a sharp pain on top of his head and crimson quickly began to drip through his white patch and down his forehead.

What ensued next was a duet of phlegm-filled cackles coming from the front door, which Liz had left wide open. Liz and Kyle turned around to see Eugenia Charpentier and Mustache Marge standing in the foyer, both holding disposable cameras.

13

"What did I tell ya, Marge?" Eugenia said, guffawing. "These two twerps are so fucking pathetic."

"Miss C.!" exclaimed Kyle, jumping off the sofa in surprise before succumbing to the gash on his crown and falling back onto the ottoman behind him. "Wh-what are you doing here?"

"GET THE HELL OUTTA MY HOUSE!" shouted Liz.

"Are your parents here, missy?" Eugenia asked Liz, angrily. "If they are, I think they'll be very interested to know you two broke into my store this afternoon."

"They-they're not here right now," said Liz, nervously.

"Turn off all the lights, Marge!"

Grunting and snorting in throaty laughter, Marge scampered around the ground floor, turning off every light Liz had turned on just a short time before.

Liz kept silent as she was unable to comprehend anything that was occurring at that moment: Kyle's howl followed by his knee-jerk reaction and the blood that resulted; then the two lesbians entering her house, uninvited, and lastly, an accusation of theft. It was all too much for Liz to take in all at once. She took a step back and simply watched, unable to react. She felt fear. She knew the demon had been near her and Kyle. It had gone for Kyle. These women had caused this chain of events, and still Liz could not bring herself to intervene. She drew back step by slowly dragging step until her back hit the wall.

"What's the matter, Harris?" said Eugenia in a patronizing tone and dangled the camera before her by its rubber strap.

Mustache Marge snorted and slapped her thighs, which echoed throughout the living room.

"Yeah," added Mustache Marge, "what's wrong, Harris? The little princess here not in the mood? She sure gave you a good one by the looks of your head!"

"Listen," said Kyle in a quivering voice that almost didn't sound like his own, "put down that camera. You don't get it. It's the flash."

"Oh, don't I get it, though?" said Eugenia, mocking Kyle. "You're pathetic, Harris."

"Pathetic!" giggled Mustache Marge.

"So goddamn pathetic. Since the first day you walked in my store. Your long hair, your head-banging, *mental* head music, your fucking skateboard and your skunk-do. Everything about you makes me sick. And now you think that just 'cause you got your bitch knocked up, you can steal from me to take care of things?"

"I-I wasn't stealing from you, Miss C.," pleaded Kyle while Liz still stood frozen against the wall. "Please put the camera down."

"Scared of this are you, Harris?" growled Eugenia with Mustache Marge still hooting loudly behind her. In fact, Marge was laughing so hard now, she couldn't swallow and so needed to cover her mouth to keep from drooling all over herself. Her own disposable camera was hooked onto her fat wrist and dangled below her chin.

"I've always said it," continued Eugenia. "'Oh, Harris is a goddamn loser', I used to tell my customers. 'But I keep him on because his father's a typical unemployed Irish drunk, and his mother bags groceries at the Shop 'N' Save.' No one ever believed it, though. No one ever gave *me*, Eugenia Charpentier, proprietor of Big Jake's Photorama, the benefit of the doubt."

As if the cocktail of Eugenia's cruel words and the maddening sounds emanating from Mustache Marge's mouth served as nourishment for her famished courage, Liz's courage was galvanized. She pushed off the wall with her elbows and rushed the two women.

"SHUT-UP-YOU-TWO-ASSHOLES!" screamed Liz.

Liz's intention to stifle the two women worked in that they turned their attention from Kyle to her instead, and stood there for a moment, stupefied with mouths hanging open. Had Liz continued her verbal assault, she probably could have bought Kyle a few more seconds to collect himself. But Liz's aggressive approach to the women worked better than she expected, surprising even herself. Once again she lost any ability to move or speak.

"WHO ARE YOU CALLING AN ASSHOLE, MISSY?" yelled Eugenia and got in Liz's face.

Instinctively looking out for her own wellbeing, Liz's courage quickly returned.

"I'm not afraid of you, you know," said Liz, confidently, and stood as tall as she could against Eugenia's massive frame.

"You ain't, huh?" said Eugenia. "But your little sissy boy over there sure is. And you clocked him a good one. So I guess that means you wear the pants in the relationship."

Liz tightened her fist at these words.

Strangely, Mustache Marge kept quiet and just watched.

"So," Eugenia continued, "you like to be butch, huh?" She looked Liz up and down. "How 'bout you show me just how butch you can be."

Eugenia drew closer to Liz, much to the chagrin of Mustache Marge who, at this point, only blurted out a little squeak. Liz seized her chance. She swung back her arm and sent her fist forward, landing it right between Eugenia's eyes. Eugenia stumbled back and Mustache Marge grabbed Liz.

"BITCH!" shouted Mustache Marge and threw Liz to the ground.

Liz fell onto a half-empty moving box and hit her head against the floorboard that left her nearly unconscious.

"You little witch," said Eugenia as she took her hand away from her nose to survey the slow river of blood that collected on her fingers. "I'm gonna take care of you. Oh, am I gonna take care of *you*. Right after I finish up with your little wuss."

Eugenia turned to Kyle, who had since managed to get to his feet, though he was still badly injured. The gash in his head had yielded enough blood to cover nearly his entire forehead and was trickling down into his eyes.

"Ok, Harris," growled Eugenia as she aimed the camera in his direction. "Get ready to look your most pathetic. I'm gonna even pin this one up on the community board at the Photorama, along with your pink slip, which I'll stick right underneath it!"

"Wait, Euge!" shouted Mustache Marge, as she tried yanking off the camera's strap from her fat wrist before just pulling the cord until it snapped. "Let me get you taking this shot of bloodied Harris and his little bitch squirming on the floor behind you. We'll add it to the community board too!"

"Yeah," Eugenia grinned, deviously. "I'll be known as the one who brought down Harris!"

Mustache Marge stood to the left of her partner, made sure the flash was set to *on,* squeezed one eye shut and with the other, peered through the tiny window. With Eugenia, Kyle and Liz all in view, she squeezed the shutter and the dim room came alive with a bright flash of light. Liz and Kyle looked to see where the image of the demon would appear. It stood behind Eugenia, its claws engaged and only inches from the back of her neck. Since Marge had relied on the little window to focus on the shot, she didn't see the image of the demon.

"Where's your monster *now,* Harris?" chortled Eugenia.

Liz and Kyle hastily exchanged glances. The demon tended to be *in* the path of the flash. Logic suggested that if Eugenia snapped the shot of Kyle, the demon could be over him next, ready to strike him again. It might only take one shot, or two. They didn't know how many they needed to stop Eugenia. Somehow Liz and Kyle needed to get Marge to take another photo.

Liz thought of a plan, and she prayed that Kyle would catch on. She feared that their very lives depended on it.

"Oh, Eugenia!" said Liz, getting up slowly. "You sure outdid yourself."

Eugenia double blinked, her face producing a bewildered look.

"You got us. I'm preg…knocked up, as you say, and you're so right. Kyle *is* pathetic."

Kyle frowned at Liz. She widened her eyes at him and motioned with her head to the two women.

"Pathetic, pathetic, pathetic," continued Liz. "Tsk, tsk, tsk. I even had to help him find my hole."

Mustache Marge cackled loudly.

"And to think, you've got Kyle groveling before you. Begging you to spare his job. Aren't you, Kyle? Aren't you groveling to Eugenia?"

"Ah, right!" exclaimed Kyle, falling to his knees and clutching his hands together. "Oh, please, Miss. C! Please spare my job! My family'll starve! Oh, kind, generous and...*beautiful* Miss C.!"

"Beautiful?" said Mustache Marge.

"Shut up, Marge!" scolded Eugenia. "Well, now, that's more like it, Harris. That's right. Beg me for your job back."

"This would be a photo for the books in my opinion!" said Liz, looking to Mustache Marge. "Poor white trash Kyle Harris begging the benevolent Miss Eugenia Charpentier, proprietor of Big Jake's Photorama in Allendale, New Jersey! What a photo that will make on your community board! I'm sure people will come from miles and miles to shop in your store, just to see that photo on your board! Wouldn't that make for a great picture, Marge? Kyle begging and pleading in front of Eugenia?"

"Yeah!" said Mustache Marge and aimed her disposable camera up at Eugenia.

"Oh, please, Miss C.!" continued Kyle in a beseeching tone.

"Make it a good one, Marge," ordered Eugenia.

"Oh, and don't forget the flash!" added Liz.

"Shut your mouth, missy," snapped Mustache Marge. "I know how to use a camera."

Mustache Marge aimed her disposable at Eugenia and Kyle, who had since backed up two feet from where his employer was standing. Marge made sure the flash was on, brought the camera's little window to her left eye and squeezed the right one tightly shut.

Click!

Kyle jumped out of the way of the flash as it momentarily lit up the room and the beast appeared in the same spot as a minute before. This time Liz and Kyle saw its claws dig deeply into both of Eugenia's carotid arteries. Blood gushed out of her neck as she looked toward Mustache Marge, whose face had been sprayed with the former's blood. Eugenia looked at her partner with a look half of confusion, half of horror before ultimately collapsing face-first onto the floor. Without so much as a word, Marge dropped her camera. Liz leaped for it, nearly stepping on Eugenia. With her lover dying before her, Marge was too confused and frightened to do anything. Liz got the camera and aimed it at Marge, who knelt slowly down beside Eugenia and gently stroked her hair.

"Euge? Euge?"

Eugenia Charpentier was dead.

"Get outta here!" shouted Liz. "Or say cheese, bitch."

Mustache Marge finally began to clue into what was happening, although she wasn't going to let bygones be bygones. In her eyes, Liz and Kyle had killer her beloved. She stumbled to her feet and assumed an attack position like a sumo wrestler about to fight his opponent.

"You dirty little twerps," croaked Mustache Marge. "I'll kill you's for this!"

She lunged for Liz, at which point Kyle ducked and shouted, "Take it, Liz!"

Liz clicked the shutter and the flash immediately ensued. Kyle and Liz saw the figure of the demon just beside Marge. Liz clicked the camera's shutter button again. In an instant, Marge's progress was cut short. She heaved forward, moaning loudly. An enormous amount of blood spewed from her mouth, and then she collapsed onto her knees before also falling face-first to the floor. As Kyle and Liz saw it, the demon had sunk its razor-sharp teeth into Mustache Marge's side, biting off a large chunk of her considerable torso.

Kyle fell down, beginning to succumb to the excessive loss of his own blood. Liz dropped the camera and stumbled over the two bodies in an effort to catch him.

"I gotta get you to the hospital," she said, taking the red bandana that Kyle had tied to one of his thighs and pressed it against his wound.

Just then the two of them stopped and sniffed the air around them. They looked back toward the direction of the kitchen. Then they looked slowly back at each other, almost serenely.

"The house," said Kyle, weakly.

"I know," said Liz. "I forgot to shut off the pilot."

"That's not what I mean." he answered. "The demon, he didn't follow the Rempleys. He stayed here. It's the house; the land it's connected to. Not the people who live here."

Liz thought about what Kyle had said. The smell of the gas was beginning to make her head pound, and she started to feel the effects of nausea and lightheadedness.

"We gotta decide quick," he urged her. "It would mean giving up everything you have."

Liz pondered what Kyle meant and then widened her eyes at him. She understood what he meant.

"Well," she said, "that's what they have insurance for, right?"

"Quick." he whispered, choking from the fumes as his eyes began to roll back. "We don't have much time. Remember, Liz, it's the house that it's connected to, not the people. Your parents would never sell this house now. Not in a million years. And we've got two dead bodies in here we can't explain."

Liz put two fingers up to Kyle's lips.

"You don't need to convince me."

Kyle nodded and they made their way toward the door.

"How are we gonna explain Eugenia and Marge?" she asked.

"We don't." he replied. No one saw us come in. No one will see us go out. Your neighbors' houses are separated by trees and bushes. Remember what Rempley said about neighbors? One of the fringe benefits of living in the suburbs."

Kyle instructed Liz to close the bay window.

"So what do we do now?" asked Liz, propping Kyle's arm on her shoulder and helping him to the foyer.

"We just walk. And keep on walking. Hopefully something will ignite the air."

Kyle looked down at the bodies of Eugenia and Mustache Marge and one of the two disposable cameras lying in a pool of blood. Just then, an idea popped into his head.

"I got it!" he said, sounding like his strength had returned.

He instructed Liz to bend down and hand him the disposable camera, which lay beside Eugenia's ass. She didn't ask questions, realizing that time was of the essence. She bent down, grabbed the camera and handed it to Kyle.

"A Stratometer Waterproof camera!" he said, triumphantly. "Perfect!"

"What are you doing?" asked Liz, intrigued, but looking over her shoulder toward the kitchen, fretting the gas that was continuing to slowly poison the air around them.

"These cameras are equipped with a timer mechanism, which is powered by the battery." replied Kyle. "They're designed for kids, mostly, who wanna take group pictures underwater. The beauty of this one is that even though it only comes with thirty-six exposures, the timer will keep it flashing every few seconds even after the last of the exposures is done. I know because some friends and I used one as a strobe light one night while we were getting ston…"

Kyle stopped and gave Liz a look as if to say, *nevermind.*

He fidgeted with the flash setting and set the timer to go off in ten second intervals.

"Done!" he said and set it back down by Eugenia's ass. "We've got fifteen seconds before the first flash. Let's go!"

"What good will that do?" demanded Liz.

"The air is becoming increasingly flammable. The flash will act like a static charge and should ignite. I just hope the damage is complete so there's no chance your folks will rebuild."

"Kyle, you're a genius!" Then Liz contemplated the last thing Kyle had said about hoping the fire would completely destroy everything. "Flammable. Wait! The tank in the basement. I remember my dad commenting on the Rempley's generosity. He told my mom that they had filled up the oil tank before the closing."

"Perfect!" cheered Kyle. "That'll keep the fire burning hot enough to char everything in this place!"

They hurried out of the house. Liz grabbed the knob to the front door and looked back, hesitating a bit. Then she realized all that was at stake. The demon wouldn't stop. He was growing stronger, just like Rempley had said. She had her mother, her father and her twin brothers to think about. She was doing the right thing, she thought. As bad as it seemed, there wasn't any other solution. And what's more, no one would believe them about any of this. Demons coming to life just from the flash of a camera? Who was to say the Rempleys would corroborate their story? And the two bodies inside were an issue. With their remains charred beyond recognition, the police would have little if anything to go on. Only after Eugenia Charpentier and Mustache Marge were listed as missing persons would they be identified. Then the next question would be, *"why were the two women in the Brentwood house in the first place?"* It would simply be a case whose outcome would be purely speculation. And it wouldn't be the first time that ever happened.

Liz pulled the door tightly shut and as she and Kyle stepped off the last of the front stairs, the first flash lit up behind them, lighting up the front yard. Liz didn't want to look back. By the time they made it to the sidewalk, another flash ensued. Kyle had been looking over his shoulder the whole time and, with the help of the flash, saw the demon standing in the bay window. It stared angrily at them momentarily before disappearing along with the second flash. He never told Liz what he'd seen. He worried that such an image would haunt her until the end of her days. He was looking out for her now. He planted a kiss on her temple and she leaned her head into his lips.

Regardless of what her parents' reaction would be, Liz knew everything was going to be all right. In a way she felt grateful for everything that had happened. Not that she took comfort in the fact that two women, miserable as they were, had lost their lives and that their deaths would be covered up in a tragedy that involved her new home. But knowing that she emerged from a nightmare with someone who had shared it with her every step of the way gave Liz Brentwood comfort, much-needed comfort she had longed for, ever since she'd left California. A comfort she'd shared with Rob Hornsby, a feeling she had no inclination she'd ever feel again in her life.

She had hope now.

Good over evil.

The seventh flash gave way to an explosion louder than Liz or Kyle had ever known. Although already at the corner of Liz's street, the blast had caused Kyle to lose what balance he had and he brought Liz down with him. They fell hard onto the concrete. As the fiery debris from the explosion shot outward, landing all around them, the two teens embraced tightly and kept their heads down. Soon all was quiet, save for the crackling of the massive inferno that now engulfed the former property of 11 Grover Road. Slowly Liz and Kyle rose to their feet and saw that all that remained of the house was a large pile of blazing kindling. The destruction had been exactly what Kyle had hoped for, as the blast utterly leveled the house. As the two made their way out of Ho-Ho-Kus, the conflagration behind them lit up the night.

"What the hell happened to you?" asked Paul Brentwood as he, Patricia and young Sean saw a filthy Liz practically dragging a boy none of them had ever seen before into the emergency room of Hackensack University Medical Center.

"I had a feeling you'd be here," joked Liz, helping Kyle to a seat and then kissing him on the cheek. "I need to tell the receptionist that we need to see a doctor."

"Elizabeth," scolded Patricia, "what's going on here? Where were you? And who is this young man?"

"Mother," began Liz, "you and dad are just gonna have to trust me."

****

At dawn, Paul Brentwood hung up the public pay phone in the emergency room lobby and rejoined his family. One of the Brentwood's new neighbors on Grover Road, with whom Paul had left word in case Liz showed up back at the house, had left Paul a rather urgent voicemail.

"I hate to tell you this, Paul," stated the voice of Lloyd Green, "but your house just exploded. I think you need to get over here quick."

"Thank God Liz wasn't in it when it blew." muttered Paul to Patricia. "Or any of us for that matter. Jared's broken arm was a blessing in disguise. What could it have been, I wonder? The boiler? All that oil. It could have sprung a leak that ignited somehow. Or the electrical wiring in that frigging thermostat. No matter how it happened, every last bit of our property is gone."

"Paul. We're alive and that's all that matters!" cried Patricia. "And Liz! Thank God you showed up here before your father checked his voicemail, baby!" She hugged her daughter tightly. "The thought of losing one of my children…"

"I know, mom," Liz said, and pressed her nose deeply into her mother's breast. "I don't like worrying you."

"Are you going to go back to the house?" began Patricia, and then frowned. "I mean, go back to the…uhm…oh, God, I don't know what to call it."

"Who were you talking to, daddy?" asked Jared as Sean drew a smiley face on his arm's cast.

"The chief of police *and* the fire marshal," answered Paul, looking at Liz and Kyle, who'd just been discharged. "They want us to head over to the police station to make a statement and fill out some paperwork."

"Everything's gone," said Patricia, mournfully. "But I'll say it again. We have each other."

"Well, at least we still have the BMW!" exclaimed Liz.

Paul turned his head slightly, narrowing his eyes at Liz and Kyle.

"You two wouldn't happen to have anything to do with any of this, would you?"

"Dad," began Liz, "I may not have been crazy about moving to New Jersey, but do you really think I'd feel so strongly about it that I'd actually blow up our own house?"

Patricia intervened, clearing her voice and stepping between Paul and Liz.

"Liz, are you going to introduce us to your new friend?"

"It's Lizzy's new boyfriend!" said the twins together.

Kyle lowered his head and smiled in spite of himself.

"Mom. Dad." said Liz, taking Kyle's hand. "We used all our money on the cab ride over here so I'm gonna walk Kyle back to Allendale."

"WALK?" exclaimed Paul. Allendale's gotta be over ten miles from here. And, no offense, Kyle, I'm sure you're a…fine boy, but…"

"We'll be ok, dad," insisted Liz, grinning at Kyle who in turn winked at her. "We've been through a lot together these last two days."

"Elizabeth." Patricia interrupted.

"Mother," replied Liz, "like I said, you're going to have to learn to start trusting me."

She and Kyle left the emergency room and headed out to the main road. When they were far enough away from the watchful eyes of Paul and Patricia Brentwood, Kyle took Liz by the backs of her ears and leaned forward, kissing her softly. As their lips met, Liz brought her hand up to Kyle's hair and began to caress his bandaged wound.

Kyle withdrew, wincing.

"Sorry," she said, sincerely. "Sheesh. Twenty-two stitches. Lucky that thing didn't dig any deeper, you'd be one dead skunk."

"Think we'll have a lot to tell our kids someday?" he said.

"Don't get ahead of yourself, mister," she laughed.

As the sun began rising from the east, the two teens walked north. They beamed from the thought of having the whole summer before them, but they remained silent for a long time. It was enough that they finally had the chance to simply enjoy each other's company, on a beautiful summer morning, hand in hand.

Epilogue:

The Waxing Gibbous

1

BEHOLD, LITTLE WHORE! The lunar phase I've been waiting for is at last upon us! And so, I've won! You and I are as one! You cry those tears of blood and grit your crimson-stained teeth! Chew on your tongue, and as I free one of your hands, take up the crucifix above your head and gouge out your fucking eyes! Yes, try to push me out! And as you do, feel down below how you are instantaneously shitting yourself! Let the smell permeate the room! It will repel anyone who tries to intervene!

YOU ARE MINE, CUNT!

You relax? You are now at ease? Have you surrendered your will to me? You've come to terms with the fact. Excellent!

EXCELLENT!

"Sh-sh…"

WHAT? WHAT IT THIS? SHE SPEAKS? IMPOSSIBLE!

NOT POSSIBLE!

"Sh-she h-h-hoped."

You shall not speak anymore! I have total control of you, fucking little wench!

"H-h-hope!"

WHAT? WHAT DID YOU SAY?

"H-h-ooooope!"

HOPE?

"Y-y-y-esss. L-L-Liiiiz h-h-had h-h-ooooope!"

WHAT ARE YOU TALKING ABOUT?

"Y-you said, 'She had hope now…Good over evil.' Is-isn't that w-what you said?"

You've misunderstood! You're a stupid child! You always were! You misunderstood me!

"L-Liz heard her father's voice, '*Good over evil. Good over evil. Good over evil. Good always triumphs over evil.*' You told me so yourself."

(*I'm losing my grip on her!*) *WHORE! YOU MISUNDERSTOOD, I SAY! HEAR ME!*

"Liz told Kyle, 'Good over evil. It's just something my father once told us.' She said this. It gave them hope. At the end of the story, they *beat* the demon, didn't they? They-they *won*. Their story ended happily ever after. They ended happily, *didn't they?* They had *hope*. I…I h-have hope too!"

You HAVE NO HOPE! I've drained you of it! And now you will be silent!

"Hope."

SILENCE, CUNT!

"I-I Hope!"

YOU DON'T!

"I-I *DO!*"

YOU DON'T!

"I DO!!!"

FUCK YOU!

"I hope...I hope...I hope...I hope...I...HOPE!"

NOOOOOOOOOO!!!

2

Alice Bennett

Mrs. Rodgers

December 9th, 2020

Grade 12 – Poem assignment

HOPE

On a dark winter night he came to my room
He taught me of hate, he spelled out my doom
And so I gave in, I gave into him.
He told me my future, that it would be so grim
He watched me ten years, yes one whole decade;
He took me one evening, all hope so did fade
He had a short time, a window of chance;
For the moon's waxing phase, I fell under his trance.
I could no longer move, my body was his
I thought all was over, until he told me of Liz.
I heard three tales told, of horror and gore.
Once ended the first, my faith was no more.
Then came the second, I begged to be spared
He thus must have known I'd be ever so scared;
And then came the third, ready was I to die
And then he slipped up, but claimed it a lie.
He spoke of a hope, throughout this whole tale;
This was his mistake, which led him to fail.
He tried to renounce, told me I was wrong
But returned all my strength, my voice again strong;

He knew not of faith, of hope nor of love
That strength from God comes from heaven above.
And so did he leave, just as swift as he came
Yet I knew that my life could ne'er be the same;
Although I kept silent, until now never spoke
Of this terrible dream from which I awoke.
I now choose to tell, in my own private way;
Through words in a poem I shall have my own say
This nightmare has taught me the meaning of life
And when I am older and finally a wife,
I shall remember the teachings from rabbi to Pope
That in this life one needs love, peace, faith and hope!

Perpetual hope!

Printed in the United States
by Baker & Taylor Publisher Services